PRAISE FOR THE NOVELS OF SHERRY HARRIS

Praise for *The Gun Also Rises*

"A roller-coaster of a mystery penned by a real pro. This series just gets better and better. More, please!" —*Suspense Magazine*

"Author Sherry Harris never disappoints with her strong, witty writing voice and her ability to use the surprise effect just when you think you have it all figured out!"—*Chatting About Cozies*

"This series gets better with every book, and *The Gun Also Rises* continues the trend. If you haven't started this series yet, do yourself a favor and buy the first one today."—*Carstairs Considers*

Praise for *I Know What You Bid Last Summer*

"*I Know What You Bid Last Summer* is cleverly plotted, with an engaging cast of characters and a clever premise that made me think twice about my shopping habits. Check it out."—*Suspense Magazine*

"Never one to give up, she (Sarah) continues her hunt for the killer in some unlikely and possibly dangerous places. Fans of Harris will appreciate both the clever mystery and the tips for buying and selling at garage sales."—*Kirkus Reviews*

"Each time a new Sarah Winston Garage Sale Mystery releases, I wonder how amazing author Sherry Harris will top the previous book she wrote for the series. I'm never disappointed, and my hat's off to Ms. Harris, who consistently raises the bar for her readers' entertainment."—*Chatting About Cozies*

Praise for *A Good Day to Buy*

"Sarah's life keeps throwing her new curves as the appearance of her estranged brother shakes up her world. This fast-moving mystery starts off with a bang and keeps the twists and turns coming. Sarah is a likable protagonist who sometimes makes bad decisions based on good intentions. This ups the action and drama as she tries to extricate herself from dangerous situations with some amusing results. Toss in a unique cast of secondary characters, an intriguing mystery, and a hot ex-husband, and you'll find there's never a dull moment in Sarah's bargain-hunting world."—*RT Book Reviews*, four stars

"Harris' fourth is a slam dunk for those who love antiques and garage sales. The knotty mystery has an interesting premise and some surprising twists and turns as well."—*Kirkus Reviews*

"The mystery of the murder in *A Good Day to Buy*, the serious story behind Luke's reappearance, the funny scenes that lighten the drama, the wonderful cast of characters, and Sarah's always superb internal dialogue, will keep you turning the pages and have you coming back for book #5."—*Nightstand Book Reviews*

Praise for *All Murders Final!*

"There's a lot going on in this charming mystery, and it all works. The dialogue flows effortlessly, and the plot is filled with numerous twists and turns. Sarah is a resourceful and appealing protagonist, supported by a cast of quirky friends. Well written and executed, this is a definite winner. Bargain-hunting has never been so much fun!"—*RT Book Reviews*, four stars

"A must-read cozy mystery! Don't wear your socks when you read this story cause it's gonna knock 'em off!"—*Chatting About Cozies*

"Just because Sherry Harris's protagonist Sarah Winston lives in a small town, it doesn't mean that her problems are small. . . . Harris fits the puzzle pieces together with a sure hand."—Sheila Connolly, Agatha- and Anthony-nominated author of the Orchard Mysteries

"A thrilling mystery. . . . Brilliantly written, each chapter drew me in deeper and deeper, my anticipation mounting with every turn of the page. By the time I reached the last page, all I could say was . . . wow!"—*Lisa Ks Book Reviews*

Praise for *The Longest Yard Sale*
"I love a complex plot and *The Longest Yard Sale* fills the bill with mysterious fires, a missing painting, thefts from a thrift shop and, of course, murder. Add an intriguing cast of victims, potential villains and sidekicks, an interesting setting, and two eligible men for the sleuth to choose between and you have a sure winner even before you get to the last page and find yourself laughing out loud."—Kaitlyn Dunnett, author of *The Scottie Barked at Midnight*

"Readers will have a blast following Sarah Winston on her next adventure as she hunts for bargains and bad guys. Sherry Harris's latest is as delightful as the best garage sale find!"—Liz Mugavero, Agatha Award–nominated author of the Pawsitively Organic Mysteries

"Sherry Harris is a gifted storyteller, with plenty of twists and adventures for her smart and stubborn protagonist."—Beth Kanell, Kingdom Books

"Once again Sherry Harris entwines small-town life with that of the nearby Air Force base, yard sales with romance, art theft with murder. The story is a bargain, and a priceless one!"—Edith Maxwell, Agatha-nominated author of the Local Foods mystery series

Praise for *Tagged for Death*
"*Tagged for Death* is skillfully rendered, with expert characterization and depiction of military life. Best of all Sarah is the type of intelligent, resourceful, and appealing person we would all like to get to know better!"—*Mystery Scene Magazine*

"Full of garage-sale tips, this amusing cozy debut introduces an unusual protagonist who has overcome some recent tribulations and become stronger."
—*Library Journal*

"A terrific find! Engaging and entertaining, this clever cozy is a treasure—charmingly crafted and full of surprises."—Hank Phillippi Ryan, Agatha-, Anthony-, and Mary Higgins Clark Award–winning author

"Like the treasures Sarah Winston finds at the garage sales she loves, this book is a gem."—Barbara Ross, Agatha Award–nominated author of the Maine Clambake Mysteries

"It was masterfully done. *Tagged for Death* is a winning debut that will have you turning pages until you reach the final one. I'm already looking forward to Sarah's next bargain with death."—Mark Baker, *Carstairs Considers*

The Sarah Winston Garage Sale Mysteries
by Sherry Harris

From Beer to Eternity

Sherry Harris

KENSINGTON BOOKS

www.kensingtonbooks.com

To Bob
For making life an adventure no matter where we live
and
To Clare
The angel on my shoulder

Heritage Businesses

Sea Glass—owner, Vivi Jo Slidell
Briny Pirate—owner, Wade Thomas
Redneck Rollercoaster—owner, Ralph Harrison
Russo's Grocery Store—owner, Fred Russo
Hickle Glass-Bottom Boat—owners, Edith Hickle,
    Leah Hickle, Oscar Hickle
Emerald Cove Fishing Charters—owner, Jed Farwell

CHAPTER 1

Remember the big moment in *The Wizard of Oz* movie when Dorothy says, "Toto, I've a feeling we're not in Kansas anymore?" Boy, could I relate. Only a twister hadn't brought me here; a promise had. This wasn't the Emerald City, but the Emerald Coast of Florida. Ruby slippers wouldn't get me home to Chicago. And neither would my red, vintage Volkswagen Beetle, if anyone believed the story I'd spread around. Nothing like lying to people you'd just met. But it couldn't be helped. Really, it couldn't.

The truth was, as a twenty-eight-year-old children's librarian, I never imagined I'd end up working in a beach bar in Emerald Cove, Florida. In the week I'd been here I'd already learned toddlers and drunk people weren't that different. Both were unsteady on their feet, prone to temper tantrums one minute and sloppy hugs the next, and they liked to take naps wherever they happened to be. Go figure. But knowing that wasn't helping me right now. I was currently giving the side-eye to one of the regulars.

"Joaquín, why the heck is Elwell wearing that armadillo on his head?" I asked in a low voice. Elwell Pugh sat at the end of the bar, his back to the beach, nursing a beer in his wrinkled hands. I had known life would be different in the Panhandle of Florida, but armadillo shells on people's heads?—that was a real conversation starter.

"It's not like it's alive, Chloe," Joaquín Diaz answered, as if that made sense of a man wearing a hollowed-out armadillo shell as a hat. Joaquín raised two perfectly manicured eyebrows at me.

What? Maybe it was some kind of lodge thing down here. My uncle had been a member of a lodge in Chicago complete with funny fez hats, parades, and clowns riding miniature motorcycles. But he usually didn't sit in bars in his hat—at least not alone.

Elwell sported the deep tan of a Florida native. A few faded tattoos sprinkled his arms. His gray hair, cropped short, and grizzled face made him look unhappy—maybe he was. I'd met Elwell when I started working at the Sea Glass. I already knew that Elwell was a great tipper, didn't make off-color comments, and kept his hands to himself. That alone made him a saint among men to me, because all three were rare when waitressing in a bar. At least in this one, the only bar I'd ever worked in.

It hadn't taken me long to figure out Elwell's good points. But I'd seen more than one tourist start to walk in off the beach, spot him, and leave. There were other bars farther down the beach, plenty of places to drink. So, Elwell and his armadillo hat seemed like a problem to me.

"Elwell started wearing it a few weeks back," Joaquín

said with a shrug that indicated *what are you going to do about it.* Joaquín's eyes were almost the same color as the aquamarine waters of the Gulf of Mexico, which sparkled across the wide expanse of beach in front of the Sea Glass. With his tousled dark hair, Joaquín looked way more like a Hollywood heart-throb than a fisherman by morning, bartender by afternoon. That combination had the women who stopped in here swooning. He looked like he was a few years older than me.

"It keeps the gub'ment from tracking me," Elwell said in a drawl that dragged "guh-buh-men-t" into four syllables.

Apparently, Elwell had exceptional hearing, or the armadillo shell was some kind of echo chamber.

"Some fools," Elwell continued, "believe tinfoil will stop the gub'ment, but they don't understand radio waves."

Great, a science lesson from a man with an armadillo on his head. I nodded, keeping a straight face because I didn't want to anger a man who seemed a tad crazy. He watched me for a moment and went back to staring at his beer. I grinned at Joaquín and he smiled at me. Joaquín didn't seem concerned, so maybe I shouldn't be either. I glanced at Elwell again. His eyes always had a calculating look that made me think there was a purpose for the armadillo shell that had nothing to do with the "gub'ment," but what did I know?

CHAPTER 2

"Whatta ya gotta do to get a drink round here?" a man yelled from the front of the bar. He was one of two men playing a game of rummy at a high top. They were in here almost every day.

"Not shout for a drink, Buford," Joaquín yelled back. "Or get your lazy as—" he caught himself as he glanced at Vivi, the owner and our boss, who frowned at him from across the room, "asteroid up here."

Vivi's face relaxed into a smile. She would have made a good children's librarian considering how she tried to keep things PG around here. Joaquín tilted his head toward me. I took a pad out of the little black apron wrapped around my waist and trotted over to Buford.

"Would you like another Bud?" I asked Buford. "Or something else?"

"Sure would," Buford said. There was a "duh" note in his voice suggesting why else would he be yelling to Joaquín.

"Another Maker's Mark whiskey?" I looked at Buford's card playing partner as I wrote his beer order on my pad.

"You have a good memory," he said looking at his half empty glass. "But I'm good."

Good grief, I'd been serving him the same drink all week, I'd hoped I could remember his order. I made the rounds of the other tables. By each drink I wrote a brief description of who ordered it: beer, black hair rummy player; martini, dirty, yellow Hawaiian shirt; gin and tonic, needs a bigger bikini. I'd seen way more oiled-up, sweaty, sandy body parts than I cared to in the week I'd been here. Not even my dad, a retired plumber, had seen this many cracks at a meeting of the Chicago plumbers union.

Those images kept haunting my dreams, along with giant beach balls knocking me down, talking dolphins, and tidal waves. I'd yet to figure out what any of them meant—well, maybe I'd figured out one of them. But I wasn't going to think about that now.

Nope, I preferred to focus on the scenery, because, boy, this place had atmosphere—and that didn't even include Elwell and his armadillo shell hat. The Sea Glass Saloon I'd pictured before I'd arrived had swinging, saloon-style doors, bawdy dancing girls, and wagon-wheel chandeliers. This was more like a tiki hut than an old western saloon, though thankfully I didn't have to wear a sarong and coconut bra top. I could fill one out, but I preferred comfortable tank tops. Besides, the Gulf of Mexico was the real star of the show. The whole front of the bar was open to it, with retractable glass doors leading to a covered deck.

The Sea Glass catered to locals who needed a

break from the masses of tourists who descended on Emerald Cove and Destin, the bigger town next door, every summer. Not that Vivi would turn down tourists' money. She needed their money to stay open, as far as I could tell.

Like Dorothy, I was up for a new adventure and finding my way in a place that was so totally different from my life in Chicago. I only hoped that I'd find my own versions of Dorothy's Scarecrow, Tin Man, and Cowardly Lion to help me on the way. So far, the only friend I'd made—and I wasn't too sure about that—was Joaquín. He, and everybody, seemed nice enough, but I was still trying to adjust to the relaxed Southern attitude that prevailed among the locals in the Panhandle of Florida. It was also called the Emerald Coast, LA—lower Alabama, and get this—the Redneck Riviera.

You could have knocked me over with a palm frond when I heard that nickname. The chamber of commerce never used it, nor would you see the name in a TV ad. But the locals used it with a mixture of pride and disdain. Some wanted to brush it under the proverbial rug, while others embraced it in its modern-day form—people who were proud of their local roots.

The Emerald Coast stretched from Panama City, Florida, fifty miles east of here, to Pensacola, Florida, fifty miles to the west. The rhythm and flow was such a contrast from the go, go, go lifestyle in Chicago, where I'd lived my entire life. The local attitude matched the blue-green waves of the Gulf of Mexico, which lapped gently on sand so white you'd think Mr. Clean came by every night to tidy up.

As I walked back to the bar Joaquín's hips swayed to the island music playing over an old speaker system. He was in perpetual motion, with his hips moving like some suave combination of Elvis and Ricky Martin. My hips didn't move like that even on my best day—even if I'd had a couple of drinks. Joaquín glanced at me as he added gin, tonic, and lime to a rocks glass. I'd learned that term a couple of days ago. Bars had names for everything, and "the short glasses" didn't cut it in the eyes of my boss, Vivi Jo Slidell. And yeah, she was as Southern as her name sounded. I watched with interest as Joaquín grabbed a cocktail shaker, adding gin, dry vermouth, and olive brine.

"Want to do the honors?" Joaquín asked, holding up the cocktail shaker.

I glanced at the row of women sitting at the bar, one almost drooling over Joaquín. One had winked at him so much it looked like she had an eye twitch, and one was now looking at me with an openly hostile expression. Far be it from me to deprive anyone from watching Joaquín's hips while he shook the cocktail.

"You go ahead," I said with a grin and a small tilt of my head toward his audience. The hostile woman started smiling again. "Have you ever thought about dancing professionally?"

"Been there, danced that," Joaquín answered.

"Really?" the winker asked.

"Oh, honey, I shook my bootie with Beyoncé, Ricky Martin, and Justin Timberlake among others when I was a backup dancer."

"What are you doing here, then?" I was astonished.

"My husband and I didn't like being apart." Joaquín started shaking the cocktail, but threw in some extra moves, finishing with a twirl. "Besides, I get to be outside way more than I did when I was living out in LA. There, I was always stuck under hot lights on a soundstage. Here, it's a hot sun out on the ocean. Much better." He winked at the winker, and she blushed.

The women had looked disappointed when he mentioned his husband, but that explained Joaquín's immunity to the women who threw themselves at him. He didn't wear a ring, but maybe as a fisherman it was a danger. My father didn't wear one because of his plumbing, but he couldn't be more devoted to my mom.

"Put three olives on a pick, please," Joaquín asked. While he finished his thing with the shaker, I grabbed one of the picks—not the kind for guitars; these were little sticks with sharp points on one end—fancy plastic toothpicks really. Ours were pink, topped with a little flamingo, and I strung the olives on as Joaquín strained the drink into a martini glass.

"One dirty martini," Joaquín said with a hand flourish.

I popped open a beer and poured it into a glass, holding the glass at an angle so the beer had only a skiff of foam on the top. It was a skill I was proud of because my father had taught me when I was fourteen. Other fathers taught their daughters how to play chess. My friends knew the difference between a king and a rook. Mine made sure I knew the importance of low foam. You can guess which skill was more popular at frat parties in college.

As I distributed the drinks, I thought about Boone Slidell, my best friend since my first day of college. The promise that brought me here? I'd made it to him one night at the Italian Village's bar in downtown Chicago. We'd had so much fun that night, acting silly before his deployment to Afghanistan with the National Guard. But later that night he'd asked me, should anything happen to him on his deployment, would I come help his grandmother, Vivi. He had a caveat. I couldn't tell her he'd asked me to.

"Yes," I'd said. "Of course." We'd toasted with shots of tequila and laughter, never dreaming nine months later that my best friend in the world would be gone. Twenty-eight years old and gone. I'd gotten a leave of absence from my job as a children's librarian and had come for the memorial service, planning to stay for as long as Boone's grandmother needed me. But Vivi wasn't the bent-over, pathetic figure I'd been expecting to save. In fact, she was glaring at me now from across the room, making it perfectly clear that she neither needed nor wanted my help. I smiled at her as I went back behind the bar.

Vivi was a beautiful woman with thick silver hair and a gym-perfect body. Seventy had never looked so good. She wore gold, strappy wedge sandals that made my feet ache just looking at them, cropped white skinny jeans, and an off-the-shoulder, gauzy aqua top. I always felt a little messy when I was with her.

"A promise made is a promise kept." I could hear my dad's voice in my head as clear as if he were standing next to me. It was what kept me rooted here, even with Vivi's dismissive attitude. I'd win her over sooner or later. Few hadn't eventually succumbed to my winning personality or my big brown eyes. Eyes that various men had described as liquid chocolate, doelike, and one jerk who said they looked like mud pies after I turned him down for a date.

In my dreams, everyone succumbed to my personality. Reality was such a different story. Some people apparently thought I was an acquired taste. Kind of like ouzo, an anise-flavored aperitif from Greece, that Boone used to drink sometimes. I smiled at the memory.

"What are you grinning about?" Joaquín asked. Today he wore a neon-green Hawaiian shirt with a hot-pink hibiscus print.

"Nothing." I couldn't admit it was the thought of people succumbing to me. "Am I supposed to be wearing Hawaiian shirts to work?" I asked. He wore one every day. I'd been wearing T-shirts and shorts. No one had mentioned a dress code.

"You can wear whatever your little heart desires, as long as you don't flash too much skin. Vivi wouldn't like that." He glanced over my blue tank top and shorts.

"But you wear Hawaiian shirts every day," I said.

"Honey, you can't put a peacock in beige."

I laughed and started cutting the lemons and limes we used as garnishes. The juice from both managed to find the tiniest cut and burn in my fingers. But Vivi—don't dare put a "Miss" in front of "Vivi," despite the tradition here in the South—wasn't going to chase me away by assigning me all the menial tasks, including cleaning the toilets, mopping the floors, and cutting the fruit. I was made of tougher stuff than that and had been since I was ten. To paraphrase the Blues Brothers movie, I was "on a mission from" Boone.

"What'd those poor little limes ever do to you?"

I looked up. Joaquín stood next to me with a garbage bag in his hand and a devilish grin on his face. He'd been a bright spot in a somber time. He smiled at me and headed out the back door of the bar.

"You're cheating," Buford yelled from his table near the retractable doors. He leaped up, knocking over his chair just as Vivi passed behind him. The chair bounced into Vivi, she teetered on her heels and then slammed to the ground, her head barely missing the concrete floor. The Sea Glass wasn't exactly fancy.

Oh, no. Maybe incidents like this were why Boone thought I needed to be here. Why Vivi needed help. The man didn't notice Vivi, still on the floor. Probably didn't even realize he'd done it. Everyone else froze, while Buford grabbed the man across from him by the collar and dragged him out of his chair knocking cards off the table as he did.

I put down the knife and hustled around the bar. "Buford. You stop that right now." I used the firm voice I occasionally had to use at the library. Vivi wouldn't allow any gambling in here. Up to this point there hadn't been any trouble.

Buford let go of his friend. I kept steaming toward him. "You knocked over Vivi." I lowered my voice, a technique I'd learned as a librarian to diffuse situations. "Now, help her up and apologize."

He looked down at me, his face red. I jammed my hands on my hips and lifted my chin. He was a good foot taller than me and outweighed me by at least one hundred pounds. I stood my ground. That would teach him to mess with a children's librarian, even one on a leave of absence. I'd dealt with tougher guys than him. Okay, they had been five years old, but it still counted.

He turned to Vivi and helped her up. "I'm sorry, Vivi. How about I buy a round for the house?"

Oh, thank heavens. For a minute there, I thought he was going to punch me. Vivi looked down at her palms, red from where they'd broken her fall. "Okay. But you pull something like that again and you're banned for life."

CHAPTER 3

I expected a thanks from Vivi—that wasn't asking too much, right?—but she swept by me to the back, and I heard her office door close. Soundly. Winning her over, figuring her out for that matter, wasn't going to be easy. Joaquín had returned and looked at me, eyes wide. I took more orders and he started mixing drinks—not that there were that many people in here midafternoon. I was more of a beer and wine drinker, so I'd only made a couple of cocktails since I'd started here. And always under Joaquín's watchful eye, so I stood aside again today. Because the drinks were on Buford's tab, everyone had ordered expensive gins, bourbons, and rums. Buford complained loudly about that, but everyone ignored him.

I probably wasn't the best person to work in a bar because the smell of whiskey nauseated me. That was thanks to a bad experience in high school instigated by my two older brothers, who thought they were hilarious. They weren't. Instead of thinking about that,

I focused on Joaquín's strong hands. They were a blur of motion as he fixed the drinks. In no time, everyone was back in their seats, most facing the ocean. Except for the women at the bar, who continued to flirt with Joaquín. And Elwell, who nursed his beer.

Fans whirled and wobbled above, causing the warm ocean breeze to mingle with the arctic air blasting from air conditioners in the back of the bar. The resulting mix made it quite pleasant in here. I added lemons, limes, or cherries to garnish the drinks, as instructed by Joaquín.

"Good work, by the way," he said.

"I just stood out of your way and watched." Being praised for adding fruit to drinks was demoralizing after finishing college, getting a master's degree in library science, and working in the library full-time.

"I meant with Buford." Joaquín pointed at the man who'd knocked over Vivi.

"Vivi didn't seem to think so."

Joaquín turned his beautiful eyes to me. "She doesn't like to think she needs help. If she could run this place by herself, she would. But deep down, she's grateful."

"Yeah, deep, deep down." But it must be why Boone wanted me to come here. When we were in college, where we'd met, he spent all his holidays and summers working here. He loved this beach and his grandmother. The beach I understood. Maybe his grandmother would grow on me. Or me on her.

Elwell cocked his head toward me. The armadillo shell didn't move. "What's keeping you here?"

I guess he'd overheard my conversation with Joaquín. "I'm waiting for a part for my car." I shrugged.

"Finding parts for a vintage car isn't easy or cheap. And they take forever to arrive." It was a big fat lie. The one I'd been telling over and over. It was what convinced Vivi to let me work here after Boone's memorial service once I realized things weren't going the way I'd planned.

I'd inherited my vintage Volkswagen Beetle from my grandmother. It was actually fine, but Vivi didn't need to know that, or anyone else for that matter. "It's limping along for now, but no way would it make it all the way back to Chicago." I was almost starting to believe my cover story. I'd had to do *something* when I realized Vivi didn't want me here and Boone did. Talk about a conundrum.

Elwell studied my face, which I knew would give away nothing—*thanks, brothers.* Their years of torment turned "show no pain" into my personal motto, and had enabled me to quickly end their one-sided tickle wars when I was a kid.

I served the drinks. My last stop was at Buford and his partner's table. They were back to playing cards as if nothing had happened. I dropped off Buford's beer. His shaggy-haired partner cleared his throat and narrowed his eyes at Buford.

Buford turned to me. "My apologies." He shrugged. "I don't normally let things get to me. No hard feelings?"

"I have two brothers. I learned long ago that hard feelings are a waste of time."

Buford ducked his head. "Thanks." Then he busied himself shuffling a deck of cards.

I bused the tables, taking dirty glasses back to the kitchen behind the bar. It was more of a kitchenette

than an actual kitchen, with an industrial-strength
dishwasher and a refrigerator/freezer combination.
We didn't serve food. We left that to the Briny Pirate,
the restaurant next door, which delivered the food
here. Wow, I was already thinking of this place in
"we" terms. Well, that would be short-lived. Eventually, I'd click my heels and return home to Chicago,
just as soon as I gave Vivi the help she didn't want. As
I returned to Joaquín's side, a group of sunburned
beachgoers came in. At least the Sea Glass was never
dull.

At nine thirty I stood on the deck of the Sea Glass,
holding a broom. The last customer had left reluctantly a few minutes before. Our hours, unlike most
bars, were from eleven a.m. to nine p.m. No late-
night, wild crowds, bands, or karaoke here. Joaquín
had told me it cut down on the number of obnoxious
drunks and fights. And when Vivi's grandfather
opened the bar it mostly served fisherman. They left
by nine because they had to be up early. No one had
ever bothered to try anything different. It was fine
with me.

The Gulf stretched out before me, the half-moon
played hide-and-seek with fast-moving clouds, the
waves sucking, lapping, softly whooshing in and out.
I was antsy. I'd landed here in July, the height of the
summer tourist season, so I hadn't been able to find
a place to stay. At least no place I could afford for
long, or that was close enough that my whole "car
needs a part" story held up.

I'd spent one night in a high-end hotel, but my

savings wouldn't take very much of that. And I'd
spent one night in a dive motel. My sanity wouldn't
take much of that. It had been like a scene out of a
bad movie, only real—loud music, louder arguments,
and what sounded like a drug deal going down right
outside my door. Do I know how to live life to the
fullest or what? Two nights I'd slept in my car in
small increments in well-lit parking lots. Moving
from one lot to another in a game of keep-away, trying to stay ahead of the security guards or deputies
who might shoo me away or, even worse, arrest me
for loitering. Vivi had taken pity on me and hired
me, but I had no confidence she'd bail me out.

Okay, she probably would. But still, I had my
pride. That's why I wasn't sleeping in the parking lot
east of the Sea Glass. It would have been safer, but I
didn't want Vivi to find out about my accommoda-
tions problem, even knowing that whole pride goeth
before a fall thing. I'd been searching for an apartment, but at this time of year, most were filled and
rented on weekly rates well out of my price range.

Last night I was feeling a little desperate—more
than desperate. So I'd snuck onto Boone's boat, *Fair
Winds*, parked in the marina behind the bar. It wasn't
a huge boat—a twenty-footer with a center console.
It didn't have a cabin, but did have cushioned
benches, and at least last night I could stretch out.
But it was hot under the tarp. I'd unhooked it just
enough to squeeze through and left before dawn so
no one would see me. I planned to sleep there again
tonight.

Boone had loved that boat as much as anything.
I'd seen many a picture of it. The motor was big

enough to take the boat out on the Gulf when it was calm or to tool around Choctawhatchee Bay. Boone had wanted me to come with him to visit Vivi and the boat, but we'd never made it, and now, of course, we never would. Talk about wanting to kick myself. I knew better than to put things off. I hoped I didn't have any more lessons on that topic from the universe in the future.

Loud, angry voices from the kitchen jarred me back to the present. I could tell one voice was Vivi's. The other was male. Well, this was awkward. I clung to the broom, wondering if I should check on her or grab my purse, which was sitting on a nearby table, and make a run for it. I listened for a few minutes but couldn't hear any actual words. A door slammed, and footsteps—Vivi's—crossed the kitchen toward the bar. I started sweeping sand off the deck, listening to the whack of Vivi's wedges slapping the floor, heading toward me. If footsteps could sound angry, these certainly did. They stopped right behind me.

"I didn't realize you were still here," Vivi said. She sounded short of breath.

I quit sweeping and turned to her. Perspiration shone on her brow and upper lip. She held her shoulders stiffly, but her chest rose up and down in quick, angry pants. Vivi had a bottle of bourbon in one hand, a rocks glass in the other. I'd never seen her take a drink of anything stronger than sparkling water. She set both on the nearest table.

"Just finishing up," I said. Vivi's shirt was askew, and I wondered what had happened back there, and with whom.

"You can go."

"Okay, I'll just take the broom to the back."

"I'll do it." Vivi held out her hand until I gave her the broom.

"I need to get my purse." I pointed to one of the tables. "It's right there."

"Okay. Then go out the front. I just finished mopping the kitchen floor."

Maybe that's what caused the perspiration and short breath. But I didn't think so. I grabbed my purse. "Good night."

Vivi ignored me, pouring herself a glass of bourbon. I left, slung my purse over my shoulder, walked down to the edge of the water, and plopped down in the warm sand. By now only a few stragglers remained on the beach. Soft laughs and bits of conversation drifted around. Farther to the west, because of how the shoreline curved, I could see the lights of the high-rises in Destin. The putter of a boat's engine sounded in the harbor.

I sat for fifteen minutes, hands wrapped around my knees, wondering if I should go back to talk to Vivi about the argument I'd just overheard. What would I say? We were hardly bosom buddies. I finally got up and trekked back toward my car. Vivi sat, hand on head, looking down into an empty glass as I sneaked by the Sea Glass, hoping she wouldn't see me.

The tarp snapped open way too early on Sunday morning. Sunlight slapped my face and a soft breeze had me jumping up. I looked right into the dark green eyes of a man with too long lashes that made me envy him and a stubbled face that made me want to jump him.

"What the heck?" I asked, trying to cover how flustered I was. Working around kids all the time had taught me not to swear. I squinted toward the sun and figured it must be around seven in the morning.

"You were snoring. Of course, at first I thought a wounded animal had somehow crawled up under here."

This guy was a riot. Sure, my snoring was a legend within my family, and with two older brothers, that was an accomplishment or a curse, depending on your viewpoint. But who was this guy to point it out? "Well, obviously I'm not a wounded animal, so you can just be on your way." I shooed my hands at him.

His eyes said he didn't quite believe me, and maybe he wasn't all that wrong about the wounded part. But hey, who wasn't? I sat back on the bench I'd slept on, put on my running shoes, and grabbed my purse. My hair was probably sticking out all over the place. But I didn't care. At least, I shouldn't care. When the first thing a man knows about you is that you snore like a rusty chainsaw, the prospect of a future romance is dismal—not that I was interested, even given the earlier jumping thought. Imagine my surprise when instead of leaving, he stuck out his hand.

"Rhett B—"

"For heaven's sake, don't tell me your last name is Butler." He did bear a small resemblance to Clark Gable, who'd played Rhett Butler in the movie *Gone with the Wind.* I climbed out of the boat and snapped the tarp back into place. I hoped he didn't know Vivi and wouldn't mention I was sleeping on Boone's boat. I headed down the dock.

"And you are?" he asked. His voice sent rumbles through my stomach, or maybe I was just hungry.

"Scarlett O'Hara."

His chuckle followed me. "I won't tell Vivi you were sleeping on Boone's boat. But if you keep it up, you're going to have to explain it to me." The charming Southern drawl belied the words.

Drat, he *did* know Vivi *and* that I was on Boone's boat. I didn't break stride or hurry up, too much anyway. This time there was no following chuckle.

I walked along the marina, heading toward the small parking lot on the east side of the Sea Glass, where I'd left my car. I would drive into Destin, just to the west of here, and shower at one of the beachside free showers meant for washing off sand. It wasn't ideal, but worked well enough because it was hot out. Thankfully, my brown hair was so short it was wash and go.

As I approached the back of the Sea Glass, I saw a foot sticking out behind the dumpster that served the Briny Pirate, the Sea Glass, and this side of the marina. A gnarly-looking foot in an old black sandal. I veered over to see if it was one of our customers who was drunk or had passed out. It took me a moment to get there and another moment for me to recognize Elwell Pugh because his head was turned away from me. But he hadn't had that much to drink yesterday, had he?

"Elwell?" Then I noticed his armadillo shell hat off to one side. I took another step closer. That's when I spotted a channel knife sticking out of the other side of his neck.

CHAPTER 4

I dropped my purse, screamed, and then clapped my hands to my mouth. I bent down to retrieve my purse, which had landed perilously close to Elwell's outstretched hand. I spotted blood.

A roar filled my head. I saw multiples of Elwell. Everything dimmed. I landed on my bum and skittered backward, dragging my purse until I bumped into something. Hands grabbed me under my armpits and hauled me up. I looked over my shoulder. Rhett let me go.

"He's dead." I pointed at Elwell. "Dead. Call the police," I said. My voice shook. I pressed a hand to my stomach.

Rhett moved to my side and looked down at Elwell for a few seconds, his face creased. He took my arm and gently tugged me a few feet away, leaning me up against the back of the Sea Glass. "Are you okay?" His look was all wary concern. "Stupid question. No one could be." He pulled out his phone, watching me closely while he input a number. One longer than 911.

"Delores? This is Rhett. We've got a situation over at the Sea Glass."

Situation? I snatched the phone from him. "Delores, I don't know who the heck you are, but what 'we've' got is a dead body." I gulped in a couple of breaths. My legs suddenly seemed to give up the job they were meant to do. Rhett took the phone back from me. He leaned into me so I'd stay upright. His body warm against my cold one. He felt way better pressed up against me than I wanted him to. *Way better.*

"Yeah, that's right, there's a dead body," he said. "It's Elwell." He listened for a minute. "Okay. We'll wait here." After he hung up, Rhett turned to me. He looked so calm. Maybe too calm.

"What are you doing out here anyway?" I asked.

"You're not the only one who sleeps on a boat. Although mine is a heck of a lot more comfortable than Boone's." His green eyes stared into my brown ones. "They don't need to know I found you sleeping on Boone's boat. A stranger, someone new in town, being around with Elwell dead." He paused. "It wouldn't look good for you. Far as I could tell, you were out for a mornin' stroll. I heard you scream and came to your rescue."

I wanted to argue with the "rescued." I didn't need anyone to rescue me, but waves of emotion crashed through me. I nodded. He was probably right about the police. But why would he keep that secret for me—a stranger, as he said—when it was obvious that

Elwell had been murdered. Maybe he had a secret of his own to keep.

An hour later, I stood off to one side of the action. I guess Delores was a dispatcher because the sheriff's department personnel had shown up. Someone had handed me a bottle of water. Despite the increasing heat as the sun rose, I still shivered. Rhett was talking to a sheriff's deputy, and they both kept looking over at me, which was kind of freaking me out. Okay, really freaking me out. I was a stranger in a strange land. I remember how it worked out in the book of the same name for the alien, and it wasn't pretty. The deputy asked Rhett questions and jotted notes on a small spiral notebook. An occasional phrase drifted over.

"I heard a woman scream." They both looked over at me. "No, I've never seen her before." Rhett's voice changed on that one. His cadence quickened. It sounded like a lie to me, so surely the deputy would pick up on it, but he didn't say a word. Maybe it was the good old boy network at play, or maybe the deputy didn't notice. They obviously knew each other from the way they had greeted each other and did the man handshake hug thing. "Yeah, I've been sleeping on my boat."

I'd had numerous conversations with police officers before while working as a librarian. The library where I worked was in an urban area. Homeless people used it as a place to rest, read, or use the internet. Usually we didn't have problems, but occasionally we did. Not only with them, but with men who came in to use the computers to watch porn, nannies who got in fights at story time, and kids who wandered off. But I'd never had a conversation with law enforcement officers after finding a dead man.

While I waited, the loud voices at the bar last night kept rolling through my head. Maybe Vivi had noticed Elwell and his armadillo hat were scaring off the clientele too. Or maybe they had a history I knew nothing about. Or maybe it wasn't even Elwell she had been arguing with.

Vivi had shown up thirty minutes ago. She was all decked out, strappy sandals, carefully pressed linen pants, and hair styled so perfectly, it looked like she was ready for a photo shoot. Vivi eyed me from a distance, but the deputies wouldn't let her near me. And believe me, she'd tried.

The deputy finished up with Rhett and headed over to me. I took another shaky drink of my water. Tried to gather myself. Rhett walked off in the direction of Vivi, but she turned her back to him. He hesitated, glanced back at me, and strolled out of sight. The deputy stopped in front of me and squinted. His name tag said *Biffle*.

"You doing okay? I'm Deputy Biffle. I'm with the Walton County Sheriff's Department." Officer Biffle was a beefy guy with a blond crew cut and a broad forehead. His mirrored aviator glasses reflected my anxious, round face. My short hair stuck up in all kinds of directions and my brown eyes looked scared. But his voice was kind and I relaxed just a little.

"Considering the situation, I guess I'm okay." I

tried to shut down the image of the knife sticking out of Elwell's neck, but didn't have much luck.

"Name?"

"That's Elwell Pugh." I tipped my head toward the dumpster.

"Your name?"

"Oh, sorry. Of course. I'm rattled. Beyond rattled actually." When he didn't say more, I realized I still hadn't answered his question. "Chloe. Chloe Jackson."

"Why don't you tell me what happened?"

"Well, I don't know what happened to Elwell. Not specifically. It looks like someone stabbed him," I think he rolled his eyes behind those mirrored aviators, "with a channel knife." *A channel knife is a must-have tool for any bartender that's used for making garnishes.* Joaquín's voice rolled through my head. Information he'd given me two days ago. Why was I thinking *that* at a time like *this*?

"Why don't you tell me about finding him?"

"Yes." I really needed to get Deputy Biffle on my side. I remembered I was living in the land of yes, ma'ams, and no, sirs. I'd better follow protocol. "Yes, sir." I started at the point when I'd noticed Elwell's foot by the dumpster and how Rhett had happened along. My heart pounded a little harder with the omission of sleeping on the boat and talking to Rhett.

"What were you doing out here?" he asked.

"Morning run." Thud, thud, thud went my heart. I felt like the man in the opening of Poe's "Tell-Tale Heart"—"nervous—very, very dreadfully nervous." But why should I mention it? My sleeping on the boat didn't seem relevant to Elwell's murder; it was embarrassing, and maybe trespassing. "I work at the Sea Glass. I ran on the beach and walked back along the harbor to cool down." It was true yesterday. I hoped the truth part came through and the nervous part would be chalked up to finding a dead body. Every detective novel I'd ever read said to keep your answers short, so I did. I wished he didn't have the aviators on so I could get more of a read of what he was thinking.

"You always run with your purse?"

He was observant. I'd slung it cross-body style after I'd picked it up. "Not always. I was hoping to grab some breakfast somewhere." Thank heavens I had running shoes on. At least they lent some plausibility to my story.

He jotted down notes. "How well do you know Elwell?"

"I don't really know him."

Officer Biffle looked up from his notebook.

"Elwell hangs out at the Sea Glass sometimes. He was in the bar yesterday, and I asked Joaquín—he's the bartender—why Elwell was wearing an armadillo on his head. I thought it was strange, but I'm new to the area, so maybe not." I didn't want to seem judgmental.

"It's strange."

I ran through my few observations. I left out the part about hearing Vivi argue with a man. I didn't know whether it was Elwell. Well, not for sure anyway. "Do you think it was a robbery?" That would be better—not for Elwell of course, what with him being dead and all—but for Vivi.

"We don't make snap judgments about murders."

"Good to know."

"I'll need your contact details," he said.

Oh, sugar. I gave him my cell phone number, hoping that would be enough. It wasn't.

"What's your address?" he asked after he wrote down my number.

"You can find me at the Sea Glass." I waved a hand toward it.

"I need the address. Of where you're staying."

People around here spoke more slowly than they did in Chicago. But his words were so slow it was obvious he thought I was an idiot.

"I've been moving around. It's tourist season and hard to find a place to stay. One that I can afford anyway." Maybe I *was* an idiot—I wasn't even sure Vivi was going to pay me beyond the tips I made. She'd made it clear she didn't want me around. I saw a twitch of his lips. Not the kind that foreshadowed a smile, but the kind that meant someone was angry. My oldest brother was the master of the twitch, and every part of me wanted to run like I had as a kid, but in this case I managed to stay put. Bolting wouldn't go well for me. I gave him the address of the two hotels I'd stayed at. Didn't say I hadn't been at either last night or the two nights before that. He grimaced when I mentioned the low-rent one.

"Not very safe," he said.

"I know, sir. I'm continuing my search for an apartment."

He let it go after that. Thank heavens.

"Let me know if you think of anything else." Biffle whipped out a card and handed it to me.

"Yes, sir." He turned and almost ran over Vivi. I hadn't noticed her approach because I'd been concentrating on Officer Biffle's reflective lenses the whole time. I looked around for Rhett, but he was long gone apparently. My hormones were sad, but my brain did a cheer. He didn't look like a killer, but then neither had Ted Bundy—a good-looking serial killer who had committed murders right here in the Florida Panhandle. I loved true crime in book form and on TV, which had come back to haunt me the two nights I'd slept in my car. But being involved with a real-life death I could do without. I'm sure Elwell would be the first to agree with me on that.

Biffle nodded to Vivi, skirted around her, and headed to his patrol car. I guess that meant I was free to go unless Vivi had something to say to me.

"Vivi, are you all right?" Wade Thomas rushed over to her. He owned the Briny Pirate, the restaurant next door to the Sea Glass. Not only owned it, but was the chef too, and made the best gumbo east of New Orleans—at least that's what his menu said. I hadn't had a chance to try it yet. Wade gripped Vivi's arms, staring into her eyes.

"Let's go get some coffee," Wade said.

Vivi took another look at me before she smiled at Wade. What the heck was she looking at? Hadn't she ever seen someone with messy hair before? I stepped back so they could go around me, worried thoughts moving like a school of fish through my mind. Vivi looked as put together as ever as she linked arms with Wade—not like she'd been standing around in the increasingly hot weather. Not at all like a woman who'd argued with and killed someone last night.

Not that I'd run into a lot—or any—women who had killed someone the night before. Who was I to say what they looked like?

Was I really wondering if Vivi had killed Elwell? Boone's beloved grandmother? The sweet old woman I'd moved down here to help? Well, that was the whole point, wasn't it? Vivi wasn't sweet or so old. She certainly wasn't frail. Physically, she could have done it. But heck, so could I. Or most of the patrons I'd seen at the Sea Glass. Just because Vivi argued with someone last night, it didn't make her a killer. I needed to clear my head. I needed to run.

CHAPTER 5

I headed to my car and drove to Destin, wanting to put some space between me and the dumpster behind the Sea Glass. I parked at the Crab Trap, a restaurant and bar at James Lee Park on a beautiful, wide stretch of beach. I switched to an old pair of running shoes and headed west on the beach. My brothers always teased me about my running. It had started as a way to get away from them when I was five, and as I grew older, I realized it was a way to get away from almost everything. This morning it was a way to try to unsee Elwell's corpse. It didn't take me long to figure out running wasn't working.

My legs started aching not too long into my run. I wasn't used to running in the sand, but I pushed on. There was some chub rub, as my brothers called it, going on with my thighs. I wasn't one of those lanky runner types. Most people tried to cover their surprise when I said I ran regularly. I was a basset hound born to a family of whippets. Back in the family history somewhere, there must be a sturdy plowman whose genes were passed along to me. *Thanks a lot, dude.*

Eventually, the tang of salt air, the cries of gulls, and the grace of the pelicans skimming the surf soothed me. Colorful beach umbrellas stood at attention in front of the condos I passed. Rows of chairs sat under them, two by two. The sun smacked me like someone had a magnifying glass on a grasshopper. I wasn't the only runner out here and I did the chin lift at people as I went by them. Fifteen minutes later, I turned around at what I'd heard the locals call the Old Pier. All that was left of it were a few wooden posts standing firm out in the water.

When I returned to the Crab Trap, I grabbed my toiletries, some clean clothes, an apple, and a bottle of water from my car. After I showered and dressed in the bathroom, I sat on a picnic table under a wooden pavilion and ate my apple.

I glanced around, taking in the people laying out beach towels and the gentle lapping water. It looked like paradise. But it didn't feel that way to me. What *was* I doing here? Boone. My heart clinched again at the loss of him. I missed him. Six months ago, his unit had been attacked while they were out on patrol. Boone hadn't been found, but they also hadn't found his remains. A buddy in his unit had called me to give me the news. Boone had talked a lot about me to him, and when Boone was still alive, the three of us had video chatted several times. Boone's friend had tried to reassure me. Told me maybe Boone had gotten lost in the melee and he'd turn back up. They were looking for him. But I knew in my heart at that moment Boone was dead.

I'd spent the first month after he went missing crying. Pulling it together when I was at the library with kids. Their innocent, happy faces probably saved me from a complete shutdown. With time, I realized I had to live a good life for both of us. However, being here in the Panhandle of Florida, in a place I knew Boone loved, stirred up a lot of emotions.

In some ways being here was easier, because at home everything reminded me of Boone—the bars and restaurants we'd gone to, Wrigley Field, where we watched the Cubs, the Navy Pier, where we walked and talked. At home when I had closed my eyes, I could picture him on the other end of the couch reading, chatting, watching movies with me.

Once I'd heard they'd found Boone's remains and set the burial service, I'd packed up and headed down here to pay my respects and fulfill my promise. Any other time in my adult life, if I'd found a dead person, Boone would have been the first person I would have called. Now I wasn't sure who to talk to. My parents would freak out. My brothers would be driving down here to pick me up. As much as they tormented me growing up, they'd also protected me even when I didn't think I needed protecting. Trust me, Jake Hawkensbury would never forget the night he brought me home after curfew. I shuddered at that memory. It was weeks before anyone asked me out after that incident.

I dialed Rachel, my best friend and roommate in Chicago.

"Chloe!!! I was just going to call you. I have fantastic news." Rachel sounded giddy, which was unlike her. She was a serious girl, a med student at North-western. It's why we were a good team. I got Rachel out of her shell, and she tempered my I'll-try-anything streak.

It made me smile to hear her happy voice. "What's going on?"

"Ashar asked me to marry him last night."

I was stunned. They'd only been dating for nine months. He was just . . . so . . . wrong for her. Too handsome. Big ego. Thought because he worked for the Cubs, he was God's gift. But I couldn't say any of this to her, certainly not now. "Tell me all about it. Every detail." If Rachel was happy, I would be happy for her even if it gave me ulcers. We'd met in high school and she'd always been there for me.

"He proposed during the seventh-inning stretch. We were sitting behind the Cubs dugout. Ashar leaped up on it, grabbed my hand, and pulled me up with him. I thought he'd gone mad." Her laugh tinkled across the phone line. "Then he got down on one knee and whipped out the biggest diamond I've ever seen. It was all on the jumbotron. Everyone cheered for us. And then the Cubs won. It was the perfect evening."

"If only they showed the games down here. I would have seen it."

"I'll send you a link so you can watch. You'll be my maid of honor, won't you?"

"Absolutely! I'd be honored—forgive the pun. Did you set a date?"

"Not an exact date, but sometime next winter, before spring training starts."

"That makes perfect sense."

Rachel paused. "Chloe . . ."

"What?" Was she going to confess some doubt? How could she say no when Ashar had asked her in such a public way?

"Ashar wants to move in right away. And because you're away . . ."

I was a bit surprised that Ashar would want to leave his shiny penthouse for the charming old building we lived in. But it was walking distance to Wrigley Field. "Of course," I said. Rachel's grandmother owned the apartment and I paid rent to Rachel—a much-reduced rent by Chicago standards. I'd always known I couldn't live there forever. "That makes sense."

"Ashar wondered if we could put your things in storage so he can convert your room into his man cave."

Already? I'd left most of my belongings in Chicago. "I won't be able to get back up there to pack. At least not for a few weeks."

"I'll pack for you. If you don't mind."

"Of course, not" I chirped. At least I hoped I sounded chirpy. Peppy. Maid of honor-y. I tried to put myself in her shoes. Madly in love. Wanting to move on to a new phase in her life. I'd kick me out too. "My parents have a storage unit and I'll ask one of my brothers to move my stuff once it's packed." I didn't have that much because the place had been furnished with Rachel's grandmother's things.

"Thanks for understanding. You're the best. Hey, why did you call?"

I couldn't tell her about finding Elwell when she was so happy. "I must have just sensed you had something to tell me." We hung up a few minutes later.

* * *

My thoughts turned back to Elwell. I didn't know that much about him, so I looked him up on my phone. He was the president of the Emerald Cove Chamber of Commerce. *Really?* He was supposed to be supporting local businesses, not scaring customers away by acting crazy. Could that be a motive for murder? There wasn't much else about him online. Nothing about his murder, but it had only happened a few hours ago, so that wasn't too surprising.

I headed back to my car. Maybe the mindless work at the Sea Glass would help, or maybe I'd hear something that would relieve my worries about Vivi. Because as much as I loved Boone, I couldn't imagine working for a murderer.

CHAPTER 6

That evening at closing, Joaquín lounged against the backside of the bar watching me attack a stubborn stain on the wood. He'd just closed the sliders and locked up.

"What did that stain do to you? Yesterday it was chopping the fruit, today this."

"It had the nerve to appear on Vivi's bar." I'd been thinking about my run-in with Rhett, finding Elwell, and Vivi's argument with a man last night. I attacked the spot again. "Do you know a Rhett B—"

"Rhett Barnett? Sure do, but don't let Vivi hear you saying his name in here."

Hmmm. Rhett had made it sound like he was on speaking terms with Vivi, though she did give him the cold shoulder earlier. "Why not?"

"The Slidells and the Barnetts make the Montagues and Capulets look like family friends."

"Shakespeare?" I asked.

"Just 'cause I live in the South and fish don't mean

I don't know nothin'." He said it with a fake drawl heavy with sarcasm.

"That's not what I meant to imply." Or had it been? Did I have some teensy prejudices against Southern people that up until this point I didn't realize? "I'm sorry." Joaquín was the only person who was halfway friendly to me here. I couldn't lose him as a potential friend. I needed my Scarecrow.

Joaquín raised an eyebrow. "Okay, then. By the way, the stain's been gone for a good minute. You can quit scrubbing."

I looked down, and he was right. At least I'd accomplished something today, even if it was only removing a stain. "Where's Vivi?" She'd been in this morning, but took off when Joaquín showed up at one.

"She's planning a memorial for Elwell with the other heritage businesses."

"The heritage businesses?" I asked. "What are they?"

"Any business that's been open since 1950 or before. You go back much further than that and this was just a spit of land with a couple of sandy roads leading to the beach. Then the fishing village popped up, and more people starting moving here."

"So which businesses are the heritage ones?"

"Here, of course, and the Briny Pirate. The Hickle glass-bottom boat, the Redneck Rollercoaster, the Emerald Cove fishing boat charter, and Russo's Grocery Store. They've been passed down from generation to generation."

"Most of those places are stops on the Redneck

Rollercoaster." So was the Sea Glass. I had picked up a brochure, but hadn't gone for a ride yet. Why it was called that when it was a trolley that took tourists to several local historic spots, the beach, and, of course, here, remained a mystery to me.

"You done?" Joaquín asked. "I have an early start tomorrow."

"I am." I hoped it wasn't too late to find a motel room somewhere. I needed a good night's sleep and a real shower. Maybe even room service. It sounded like heaven. My morning could be summed up as one of my favorite children's books: *Chloe and the Terrible, Horrible, No Good, Very Bad Morning*. Okay, so that wasn't quite the title, but close enough. If I stayed in a motel and Officer Biffle came back around, I'd have proof I'd stayed somewhere.

Joaquín slid a dolphin key ring with keys on it across the bar to me.

"What's this?" I asked. I couldn't imagine that Vivi wanted me to have the keys to the bar.

"It's the keys to Boone's place."

I frowned. Boone had lived in Chicago, not more than two blocks from me. Was this Vivi's way of telling me to get out? "Boone's place?"

"Yes. Vivi bought it for him years ago."

I stared at Joaquín. "Boone rented his place in Chicago." I would have known if he'd owned it.

"Not his place in Chicago. His home here."

Boone had a home here? It had been a long day. Rhett had scared the bejesus out of me early this morning, and then I found Elwell dead. Followed by

Rachel's big engagement-and-moving announcement. Throw in worrying about Vivi and working. I was starting to wonder if I was hearing things.

"Are you okay?" Joaquín raised his eyebrows in alarm.

The jury was out on that one. Boone having a place here was news to me. "Does she need me to go over there and clean or something?"

"You can stay there. I didn't know you'd been sleeping in your car."

I blushed. This was so humiliating. I lifted my chin. "I don't need charity. I'm staying at a motel tonight, and I'll find a permanent place in the morning." If I could. It was the height of tourist season, when condo rentals were as rare as snowflakes and more expensive than a private yacht. If not, maybe I'd buy a tent and camp somewhere. Although none of my childhood camping experiences had been all that great. I'd never been sure which I'd been more afraid of, a wandering bear or a psychopath I was always sure was hiding out in the woods. Needless to say, when we'd camped, I hadn't slept well.

"How did you know I was sleeping in my car?"

"I didn't. You just told me you had been."

Great. First I was humiliated and now I was tricked. "But why would you even ask me that?"

"Vivi handed me the keys and asked me to give them to you. I figured something was up."

Vivi did that? Life was full of surprises. She must have heard my conversation with Deputy Biffle and figured it out. Or Rhett had called a cease-fire to the feud long enough to tell Vivi he had found me sleeping on the boat.

"Why didn't she just give them to me herself?"

Joaquín sighed. "As I've told you, she has a good heart. It seems like it was dislike at first sight with you two, so I've become the middleman."

"That's not true. I don't dislike her." Was it? Maybe I resented that she wasn't who I thought she'd be. In my head, I'd pictured swooping in to save the day. It had been my noble cause since the day I'd heard Boone had gone missing. His grandma would be grateful. I'd be lauded. The reality was so vastly different from the notion.

"I'm fine." I pushed the keys back to Joaquín. My parents had taught me to stand on my own two feet. Moving into Boone's place seemed like taking charity.

He pushed the keys back to me. "It's what Boone would have wanted."

Boone. Of course that was true. Boone would have given his left arm to someone if they'd needed it. It's why he'd joined the National Guard.

Joaquín scribbled something on a piece of paper and handed it to me. "Boone's address."

I curled my hand around the keys. "Thank you."

"Don't thank me. Thank Vivi."

Maybe this could be a new beginning for Vivi and me. "I will."

Fifteen minutes later, I rounded one of the coastal lakes, drove down a long, tree-lined driveway, and parked in front of a one-story, concrete-block house that crouched on top of a sand dune. There were tall pine trees on the right side of the house. To the left, there was a patch of brush, scrub oak, magnolia, and then, farther off, more tall pines. I glimpsed the lights of another house through the trees. I felt like Amanda in the very first Goosebumps book by R. L. Stine, when she'd thought, "It's so dark."

I grabbed a suitcase and climbed a set of rickety wooden steps. I had to use the flashlight on my phone to see. I could hear the slap of waves, but nothing else. No cars. No sirens. No conversations. It was creepy for a city girl like me. The soft tang of salt-water mingled with the fresh pine scent as I un-locked the heavy wooden door. It complained a bit as I forced it open. I flipped on a light, took two steps inside, and stopped. The whole back side of the house was glass windows and one door looking out on . . . was that the *Gulf*? Wow. If the yellow brick road had ended here, Dorothy might have kept Kansas in her rearview mirror.

I set down my suitcase, closed and locked the front door, skirted the furniture, and unlatched the flimsy lock of the aluminum door at the back. It led to a screened-in porch that ran across the entire back of the house. The sound of the Gulf was louder here. Warm, damp air surrounded me. Even in the dark I could make out the white beach and the black Gulf beyond it.

Why hadn't Boone ever mentioned this place? I frowned and thought back over conversations about

his visits here. Remembered something about Vivi
liking her privacy, so he crashed in a family place.
He'd never mentioned it was his or that it was on the
beach.

I crossed the porch to a screen door with another
flimsy lock. I unlocked it and went out onto a set of
three steps that led to a wooden walkway. It went over
the sea grass on the dune down to the beach. The
Gulf was inky black, calm. Beautiful. After I stood for
a few minutes, I went back in, turned on more lights,
and began looking around. The house was small, but
someone had spent time updating it so the main
room was an open living, kitchen, and dining room.
There was a bedroom and bath on either side. Each
room had a ceiling fan, and I flipped them on. The
air smelled a bit musty. I found a thermostat and
turned it down so the air conditioner kicked on. As
much as I didn't like manufactured cold air, without
it, mold would soon take over. *And as a plumber's
daughter, I know: better cold than mold.*

I chose the bedroom that had sliding glass doors
out to the screened porch and tossed my suitcase on
the bed before heading to the kitchen. I opened the
refrigerator. A twelve-pack of Boone's favorite beer
was inside. I grabbed a bottle. It felt like he was wel-
coming me. I found an opener in the drawer,
popped the top off, and wandered back out to the
porch. It was furnished with a wicker chaise lounge,
couch, rocker, and coffee table. The chaise and
couch had lime-green cushions. On the other side of
the porch was a wooden porch swing. I took a swig of
my beer as I settled on a wicker couch that creaked
and popped.

"Thank you, Boone." I held up my beer in a toast. "I'll keep my promise, even though Vivi doesn't want me here." I looked out at the Gulf. "Vivi doesn't need me either. I wish I would have asked you why you wanted me here when I had the chance."

CHAPTER 7

The sky was just getting light when I woke up on Monday morning. I'd left the slider ajar so the waves would lull me to sleep. I'd stuck a yardstick in the tracks to keep it from opening too far, so I wouldn't have to worry about being murdered in my sleep. You can take a girl out of the city but . . . well, you know. Anyway, the open slider worked great, and I'd slept better than I had since I'd arrived. Of course, sleeping in a bed rather than on a boat or in my car didn't hurt. Considering what had happened to Elwell yesterday, I was surprised I'd slept at all.

I threw on jogging shorts and a sports bra, trotted down the stairs to the beach, and headed west toward the Sea Glass. I wondered how close it was as the pelican flies. To get here last night I'd had to follow the road that skirted the other side of the lake. I had a feeling it was much closer this way. The beach between Boone's house and the Sea Glass was state land protected from development, according to a small sign. The lake and a stand of tall pines must be part of the preserve too.

The sand down by the water's edge was almost as solid as concrete and much easier to run on than the soft sand above. My feet seemed to slap out Elwell Pugh, Elwell Pugh. Sanderlings—small shore birds— darted away, escaping me and the waves as I ran along. They pecked at the sand for something too tiny for me to see even when I stopped and ran in place to watch.

I passed the lake, seventy-five yards, three-quarters of a football field to my right. Compared to Lake Michigan, this was a pond that was given the grander name of lake. It was surrounded by pines on three sides. Giants protecting lily pad–covered water. Monet probably would have liked to paint the scene given the chance. I hoped there weren't any alligators in the lake. I glanced over, didn't see anything, but sped up a bit anyway, just in case any were submerged, waiting for someone like me to pass by.

Ten minutes later, I was in front of the Sea Glass. It would be fun to run to work if the weather wasn't so hot. I was already dripping with sweat. From what the locals had told me, it would cool off around October, but I would be back in Chicago by then. My boss had allowed me to take a leave of absence, but it wouldn't last forever. We'd left it vague—a few weeks.

Ack, and I'd have to find a new apartment. Chicago was so expensive, it wouldn't be easy to find something close to my library on what I made. I supposed I could live out in the suburbs in one of my brother's basements for a bit if worse came to worse.

They both had lovely wives and kids, but the commute would be awful. And my brothers still treated me like I was nine.

I kept running. Fishing boats dotted the horizon, glowing pink in the early light. I wondered if Joaquín was out there. I glanced toward the harbor. I couldn't see Boone's boat because the Briny Pirate and the Sea Glass blocked my view.

Rhett could be back there. Oh, I was curious about him—in a curiosity-killed-the-cat kind of way that probably meant trouble for me. I'd been down that road before with a handsome man. After I'd been dumped, I had ended up engaged to a very nice but very boring man. Then I had come to my senses. In fact, Boone helped me come to my senses. I'd broken off our engagement, but I'd hurt the man deeply.

I didn't want to go through that kind of drama again any time soon, not as the dumper or the dumpee, so I'd stay far away from Rhett. Although a little flirting wouldn't hurt, would it? I wasn't going to be around *that* long. No chance of getting my heart broken because I didn't give it easily anymore. I rolled my eyes at myself. So much for being strong.

I came to the small pass that led from the ocean to the inlet behind the Sea Glass. This was nothing like the deeper, wider East Pass in Destin I'd heard about at the bar. I had quickly learned that people talked a lot in bars. While libraries aren't the quiet places they once were, they had nothing on a bar. Liquor, loose lips, and all that.

I turned back to the east and decided to run along

the harbor to check out the boats to see if I could figure out which one was Rhett's. See? Cat—curiosity—
sometimes I couldn't help myself. I powered my way
through the soft sand between the water's edge and
the cement walkway that ran along the marina. Once
on the walkway, I slowed my pace so I could read the
names of the boats—*Fish You Were Here, Sea Who Laughs
Last, Sail and Fair Well, Tuna the Music Up, The Codfather.*
It didn't take long to realize that unless Rhett was
standing on his boat waving at me, I wouldn't be able
to figure out which one was his.

Also, a lot of the slips were empty. Dawn was prime
fishing time because that's when the fish themselves
were feeding. The boats still at dock ran the gamut of
small fishing boats like Boone's to sailboats to cabin
cruisers. The big fishing operations were over in Destin Harbor.

I shuddered as I came along the dumpster behind
the Sea Glass. At least it was free of bodies this morning. I stopped while I sucked in gulps of humid air
and looked around for security cameras. Maybe that
would give some insight into what happened yesterday. There was one behind the Briny Pirate and one
on the back of the Sea Glass. Both looked weathered,
like they'd been there a long time. The one on the
Sea Glass pointed straight down. It wasn't going to
help anyone. I hoped the sheriff's department would
find Elwell's killer quickly. Up until yesterday morning, this place had seemed so peaceful after Chicago.
Almost innocent.

The back door of the Sea Glass popped open. Vivi
came out. All dressed and decked out at this hour of

the morning. Her gold flats even matched her gold purse. And here I was in an old sports bra, covered in sweat, with my hair sticking to my skull. Nothing like impressing the new boss. She looked surprised to see me, but covered it quickly.

"Here," she said. Vivi tossed me a set of keys. "Open up at eleven and do the best you can until I get back or Joaquín shows up."

The best I could? Was she serious? If someone wanted something fancier than a beer, I'd be toast. "Where are you going to be?"

Vivi gave me a look that said *mind your own business* and walked to the parking lot. I watched as she climbed into a sleek, silver Mercedes. Then I remembered I hadn't thanked her for the keys to Boone's place.

I raced over to the side of Vivi's car. She rolled down the darkly tinted window. "What?"

"Thank you for the keys to Boone's place. Let me know how much I owe you for rent."

Vivi looked at me, opened her mouth, buzzed up the window, and peeled out of the parking lot.

I looked after her for a moment before heading down to the water to run back to Boone's. What the heck did that reaction mean? Trying to figure out Vivi was harder than running in soft sand.

About the time I came even with the lake, the sun burst over the horizon. There were just enough clouds that the beauty of it made me catch my breath. I slowed down and decided to walk the rest of the way back to cool down. I looked for shells, as did other people, but shells were few and far between here. And I hadn't seen a bit of sea glass, which made me wonder how the bar got its name. Two sandbars stretched along the beach in this area, which meant most of the shells were on the other side of the second sandbar. Maybe sea glass was there too. That's also where sharks were occasionally spotted. One of these days I'd swim out there, but not now. Dawn meant feeding time for sharks too, and I didn't want to be a shark's breakfast.

Once I got back to Boone's place, I noticed there were surfboards, paddleboards, beach chairs, and a kayak tucked under the elevated screened porch. Oh good, toys to play with. I hauled the rest of my things out of my car and into the house, along with a bag of assorted snacks I'd purchased a couple of days before. I grabbed another apple, took it out to the porch, and flopped onto the wicker chaise. Then I looked up how to make different tropical drinks on my phone and prayed that Joaquín would show up early.

I unlocked the back door to the Sea Glass just after ten. It was weird to be here alone because the place was usually so full of life. That made me think of Elwell again. I stopped to listen for a moment. The refrigerator hummed, but I didn't hear anything else. No one was waiting around to kill me too. Faint smells of beer, lemon cleaner, and salt air combined in a not-unpleasant scent. I flipped on lights, headed through the small kitchen, out to the bar. The water was dazzling today. People had already set up umbrellas on the beach, and a Frisbee game was in full swing.

I'd never opened before and I had no idea what I was supposed to do, setup wise. Getting the register up and running seemed like a good first step. I flipped it on, and a start screen came up, asking for a password. Great. I remembered Joaquín had restarted it the other day as I watched. Concentrating on that image, I gave it a couple of tries. It bloomed to life after I'd typed in a combination of the words "Sea Glass" and Boone's birthday. This system not only allowed us to ring up orders, but tracked everything from our hours to repeat customers to sales figures.

An array of folders came up. One said "security." I hesitated for a moment before opening the folder. *You are not being nosy. You are being helpful.* I repeated that to myself a few times. I didn't believe it for a minute. There were two cameras. One in here that I hadn't noticed hidden in a corner. It showed the cash register and the interior of the bar.

I glanced over my shoulder and spotted the camera in the shadows of the back right corner. At this very moment, it was recording me opening this folder. It took all my strength not to wave to it. Hopefully, Vivi only watched the recordings if there was some reason to. But just in case, I moved my body until it blocked what I was doing on-screen.

The other camera was the one I'd noticed that pointed straight down at the ground. The picture was cloudy. The lens was probably coated with salt spray. I'd noticed since I'd arrived in Emerald Cove that I had to clean off my windshield more frequently because of the salt air. The shot didn't even show the area near the back door, which I figured was what it was supposed to do.

Each day seemed to have its own file within the folder. I clicked on the one for the day before yesterday, hoping I could find proof that Vivi was arguing with someone other than Elwell. That way, if the police came after her, she'd have proof . . . of what? Proof she was angry with someone else? Proof she had a temper? I shrugged. Would that be better than nothing—or her arguing with Elwell?

But that was not to be. The camera pointed straight down. I kept watching, hoping it had captured something. Zippo. The camera occasionally moved, like the wind pushed it a bit, but that was it. Nothing to help Vivi. Then again, there was nothing to hurt her either.

CHAPTER 8

At eleven fifteen someone pounded on the back door. I had everything like Joaquín always did. Fruit was cut and out, napkins and stirrers replenished. Glasses at the ready. I was ready, willing, and fingers and toes crossed hopefully able.

One of the regulars, a man who'd ignored me up to this point, stood outside. "Why's the door locked?" he asked as he breezed past me through the kitchen and into the bar. *Vivi!* She usually left the back door unlocked and regulars used it all the time. Easy enough for one of them to grab a channel knife on their way in or out. Heck, it didn't even have to be a regular. Anyone could have slipped in and out unnoticed. Especially because the camera wasn't working.

The man slid into a seat midway between the doors that opened to the beach and the bar. His back to the wall. His Florida Gators hat tipped back. Another regular, a woman with gray, permed hair, who'd come in the front, sat opposite him on the other side of the bar. I grabbed a notebook and approached the woman first.

"What can I help you with?" I asked.

She looked askance at me. Her skin defined the term "leathery." "Help me with?" There was a chuckle in her voice.

Oops. The "help you with" came from working at the library. But before I could correct it and ask her what she'd like to drink, she was talking.

"Well, a lot of things. My car needs vacuuming, my knee aches, and my grown kids won't move out." She paused. "Can you help me with any of that?"

Never count out a librarian when you needed something. "You might try drinking a combination of apple cider vinegar, honey, and cinnamon for the aching knees." Librarians had a lot of aches and pains from all the standing, sitting, and squatting that took place with finding and reshelving books. "I have a coupon for a free vacuuming with car wash I can give you. But you're on your own with the kids. If a drink would help, I can handle that." I hoped.

She laughed. "I'll take you up on that coupon. And a mimosa would be a great start. Thanks."

"One mimosa coming up." That I could do. I'd attended many a brunch in Chicago, where all the mimosas you could drink were included in the price. I walked over to the man.

"What can I get you to drink?"

"No offers of help for me?" He looked dead serious.

"It depends on what you need."

"I need a drink. Why else would I come in here?"

I could think of a lot of reasons—to hang out with friends, to enjoy the view, to look at Joaquín. I kept my opinions to myself. "What would you like?"

"I'll have an old-fashioned."

I waited for him to go on, pen poised. I looked up when he didn't say anything else. He stared at me. "An old-fashioned what?" I asked.

"It's a drink. An old-fashioned." He said it slowly, like I wasn't too bright. It seems like that had been happening a lot lately. "Where's Vivi and Joaquín?"

As if I knew. "Fishing and out getting things for El-well's memorial." That sounded good. "I'll get that drink for you."

I hurried behind the bar, grabbed my phone, and did a quick search of how to make an old-fashioned. I found a brief history, which I knew I should ignore but scanned quickly. I blame the librarian side of my personality. I'd been curious as a kid, to my detriment sometimes.

The word "cocktail" dated back to 1776 and supposedly came about when a woman in New York ran out of wooden stirrers and grabbed the feather of a cock's tail to use instead. Ack. That sounded disgusting. The old-fashioned was considered a classic drink, and there was some argument about whether fruit should be included and muddled, meaning you pressed the fresh ingredients—like herbs or fruit—against the sides or bottom of the glass to release the flavors. As much as I wanted to keep reading, I needed to skip ahead to the actual making instead of muddling along here.

I found the lumps of sugar and dropped one into the bottom of a rocks glass, which I just learned was also called an old-fashioned glass. I studied the liquor—or spirits, as Joaquín called them—behind the bar. Instead of the usual shelving, Vivi had the liquor in various open-fronted, staggered wooden cabinets that gave the place a homey feel. I finally found the Angostura bitters, whatever they were, and crushed the sugar and bitters together as instructed. I added two ounces of whiskey and gave it a stir. Then I garnished, as directed, with a lemon peel twist, orange slice, and maraschino cherry. It looked pretty. I was quite proud of myself.

I whipped together the mimosa, put both drinks on a tray, and delivered them, ladies first. The two customers lifted their drinks. I think I saw the man wink.

"To Elwell. May he rest in peace," the woman said.

"Unlikely. But I'll drink to that," he said.

Both took a drink and neither spit them out. Woohoo. Success. I wanted to hear whether they were going to say anything else about Elwell, so I started straightening some of the many pictures that lined the walls. Some were old advertisements. Lots of photos—many of which were black and white. Most didn't need straightening. I turned my back to the customers in an attempt to look like I wasn't eavesdropping.

"Why don't you think he'll rest in peace?" she asked.

"Too ornery. Caused too many problems while he was here." He paused, maybe took a drink. "A man must have to pay up at some point."

I took a closer look at the photo in front of me. Black and white. A young Vivi and Elwell. They looked to be in their late teens, but sometimes I found it hard to tell how old people are in old photos. They stood on the beach in swimwear, arms slung around each other. Vivi's head was thrown back, laughing. A young woman stood off to the side, arms crossed and glaring.

"Well, aren't you philosophical today, and you haven't even finished your first drink of the day," the woman said.

"Who says this is my first drink?" the man replied.

I turned to them. "This photo looks like Vivi and Elwell." The woman got up and came over to me. The man just swiveled on his barstool and squinted.

"That's them," he said. He turned back to his drink.

"High school sweethearts," the woman said. "They had a bad breakup while Vivi was in college."

"Really?" I asked. Could their argument—if it was them arguing—have had something to do with their past? More likely it had to do with him wearing that weird armadillo hat. I couldn't be the only one who'd noticed it was scaring away customers. Or was it some combination of the past and present? "How bad was their breakup?"

"So bad that it's amazing they were ever in the same room again."

Interesting. Yet Elwell had married someone else— he wore a wedding band—and hung around in the bar. Even more astonishing was that Vivi let him. She wasn't one to tolerate anyone's bull as far as I could tell. There was that old saying that time heals all wounds. Maybe time had healed theirs.

The woman went back to her seat, so I headed back to the bar. I took another peek at the history of the old-fashioned. In 1806 a cocktail was considered a drink with liquor, sugar, water, and bitters. *1806!* Jefferson was president. Cocktails had been around a long time.

I checked on my two customers. "How's every-thing?" I asked the man.

"I've had worse," he said.

Deflated, I turned to the woman. She glanced at the man. "Mine's perfect. Not watered down with too much orange juice like so many places."

"Thank you," I said.

"And 'I've had worse' is high praise from that cranky Yankee," she said. Loud enough for him to hear. I gave her a quick smile. "His forefathers left New England and came down here in the eighteen hundreds for the fishing."

I nodded politely.

"His family has been here longer than most. But somehow you can take a cranky Yankee out of New England . . ."

"But you can't take the cranky out of the Yankee," he finished for her. "Heard it a million times from you, old woman."

"And you'll hear it a million more, *old* man," she said back.

He looked at me. "At least you didn't muddle the fruit. It's an atrocity to call it an old-fashioned when people do that."

Well, my lack of muddling experience had worked well in this case.

Thirty minutes later, a group of college-aged girls stumbled in. It looked like they'd either been out all night or gotten an early start. I wasn't sure what the policy was for serving people who looked tipsy. There must be Florida laws about that, but up until now I'd just done as I was told. No decision-making necessary. I guess I'd have to wing it until Joaquín showed up.

One of the girls wore a tiara with a wedding veil attached. It sat askew on the top of her light red hair. She'd make a lovely if tipsy bride. I sure hoped this was her bachelorette party and not her wedding day. I headed over. The girls started shouting their orders. All of them wanted some kind of fruity frozen drinks. Daiquiris, margaritas, strawberry, peach. One asked for a Bahama Mama. A faint sweat dampened my forehead. I had to figure out something fast.

"Mimosas are fifty percent off this morning," I said.

"Yay," the one with the veil said. "Mimosas for everyone."

I did a happy dance in my head. And in my head, my moves were every bit as good as Joaquín's. The only downside was it would create a deficit in Vivi's revenue. I'd make up for the extra out of my own pocket. It would be so worth it.

"I'll need to see some ID." They all grumbled and complained, but I heard far worse in the library. Try telling a little old lady her time was up on Ancestry.com and that another patron was waiting for the computer. I've heard sailors with better language. Fortunately, every last one of them actually had a valid ID.

As I walked back past the other woman, I stopped. "I'll make yours fifty percent off too."

"You're quick on your feet," she said. "But Vivi isn't one to give deals to tourists."

"I'll take care of it," I said.

I quickly got out champagne flutes. I made these with more orange juice than sparkling wine. After I delivered them I took over glasses of water too. They looked like they needed to hydrate. Another group of people came in—eight couples. I was seriously questioning my life decisions and praying that Joaquín would show up. I took their orders. The men all wanted beers (thank heavens) and the women decided on the half-price mimosas. As I returned to the bar, Joaquín walked in.

I flung my arms around him. "You're here," I said. He smelled great—salt air and soap.

He gave me a quick hug before freeing himself. "Where's Vivi?"

"No idea. I saw her when I was out on my morning run. She gave me the keys and told me to open."

I could tell by how his brow crinkled that this was unusual behavior, but there wasn't time to speculate with the crowd he had. Joaquín and I worked together, preparing the beers and mimosas. They didn't use frosty beer mugs at the Sea Glass. Joaquín told me it was because as the ice melted on the mug, it would dilute the flavor of the beer. Who knew?

After I delivered the drinks I came back.

"Why in the world are mimosas so popular this morning?" he asked.

"Um, maybe because they're fifty percent off?" My voice rose at the end of the sentence.

"Vivi won't—"

"Like that. I heard." I pointed to the woman with the permed hair. "It was that or trying to figure out how to make a bunch of different frozen drinks." Some bars had frozen drink machines, but Vivi insisted that all our drinks had to be made fresh. "Don't worry. I'll make up the difference." I loaded up the tray, carried it over, and distributed drinks. Fortunately, I was used to carting books and kids around the library, so I could take the weight. The dexterity to distribute them without spilling was a new challenge. But I managed it this morning.

Joaquín and I worked well together. While he was a whiz with drinks, I was great at small talk and keeping things clean and orderly. With Vivi gone, I was more relaxed and began to enjoy myself. Working here was kind of fun.

"I got a text from Vivi." Joaquín held up his phone. "She said she's out making arrangements so we can have a memorial for Elwell tonight."

"Do you think that's what she's really doing?" Why wouldn't she be here doing that? "I don't know. But can you make up a couple of signs that say we're closed at seven for a private event?"

"Vivi's going to close for the memorial?"

"It will be plenty busy just with the locals here. No one will want curious tourists around."

I hadn't thought about *curious* tourists. I looked over the crowd. Were any of these people here because there'd been a murder? I shrugged, unlocked Vivi's office, and found cardboard and Sharpies. The office was cramped but tidy. Her desk faced a beautiful oil painting that captured the emerald color of the water. There were black and white photographs of the Sea Glass from early days, along with others of fishermen. The desk was old and scarred. The chair, modern and ergonomic. Almost seemed like a metaphor for this area—the old and new trying to work together, but not always succeeding.

I sat at Vivi's desk and quickly made three signs, two for outside and one for inside. I didn't embellish them because that seemed like it would be disrespectful to Elwell. The temptation to look through drawers was strong, but I made the difficult decision to skip that. I hung the signs and got back to work.

By three, even Joaquín looked really worried, and I assumed it was about Vivi's whereabouts, although I'd also mentioned the outside security camera was pointing straight down. He didn't say it out loud, but he'd spent a good part of the last hour looking toward the back door in between mixing drinks. He'd also made several phone calls. As far as I could tell, whoever he was calling didn't answer. I heard him muttering in Spanish a couple of times. Something about *loco*, crazy. The muttering was a first since I'd met him. That didn't bode well, and I was starting to worry too.

"Where do you think she is?" I finally asked. "I'm guessing from your demeanor this isn't normal behavior for Vivi." I didn't know her well enough to be certain what normal behavior was. I tried to remember the bits and pieces Boone had said about his grandmother. None of it included wandering off for hours without letting her employees know where she was.

"Will you go next door and check with Wade about the food for tonight?" Joaquín asked.

I looked at him for a moment. "Sure." Why should he confide in me? I hadn't been here that long. Still, I was disappointed. Joaquín was the only friend I had here—or sort of friend, apparently. I went out the front and stopped to gaze at the beach scene. Volleyball players, sunbathers, sandcastle builders, and people with metal detectors all cohabited the beach in harmony. Maybe it was just too hot to fuss about anything. A couple of Jet Skis darted around on the placid water as I made my way through the soft sand to the Briny Pirate.

It was an old wooden structure with only a small sign over the door that said, "Briny Pirate." Nothing big or garish along this strip of beach. No flashing neon signs, or many signs of any kind. It kept the natural beauty of the area the focus. Like the Sea Glass, the Briny Pirate had a deck on the ocean-facing side. I wove my way through the tables and stepped inside. The interior was decorated with fishing nets, fake gold coins, and a talking treasure box in one corner that kept kids amused. The scent of barbecue wafted in from the smoker on the west side of the building. I realized I was hungry.

Vivi sat at the four-seater bar talking to Wade, their foreheads almost touching. She had a glass of iced tea in front of her. Moisture beaded on the glass, which was only about a quarter full, so she'd been here a while or had guzzled it. I was part aggravated and part relieved. At least she was okay. Their conversation looked intense. The only words that floated over were "questioned" and "Deputy Biffle."

CHAPTER 9

Oh, no. So that's where Vivi had been. Being questioned by the deputy. The empty feeling in my stomach got worse. I hesitated interrupting, but decided I had nothing to lose by approaching Vivi. And eventually Wade would spot me. I went over and stood beside her. Wade and Vivi jerked away from each other.

"Joaquín is worried," I said, looking Vivi right in the eye. For once, she looked embarrassed. The look was fleeting.

She stood. "Wade, we'll talk later." She walked out the front door and, I assumed, headed back to the bar.

I turned to Wade. "Joaquín wanted me to check on the food for tonight. Although I'm guessing he really wanted me to come over to see if you'd heard from Vivi."

Wade smiled. He had light blue eyes in his tan and wrinkled face. The man had a resting helpful face.

"I've got brisket in the smoker and fish will be

grilled. Rolls are in the oven, coleslaw in the fridge, and the fried pickles will be hot and fresh."

I must have grimaced at the fried pickles. They sounded disgusting.

Wade laughed. "You haven't lived until you've tried my fried pickles."

"I'll try anything once. Except raw oysters." I shuddered. "I've never figured out how people can eat that slime."

Wade laughed. "We'll have to work on that too."

That wasn't going to happen. "Is Vivi okay? It sounded like she was hauled in for questioning by Deputy Biffle."

Wade's helpful look disappeared into a frown.

"I'm worried about her. Or for her," I said. "Losing Boone and now this. That's hard for anyone to take."

"I'm worried too," Wade finally said. "They kept her a long time."

"Do they think Vivi killed Elwell?"

"Vivi doesn't think so. She tried to brush off the questions as routine. But from what she told me, I'm afraid they do."

I was surprised that Wade confided in me, and I had hoped for reassurance, but his answer only increased my anxiety. When Boone asked me to come down here if anything happened to him, I'm guessing he never imagined a scenario like this. Unless Vivi had some kind of criminal background I didn't know about. What did I really know about her? Bars could be tough places, with tough customers. Maybe she had a troubled past.

"I've got a couple of Redneck specials ready to go over to the Sea Glass. Mind taking them?" Wade asked.

Apparently Wade was done answering questions about Vivi. "I'd be happy too." I'd had the Redneck special earlier in the week. Rice, corn, greens, black-eyed peas, and the meat of your choice, with just enough hot sauce for tang. I'd had the pulled pork. The serving was enough food for three meals. It had tasted like heaven surely would. Wade handed me two cardboard containers and I headed back over to the bar.

At eight that night, during Elwell's memorial service, a thunderstorm raged, my first since I'd moved here. I stood behind the bar, fascinated and jumpy, as the storm rolled across the Gulf from the horizon to the doorstep of the Sea Glass. Watching lightening on the horizon was amazing—a great show curtesy of nature. But now every bolt of lightning seemed closer than the last, and I couldn't help but jump.

It wasn't like Chicago didn't have storms. Lake Michigan could have bigger waves than I'd seen on the Gulf so far. One storm had been so bad, it destroyed a Wisconsin lighthouse by knocking it right into the lake. Many a ship had sunk in Lake Michigan. Thinking about it made me quiver. I had a history with bad storms. It's what made me so jittery now.

The Gulf's angry-looking white caps marched to the deserted beach reaching higher and higher. None of the locals, and there were a lot of them packed in here, seemed disturbed by the storm. Technically, I didn't have to work tonight, but I wanted to hear what the attendees had to say about Elwell. So far, no one had said anything that piqued my interest. Nothing that pointed to a killer. I stayed anyway because I'd rather be around people during a storm like this than alone at Boone's house huddled under blankets.

People ate, drank, and chatted. Food and pitchers of beer were sitting out on one side of the room. Folks sat at tables on the other. At Wade's urging, I tried a fried pickle. The fried coating had just a bit of spice and the dill pickle slice was crunchy. It was delicious.

Nothing formal had happened, although I saw a wireless microphone sitting on a table next to Vivi. She'd kept to herself since I'd returned from the Briny Pirate. I hadn't even had a chance to ask Joaquín if he knew she'd been questioned because we'd been slammed.

I helped Joaquín and served as needed. A woman, who looked a few years older than me, sat at the bar on the very stool Elwell had been sitting on since I started. She had dark hair that fell in sultry waves halfway down her back. I'd noticed her in here several times before because she was stunning. She usually picked some corner or other to sit in by herself and often had a paperback in one hand and a martini in the other. A dirty one.

Today, she had her back to the bar and was in her usual black—this time shorts and a T-shirt—sans book. Her skin color was just dark enough that it gave her a sultry appearance. If I was given to flights of fancy, I'd say she looked like a pirate. A lovely, intelligent-looking pirate. Her legs were crossed and she had a small tattoo of a red, yellow, and green rectangle with a starburst in the middle on her inner left ankle.

Vivi flicked on the microphone. "I'm going to pass this around. If any of y'all have anything you want to say about Elwell, now's your chance."

The microphone passed from person to person. Some people just held up their drink and said, "Rest in peace."

Buford stood up and swayed a bit. He'd been here for the past several hours pounding beers. I'd seen him hand over his keys to his rummy-playing friend about an hour earlier. "I met Elwell on the playground in kindergarten when he punched me in the nose. I punched him back and we became best friends. We played Pop Warner football together. I was the center and he was the quarterback. I took the hits, he got the glory. Kind of a metaphor for our friendship." He swayed. "Metaphor's a big word for a redneck, right?" He wiped a tear from his eye and looked up. "Elwell, you were the shark and the rest of us minnows."

What the heck did that mean? What was *that* a metaphor for? They'd been friends for a long time if they played Pop Warner together. The league started at age five.

A bleached blonde grabbed the microphone. Her eye shadow was sparkly blue, her deep, V-neck shirt showed too much wrinkled, tanned cleavage. Her face looked Botoxed to the point I was surprised she could move her lips. But move them she did.

She stood up, not too steady on her feet.

"Who's that?" I asked Joaquín.

"Gloria Pugh."

"Elwell was a son of a bitch. But he was my son of a bitch until I left him six months ago." Her voice had a pack-an-hour kind of husk to it. A couple of big diamond rings sparkled on her hands. "He was up to something, and I think one of you, sitting here pretending to be sorry, was in on it with him." She turned slowly in a big circle, looking everyone in the eye. "One of you killed Elwell."

CHAPTER 10

The room went dead silent. I glanced at Vivi, and she looked over at me in just that moment. I'm not sure what she was thinking, but she didn't look away until I did.

"And I wouldn't blame you if you did," continued Elwell's wife. "He'd become an embarrassment to me, our businesses, and our daughter. What kind of man wears an armadillo on his head? A sick one, that's who." She swayed again. There was more swaying going on than laundry hung outside in a gale. She got misty-eyed and gripped the microphone harder. "But I guess in the end I still loved him or I wouldn't be so sad." She crumpled back into her seat, sobbing. A man next to her pried the mic out of her hand. No one else had anything to say after that. At least not publicly. I noticed Vivi hadn't said anything at all about Elwell.

By nine thirty the storm had passed with the last rumbles of thunder off in the distance to the north. There was only one table full of people left, and as far as I could tell, they were the heritage business owners. The only exception was the dark-haired woman who'd been sitting at the bar earlier.

"Who is that woman?" I asked Joaquín as we cleaned up.

"Ann Williams."

That didn't tell me much. "Is she a heritage business owner?"

Joaquín let out a sexy chuckle. "Hardly."

He didn't add anything.

"What's she do?"

"She fixes things," Joaquín said.

"Oh, interesting." A handywoman. I liked it when women were in traditional male roles. "Good for her." It also explained why she was in here during the day sometimes. She probably worked when she could and didn't keep any kind of regular hours. I started putting clean glasses back on shelves below the bar.

I was distracted when I heard someone out on the deck. Rhett stepped into the bar with a silver-haired woman on his arm. She was a tiny thing but had the same green eyes as Rhett.

I nudged Joaquín. "Looks like the Montagues just showed up. Who is that with Rhett?"

"His grandmother."

Rhett's grandmother dropped his arm and strolled over to the table where everyone was sitting. She wore what looked like a flowered Lilly Pulitzer dress. The owner of the fishing charter stood and offered her a seat. She shook her head. "I won't be here that long. I just wanted to pay my respects to Elwell." Her face was wrinkled and dotted with age spots.

"You're late. But what's new about that?" Vivi said.

"At least I can let go of the past," Rhett's grand-mother answered, lifting her chin.

Whoa, what was that about? I stopped putting away glasses to watch.

Vivi looked over in my direction. "Open a bottle of champagne and bring over some coupe glasses. If Melanie wants to toast Elwell, who am I to stop her."

Melanie? Was Rhett's whole family named after characters from *Gone with the Wind*? Was his mom Scarlett and his brother Ashley? I reached for a bottle out of the small fridge under the bar.

"Get the good stuff," Joaquín said.

There were two bottles of Dom Perignon in the fridge. I liked champagne and knew that Dom was the good stuff. I grabbed them and handed them to Joaquín. He opened both bottles while I arranged the coupe glasses on a tray. Coupe glasses were more saucerlike than flutes. According to Joaquín, people argued which was better for drinking champagne out of. Personally, I didn't care. I just loved a bubbly drink. I guess Vivi was on team coupe because those were the glasses she'd requested.

Joaquín poured enough in each glass for everyone to toast. I carried the tray over to the table and distributed drinks, ignoring Rhett. And by ignoring him, I mean being aware of exactly where he was and what he was doing. In this moment, he was talking to stunning Ann Williams.

I gave the first glass of champagne to Vivi, the next to Rhett's grandmother. It dawned on me that Rhett's grandmother was in the picture I'd noticed earlier. She was the one standing off to one side, arms crossed. I finally had to look at Rhett directly when I handed him his glass. His green eyes, the intense look, made me unreasonably fluttery inside. Maddening. I turned to go.

"Oh, stay," Vivi said. "Joaquín, please bring two more glasses so you and Chloe can join us."

Joaquín complied, and Rhett somehow maneuvered around so he stood next to me. Everyone lifted their glasses. Vivi and Melanie spoke at once: "To Elwell."

As everyone else said, "To Elwell," Rhett leaned in and whispered, "To secrets." I tried to ignore the shiver his breath on my ear brought, but I couldn't. My skin grew warm and my face was probably blazing red. I glanced around, hoping no one had noticed. But Vivi and Rhett's grandmother looked first at us and then at each other—and not in a happy way. Rhett seemed unperturbed by it all. When I moved away, he started making his way around the table, shaking hands and talking. I went back behind the bar to what was starting to feel like my safe place. He looked so at ease, as if the tension I picked up on didn't exist. Maybe he was a sociopath and didn't have any normal human emotions.

When Rhett made it all the way around the table and back to his grandmother, he took her arm, and they left.

Vivi stood, so everyone else did too. "Thanks for coming."

Fifteen minutes later, after much hugging and cheek kissing among the heritage business owners, the place was empty except for Vivi, Joaquín, and me. Joaquín put barstools up on tables while Vivi swept the floors. I collected all the champagne coupes, washed them by hand, dried them, and put them away. By the time I was done, Vivi sat in her office with a glass of bourbon in her hand. I poked my head in to say good night even though it felt awkward and I never knew what kind of reaction I'd get.

"Take tomorrow off," Vivi said. "You've had a long day."

"Okay," I said reluctantly. I hadn't had a day off since I'd arrived. And wasn't sure what I'd do with myself if I did. I told Joaquín goodbye and walked out the front. As I walked to the parking lot, I could see a couple of the heritage business owners chatting there. They couldn't hear me coming as I crossed the soft sand. I stopped in the shadow of the Sea Glass, curious to hear what they were saying.

"Did you buy that bit from Elwell's wife that one of us did it?" It was Edith Hickle, the owner of the glass-bottom boat.

"I don't want to," said the man who owned Russo's Grocery Store. I thought his name was Fred Russo. "Seems like she had as good a reason as any of us."

"Yeah, all Elwell's money and property gives her about ten million reasons."

Ten million? I never would have suspected Elwell had that kind of money from the way he dressed. Armadillo shell hats must be *way* more expensive than I guessed. The two said their good nights.

"Eavesdropping?" Rhett said from behind me.

I jumped and clapped my hands over my mouth to keep from screaming. He was right behind me. Too close. His voice a whisper. Once the two heritage owners climbed in their cars, I dropped my hands and whirled around.

"What are you doing here?" I asked. I didn't manage to disguise the annoyance in my voice. At least I hoped I sounded annoyed and not scared, which might be closer to the truth. That someone could walk up behind me without my knowing it completely unnerved me. Thank heavens it was only Rhett. There was a killer on the loose.

"After I walked my grandmother to her car, I took a walk down the beach. It's a beautiful night." He gestured toward the Gulf.

"What was that toast about?"

"I wanted you to know that I wasn't going to throw you under the bus. I'll keep your secret."

"Why would you? That's what I don't understand. Even if you did say it was to protect me."

"I have my reasons."

The clouds had cleared, and the moon sparkled on the calm water. He was right about the beautiful night. "You're always around," I said.

"Get used to it. I live here. My boat's here. It's a small town. The better question is, what are you doing here?"

I started rattling off my story about my car.

"Yeah, I heard that, but somehow I don't believe it. Am I right?"

"I'm here to help Vivi. Does anything else matter?"

"Maybe not." He paused and stared down at me. "You intrigue me, Chloe Jackson." Rhett walked away toward the marina.

CHAPTER 11

I intrigued him? *Well, back at you, buddy.* I didn't
want to outright follow him—that would be too obvious—but I did want to know which boat was his. So
instead of walking behind the Sea Glass, I crossed in
front of it. The soft sand slowed me a bit. I slipped off
my sandals to make myself even quieter.

The sand was warm and dry between my toes, the
air still heavy with humidity at this time of night. I
walked in front of the Briny Pirate too, but cut between it and the two-story condominium building
next to it. At the back edge of it, I ducked out my
head and peered to the left. Rhett walked his usual
confident stride about twenty feet ahead of me. I was
just about to call out to him—enough of this sneaking-
around stuff—when someone stepped out of the
shadows behind him. I opened my mouth to yell *watch
out.*

"Rhett." A woman's voice.

Rhett turned and waited for the woman. When she
caught up, they continued on shoulder to shoulder.

They walked under one of the marina's lights, and I saw it was Ann Williams. Maybe he needed a handy-woman, and she looked pretty darn handsy—whoops—handy in her sarong skirt and bikini top. Of course they'd be a couple. They looked stunning together. I did an about-face and headed home.

You could just sleep in, I told myself on Tuesday morning. Soft light filtered in through a crack in the tan curtains. It must be just before sunup. I stretched in Boone's king size bed with its soft sheets. I'd left the slider ajar again so I could listen to the Gulf. *You don't have anywhere you have to be.* But the soft slap of the waves called to me. And if I was going to get a run in today, it had better be now, before it got any hotter.

I pulled on shorts, a tank, socks, and my running shoes—threw the tan comforter up in a hasty attempt at making the bed. I filled my reusable bottle full of water and set out walking to the water's edge. One of the many reasons I ran was because I loved to eat. Maybe I'd treat myself to something special today. I headed west again this morning, and it wasn't because of Rhett and knowing his boat was in the marina somewhere. Yeah, yeah, yeah. The man was hot. I was young and single. Although, after what I'd seen last night, maybe he wasn't. So I told myself I didn't want to be facing the sun when it burst over the horizon. With no clouds in the sky, it would be brutal.

As I ran, I thought again of Rhett's *to secrets* toast. It nagged at me. Sure, he'd told me that he wasn't going to mention my sleeping on Boone's boat. But was that just a cover story he wanted out there? Did it have anything to do with Elwell? That's the only thing that made sense to me with the little information I had. I should have just been honest with Deputy Biffle. Because now the omission was bigger and the consequences scarier. It made me look guilty of something.

A couple of dolphins broke the surface about twenty feet out. I hadn't seen any this close in before. They surfaced and dove and resurfaced. It looked like they were playing, but they were probably eating. It didn't matter. They took my mind off my woes and let me enjoy a few moments of peace. The dolphins and I kept pace together until they circled back to the east.

I ran beyond the Sea Glass and Briny Pirate to the opening between it and the condominium where I'd peered out from last night when I was watching Rhett. I walked along the marina, catching my breath, wiping sweat from my brow. Some of the slips were empty, some occupied. I came to a boat named *Scarlett*. If Rhett's family stuck to their weird obsession with *Gone with the Wind*, then surely this was his boat. It was a lot bigger, more expensive-looking boat than Boone's, with a cabin that probably had plenty of sleeping space and an upper deck with a lounge area in the front. I almost stopped in my tracks when I noticed the next boat was named *Tara*. Instead, I kept going, cut back down to the beach, and ran home.

After I showered and ate a light breakfast, I pulled out my phone and read the local newspaper. This time there was an article about Elwell's death, but no mention of the way he was murdered. There was also an obituary. He was survived by his wife, Gloria, and his daughter, Ivy. Why wasn't Ivy at the memorial last night? Elwell had lived in Emerald Cove his whole life. He owned a car dealership in Fort Walton Beach and a land development company. Elwell also managed a slew of rental properties—maybe as part of his land development company. It was hard to tell if he owned them too.

The rentals and the land development both seemed like businesses that could create a lot of conflict. Heck, maybe even the car dealership was rife with problems that could lead to murder. The sheriff should know this, so hopefully, they were following those trails already. But I couldn't count on it. I had to keep vigilant for Vivi—for Boone. I'd have to do some more digging. So far, all I'd done was read up on Elwell. I'd probably find out more by talking to people who knew him than by reading articles. And I had the day off, so it was the perfect time to do just that.

At ten fifteen, I approached a kiosk across from the large, circle-shaped town green that marked the middle of Emerald Cove. While I missed the skyscrapers, the "L," and the Chicago River, there was no doubt this town was charming. A white gazebo sat smack in the middle of the green, with a flagpole at one end and a playground at the other. Benches and picnic tables were scattered around. Live oaks provided some shade. A group of kids played tag, while a male barbershop quartet practiced in the gazebo. Two-story, brick-fronted shops, galleries, and restaurants flanked the town green. It looked a lot like the set of the TV show *Hart of Dixie*.

A road wrapped around the circle, and the town's five main streets spiked off it. I'd heard that from above it looked like a starfish, with each of the main streets one of the arms. The two lower arms led to the beach. The upper one connected to Highway 98 and went on into Destin to the west and Panama City to the east. The middle-west arm curled around one of the coastal lakes and over to the harbor. The middle-east arm ended in a housing area. Various other streets ran off the main arms.

I stood at the window of the small, wooden kiosk, smiling at a young woman with dreads.

"Help you?" she asked.

"One ticket for the Redneck Rollercoaster, please." Elwell's wife's accusation that someone in the Sea Glass had killed him hung with me. As did my concern for Vivi. A tour might give me some history of the heritage businesses.

"For ten dollars more, you can take a ride on the glass-bottom boat."

"Do I have to ride the boat today?"

"No. It's good for a week," she said.

I forked over the extra money in exchange for my tickets. I drifted over to where a group of people were waiting in a queue to board the trolley. The ticket taker was one of the men who'd been at the memorial for Elwell. His name was Ralph Harrison, and he was the owner of the trolley. He wore a turquoise shirt embroidered with small pink flamingos and had a short, graying Afro. Four people stood in front of me. Two older women and two men who looked to be in their early forties.

Ralph introduced himself to each customer, making jokes with everyone as he worked his way down the line collecting tickets. When he stopped at the group in front of me, he said, "Who do we have here?"

One of the women hooked her thumb toward the man behind her. "I'm Gladys, and that's my partner."

The man turned as pink as the flamingos on the Ralph's shirt and shook his head violently. "I'm her son," he finally managed to choke out. He pointed to the man with him. "That's my partner and that's my aunt," he said, pointing to the other woman.

The mom looked confused by her son's embarrassment.

Ralph looked back and forth at them before bursting out laughing. "You're in the right place. Get the heck on board."

Ralph turned to me as the group climbed on board. The son was trying to explain to his mother why she couldn't say he was her partner, and they all had a good laugh as they sat down.

"You're the girl who showed up at Vivi's bar," Ralph said.

After the memorial service for Boone, there'd been a gathering at the Sea Glass much like the one for Elwell, only sadder, much, much sadder. The next day, I'd shown up at the Sea Glass and told Vivi I needed a job. I needed money to pay for my car. Vivi looked like she was going to say no when Joaquín intervened.

"We need the help, Vivi," Joaquín had said.

Vivi had given a short nod, then said, "You train her. She's your problem."

Welcome to the Sea Glass, I'd thought, but at least I had a foot in the door. In the moment, I chalked up Vivi's curtness to the stress of losing Boone. Now I wasn't sure what it was about. I considered telling Ralph the truth, but decided it wasn't worth it. No one else knew the real reason I was here; why should he? "I am. I'm Chloe Jackson," I said as I handed him my ticket.

"Ralph Harrison." He stuck out his hand and we shook. "You didn't have to buy a ticket. You work for Vivi, so you're good in my eyes." He patted a couple of pockets before pulling out a piece of paper. "Here's a free coupon for a milkshake at the diner."

"Thank you." I boarded and took the seat right behind the driver's. The benches were hard wood, the large windows wide open. Maybe I could strike up a conversation and find out more about Ralph and any connections he might have to Elwell.

A few minutes later, Ralph climbed into the driver's seat. Our eyes met in the rearview mirror. He started the trolley and put on a headset so he could talk as he drove. So much for hoping we could talk. It would be hard enough to find out anything about Ralph, much less Elwell. After a safety briefing—keep your hands in the trolley and don't stand up—we took off around the circle with a jerk.

"Our first stop will be the beach. Finest sand in the whole wide world, and the whitest too. This sand used to be quartz from the Appalachian Mountains, which is why it sometimes squeaks when you walk.

Emerald Cove was settled by New Englanders. Back then, they weren't so much attracted by the mild winters and the clear water but by the abundant fishing. If y'all have any questions, just shout them on out."

"Why's it called the Redneck Rollercoaster?" someone asked.

"That's a mighty fine question," Ralph answered. He made it sound like no one had ever asked him that before. "When my grandpappy started this business, we didn't understand the importance of the dunes, how fragile they are, or how important the seagrass is to their health. Folks would come out here in jeeps and drive over the dunes. Some dunes were so tall and dropped so low, it felt like a roller-coaster. Cheap entertainment, and a hell of a good time when you're a teenager."

Ralph's voice had changed just a bit as he talked about the history. It sounded more tense to me. Even though I could see his smile in the big rearview mirror as he said the words.

Ralph pulled over by the dunes. "Great photo op here, folks. Stay on the walkways and off the dunes. We'll take a ten-minute break."

People climbed off, but I stayed on. "I feel like there's more to the story, Ralph."

He flipped off the mic and turned to me. "Aren't you a perceptive thing. I guess the drinks last night didn't leave me in top form."

"Are you going to tell me the rest?"

Ralph rubbed his forehead. "This is the South."

"Segregation?" The book I'd read about this area had mentioned whites-only beaches and venues.

"Yep. My grandfather and his friends weren't welcome at the whites-only amusement parks along the Panhandle, so they made their own fun."

"Maybe people need to hear that."

"People are here to get away. Not for a history lesson. But if you are interested in history, I've got a story for you."

"I'm all ears."

"Back in the sixties, they brought a lot of pot from Mexico up here by boat. So much that when the Coast Guard went out after them, they'd just toss it overboard and skedaddle." Ralph smiled at some far-off memory. "The bales of pot would wash up on shore or bob around close enough for fishermen to get them. They called it the save-the-bales campaign."

"No way. Really?"

He chuckled. "Really. Now, I'm not saying I ever saved any bales. Just that I heard about them." He reached in a cooler and got out a bottle of icy-cold water. "Want one?"

"Yes, please. What's the real reason you call it the Redneck Rollercoaster?" My Northern prejudice might be coming in to play again. I'd always pictured rednecks as being white guys in baseball caps and hunting gear.

"Being a redneck is a state of mind. Just like all people from—where'd you say you came from?"

I hadn't. "Illinois."

"Just like all people in Illinois aren't the same, neither are rednecks. I'm from a long line of Southern hunters with grannies who cooked collard greens and shrimp and grits. Rednecks make do with what they have. That's where the name really came from. Can't ride a real roller coaster. You make the best of what you have. And let me tell you, flying over the top of the dune was a heck of a lot of fun."

"Things have changed a lot," I said. "But all of you heritage owners have remained close." I wondered how Elwell fit in with the group. What his background was.

"It was a lot different back then. No one thought these beaches with their scrub oak were worth much. Couldn't have been more wrong about that. There were barely any paved roads to Emerald Cove, or Destin, for that matter." He tipped back his head and drank the rest of the water in a few large gulps. "All of us owners were close. Are close."

"It seems like you were all close to Elwell even though he wasn't one of the heritage business owners.

"That's true. Elwell, though," he paused and shook his head, "now that boy had some problems and pissed off the wrong people."

Before I could ask more, he rang a bell and flipped his mic back on. "Getch your heinies back on board."

Ralph's good old boy routine hid a shrewd mind and a painful past. While some people used the trolley as a hop-on/hop-off, I stayed on for the full circuit, but Ralph didn't share anymore information with me.

At one point, fighter jets drowned out his narration. "That's the sound of freedom, folks," Ralph said when he could be heard. "We have two nearby Air Force bases. Eglin, where the jets live, to the north, and Hurlburt, home of Air Force Special Forces, to the west."

The heritage businesses were all within five miles of each other. Most were close to the beach, which made sense because at the time they opened, fishing was the big draw. When we got back to the center of town, I stood.

"Hold up a minute while everyone unloads," he said to me.

He jumped down and helped people off as needed. He turned to the woman who'd made the partner comment earlier. "You and your partner have a good stay, ya hear?" He patted the son on the back, and they all had another chuckle. Once everyone was off, I climbed down. Ralph held out his hand and I placed mine in it for the last step. But once I was off, he didn't let go. He tightened his grip to firm but not quite hurting.

"What are you really doing at Vivi's?" he asked. "Most people don't just show up some place and start working whether they're welcome or not."

How'd he know I wasn't welcome? It made me wonder what Vivi had been saying about me. "I . . ." I told him the same story I'd told Vivi about my car. "Fixing a vintage Beetle is expensive. I didn't have the money for the repairs." I was an adept liar. It came from working around kids all the time. My friends gasped in horror when I said that, but I always pointed out that kids get lied to all the time— Santa Claus, Easter Bunny, Tooth Fairy, Elf on the Shelf. I'm proud to say I wasn't above doing it at the library when absolutely necessary to prevent a catastrophe.

"I thought you had some fancy job back home."

Word about me had spread fast. "I'm on a leave of

absence." Not that working in a library was exactly fancy. "Boone was my dear friend. My best friend. I couldn't miss his memorial service." Tears threatened, so I looked down and blinked hard before I looked back up. I wished I could take back my promise to Boone. I wished I were back at my job in the library, wiping snotty noses and recommending books. *That* job was like being Santa Claus. Finding the right book for the right child was a great gift. To see their shiny, happy faces at story time brought me joy.

According to my dad, wishes were for the weak. You had to make your own destiny. Right now, my destiny was here, working in the bar was interesting, and I was learning a lot. I could do a lot worse than being at the beach for part of the summer.

Ralph was still holding my hand in his large one. I pulled mine away. "Boone was my friend," I said again as I walked off. I understood where Ralph was coming from. He was trying to protect his friend. Boone would have done the same for me. But that didn't mean I was going to start spilling my emotional guts to someone I barely knew. Trust would have to be a two-way street.

A few minutes later, I drove to Fort Walton Beach, impatient with all the traffic. It was gorgeous out; everyone should be at the beach. I finally found Pugh Motors. It was a used-car dealership in a rundown-looking building, but the lot was full of Cadillacs, SUVs, and trucks. All of them sparkled in the sunlight as a breeze snapped banners hanging on poles. I parked the car and got out. I went over to a massive, jacked-up pickup, wondering how the heck someone even climbed into it. The wheels were almost as tall as I was.

"Interested in a truck?" a woman asked.

I turned to find a woman in a pretty teal sundress standing there. She was in every way the opposite of what I expected a used car salesperson to be. "I drive a vintage Beetle." I gestured toward my car. "I'm guessing this gives one an entirely different view of the world. I'd need a ladder to get in."

The woman laughed. Her gray hair curled around her chin. "I figured the guy who owned it was compensating for something. His wife made him trade it in for a minivan."

Now it was my turn to laugh.

"You look more like a sports car. Convertible."

"It would be fun, but my skin would fry."

"Stick around long enough and you'll get a good base coat of Florida sunshine on that milky white skin."

"I hope so. I usually just turn shades of red."

"What can I help you with?"

I didn't think she'd be offering me any financial information about the dealership, which is what I really wanted to know. But before I had time to come up with something, she continued on.

She leaned in a little and dropped her voice. "I can give you a heck of a deal today and a great trade-in." She glanced back at the building. "My manager's out, and by the time he's figured out what we've done, you'll be long gone, sitting pretty in a brand-new used car."

So, she might look different from a typical used car salesperson, but she talked just like one. Today-only specials, along with 'the manager's out' were red flags for scams. Had Elwell known what was going on here or not? "I was hoping to speak to Elwell. He always promised me if I needed a car that he'd give me a great deal and five hundred above the blue book price for my Beetle."

A flash of sadness erased the friendly salesperson expression. "I'm sorry to tell you this, but Elwell passed." She really did look sorry.

I clasped a hand to my chest. "Heart attack?" It seemed as good a choice as any, and Elwell had had a paunch.

"He was murdered."

"Oh, my. Have they caught the person who killed him?" I glanced over my shoulder like I was afraid the murderer was right behind me.

"No. But my cousin works at the Walton County Sheriff's Department, and they have a high degree of confidence that the owner of the bar Elwell was found behind did it. They hope to make an arrest soon."

CHAPTER 12

Noooooo. I made an excuse or maybe a bunch of them. I was so shocked by what she had said, I wasn't sure what I had said, but soon I was back in my car heading toward Destin. I didn't want to sit in Boone's house all by myself worrying, so I parked at Destin's harbor and strolled around. Big yachts moved out of the harbor and toward the East Pass. From there, they could head south to the Gulf or north to Choctawhatchee Bay. There were all kinds of tourist lures here, from pirate tours on sailboats to beach art to restaurants and bars. The signs for parasailing tempted me, but then I saw one for Jet Skis and, to quote my dad's favorite movie, *Top Gun*, I "felt the need for speed."

After a safety briefing and a quick how-to-use-the-Jet-Ski lesson, I was chugging up the East Pass toward the harbor. I passed under the Destin Bridge that linked Destin to Okaloosa Island. The bridge I'd driven over to get to Fort Walton Beach and back. Traffic was still slow. After I got through the no-wake zone, I cranked the throttle. Moments later, I was flying. Well, it felt like it anyway. The water was clear, with just a little chop from a breeze. I headed away from the crowds, and soon, I was spinning and enjoying the slap of wind in my face. Alive. Free.

Eventually, I slowed down and headed back toward the pass. Northwest of the Destin Bridge, I spotted a huge group of boats, what looked like a floating restaurant and bar, and kids bouncing on a huge, inflated trampoline. This was the area locals called Crab Island. I'd seen it from the bridge but never from this vantage point. It wasn't an island at all but a shallow spot in Choctawhatchee Bay that had become popular with boaters.

I drove closer, weaving around boats and people until I smelled fried something wafting across the air. It made me hungry, so I pulled up to the restaurant, tethered the Jet Ski to it, and climbed onto the dock. I ordered a grouper sandwich, fries, and a beer. Once I got my order, I took it back to my Jet Ski and puttered to an empty spot that was prime for watching the party and eating my food.

Different types of music fought with one another; country and rap seemed to be winning out. People floated in the water—some on their backs and some on rafts—with coolers floating next to them. Half of them looked like their sunburns had burns, another quarter were bronzed to perfection, and quite a few looked like they'd had more than one drink. I spotted Elwell's wife, Gloria, lounging on a pontoon with a group of people. She had a full martini glass in her hand. Her head was thrown back, and her deep, throaty laugh drifted across the water. She sure didn't look too broken up for a woman who'd just accused a group of presumed friends of murdering her husband.

I motored slowly over to the vicinity of her pontoon. I kept my back to her, not that she'd recognize me out of the context of the bar. I strained to listen to bits of conversation while I ate. The grouper was nicely spiced and tender, the fries hot and crispy. The beer went down a little too easily. I wished I had another one, even though I didn't believe in drinking and boating. I'd seen and heard enough about boating accidents on Lake Michigan.

"It's complicated."

That sounded like Elwell's wife.

"Of course I'm sad, even though we weren't living together. We talked almost every day. But I told him I wasn't coming home until he quit wearing that damned armadillo shell on his head."

"Why was he wearing it?" a man asked.

I risked a glance. The man had his hand on Gloria's thigh. She didn't seem to mind.

She leaned in toward him. "He thought it made him more virile, but trust me, it didn't." The man's mouth dropped open in surprise and he laughed. Ack. I could have gone *forever* without hearing that. Elwell's wife started to turn her head in my direction. I started up the Jet Ski and headed back toward the harbor.

All I'd learn today was that Ewell had pissed off some people, which I'd heard before, that his dealership was possibly shady, Vivi might be suspect number one, and that Elwell had explained to his wife why he was wearing the armadillo shell. Although his explanation to me was something different. Thank heavens.

Nothing I learned was enough to save Vivi, if she was going to need saving. If only there was a book at the library on how to catch a killer. I'd started reading mysteries as a kid, when my grandmother handed me a Nancy Drew. I still devoured mysteries today. But nothing I'd ever read had prepared me for this. I needed to know who killed Elwell because I needed it not to be Vivi. Then I'd be off the hook and could go back to Chicago to a place where I fit in.

After I returned home, I napped. Being out in the hot sun had been exhilarating but had worn me out. After I woke, I showered and headed back to Destin around nine. I didn't want to sit at Boone's house and mope about being alone, so I'd looked up some bars—after all, I was only twenty-eight. I settled on a place called AJ's, with its outdoor deck and self-described happening scene. The rest of the evening passed in a blur of dancing and flirting with Air Force personnel and locals. I passed on the invitations to go home with someone. The attention was flattering, but I wasn't desperate—not yet anyway. In the end, none of it could chase away my anxiety about Vivi's possible arrest. Nor did it help me figure out what to do next.

Banging on my back-porch door woke me up Wednesday morning. I opened one eye, grabbed my phone, and squinted at it: seven a.m. Whoever was out there was rattling the door so hard, I was afraid it would fall off. It wasn't that sturdy in the first place. A man was yelling my name too. I rolled out of bed, threw on a T-shirt and shorts, and ran a hand through my short hair as I stumbled out through the sliding glass door.

Rhett Barnett stood there on the other side of the screen door. He wore running shorts. A T-shirt was slung over one shoulder and his tanned chest gleamed with sweat. My mouth was dry. Please God let it be from last night's festivities—a little too much wine and dancing, not enough water—and not from the sight of Rhett. Because after seeing him with Ann the other night I needed to keep my emotions and my hormones in check. No more handsome guys with girlfriends. Been there, made that mistake, wouldn't do it again.

"What are you doing here?" I asked. My voice growled and crackled out of me. Darn, dry mouth. I kept the door between us.

He pulled on the door again, and it came off its flimsy hinges. "Sorry. I'll fix it."

I flashed to a picture of him with a carpenter's belt slung low on his hips, rehanging the door. I blinked twice to rid myself of the image. I stepped back as he came in. He looked down at me, concern in his eyes, laugh wrinkles deepening, but not because he was smiling.

"It's Vivi," he said. His chest rose and fell rapidly. He must have run over here from somewhere.

"What? Is she okay?" Thoughts of heart attacks and accidents chilled me.

"She's been taken in for questioning. For Elwell's murder."

I stared at him. "They questioned her Monday too." Vivi being questioned twice was worrisome.

"They did?" Rhett frowned.

"Come in. I'll make coffee." I desperately needed to do something while I processed what he'd just said. He followed me through the slider into my bedroom. It looked like I'd wrestled the sheets and comforter into submission. A paperback by Laura Lippman was sprawled on the floor. We crossed the living room to the kitchen. My hands shook and my heart rumbaed as I made the coffee and thought about Vivi. While the old coffee maker gurgled, I turned to Rhett.

"How do you know she was taken in?" This was no time to have my thoughts be so sluggish. Maybe the Dolores he'd called when I'd found Elwell told him. I poured a glass of water and chugged it. "Water?" I asked when I was finished.

"Yes, please." I grabbed him one of the old Mason jar glasses and filled it. He drank. The smell of coffee pushed away the masculine scent of Rhett, much to my relief. I wished he'd put his shirt back on. That chest was distracting. And the abs. So many abs. Mine were all hidden behind a small roll of fat.

"Vivi?" I asked again. "It's not surprising she was questioned. Elwell was found right behind the Sea Glass, and they had a history." I paused. "It's not great that they are questioning her again, but you seem very upset about it. Why?"

"Because they didn't just ask her to answer questions. A deputy came and picked her up this morning as she was heading into the Sea Glass."

I frowned. That didn't sound good. "Do you think they're going to arrest her?"

Rhett put down his water glass and pulled his T-shirt back on. *Thank you, sweet baby Jesus.* I'd only been here a week and I was already thinking in Southern phrases. Maybe now my heart rate would quit the dance it had been doing.

"I think it's likely they'll arrest her."

"That's not what I wanted you to say."

Rhett looked in my eyes for a moment. "It's not what I wanted to say."

"It's terrible," I said. Worse than terrible. I couldn't let this happen. But before I figured out my next step, I needed caffeine. I took two cups off the mug tree on the counter and filled them with coffee. "I don't have any sweetener or cream."

"Black's fine." He took the cup from me and drank a bit. "Terrible describes it."

"My coffee?" Great now he didn't like my coffee. I was renown in Chicago for my coffee-making skills. That might be a tiny exaggeration, but I could make a decent cup. Rachel always liked it.

"No. The situation with Vivi is terrible. The coffee is great."

I sipped some confirming that it was indeed great. "Why did you come to tell me?" Now that I'd gotten over the initial shock of the news, the sight of a shirtless Rhett, and I'd had a bit of coffee, my brain seemed to be slowly kicking back into gear.

"I was coming back from a run when I saw Vivi with the deputy. She asked me to let you know. Joaquín is out on his boat. Vivi said someone had to open."

What the heck? That's what Vivi was worried about? Not the fact that the deputy was going to haul her off? Even with the Vivi distress, I couldn't help but feel a little disappointed that Rhett wasn't here because he wanted to be the one to tell me the news. "She was taken in for questioning for murder and she's worried about the Sea Glass?" I took a long drink of my too-hot coffee. *Show no pain.*

"It's her baby. Especially now that Boone is gone. The heritage business owners are her family."

He knew a lot about Vivi, considering the feud. "Is there any way to get hold of Joaquín?" He'd be better equipped to deal with this.

"I tried his cell phone but didn't reach him. He should return in an hour or two. I'll watch the dock for him."

Interesting that he had Joaquín's cell phone number. "She'll need a lawyer. Money for bail." I didn't think she'd had a lawyer with her yesterday, but she should if she was back for another round. Wade would probably know if she had a lawyer.

"Don't get ahead of yourself. They may just be trying to intimidate her."

"Then they obviously don't know who they are dealing with."

CHAPTER 13

A smile crossed Rhett's face for the first time since he'd yanked the door off its hinges. "You don't seem surprised by this."

I thought of the angry voices I'd heard. What the woman at the dealership had said. I guess I wasn't all that surprised, but I wasn't going to admit that to Rhett. "Thanks for coming over," I said. "I'll drive over in a little while and open up." Drat. I smacked my forehead. I'd taken a ride share home last night instead of risking driving after a few glasses of wine. Ouch. I rubbed my hand to my forehead. Smacking myself was stupid after partying last night.

Rhett looked at me curiously. "What's that about?"

"My car's at AJ's. I have to go get it."

"I'll run home, get my car, and drive you to yours. It'll give us both a chance to clean up."

"Don't you have to be at work?" I asked.

"My hours are flexible."

Rhett didn't add anything about why, and this didn't seem like the time to question him, when Vivi was in trouble. Though I was curious about what he did for a living.

"Okay. Thanks." A ride would mean fraternizing with the enemy, but in this case, it would make my life easier and save me some money. Besides, he wasn't my enemy; he was Vivi's. I followed him to the back and watched him run off in strong strides. I fanned myself a little. It was wrong to appreciate him at a time like this. Just wrong. Think of Ann. The beautiful babies they'd make.

I walked to the bathroom to get ready and gasped when I looked in the mirror at the mascara under my eyes and my disheveled hair. Lovely. But what did I care? Hot guy, me looking like something that washed up on shore, and not in an alluring, mermaid way. No big deal.

He was off-limits because I'd sworn off hot guys, Rhett was with Ann, and because Vivi didn't like his grandmother. If we were *West Side Story*, he was the Jets and I was the Sharks. It wouldn't end well. But accepting a ride to my car so I could get back and open the bar—that would be okay. It wasn't a big deal. Really, it wasn't.

I powered through my shower routine. My short hair could dry on its own, although it took a bit longer in the humidity and had more waves than normal. A bit of mascara, eye shadow, and lipstick helped me look way better than I had before. Another pair of shorts and a fresh, scoop-necked T-shirt completed my look.

* * *

Twenty minutes later, we were headed out in Rhett's BMW convertible. He had the air conditioner on to counteract the beating the sun was giving us. A BMW and a boat. I wondered if he was a gambler, like Rhett Butler in *Gone with the Wind*, if he'd inherited money, or if he was some kind of consultant who set his own hours.

"How'd you end up at AJ's?" Rhett asked as he pulled out of Boone's drive.

"Google. It was on a list of best bars in Destin. You sound a little judgy about my choice."

"I've got nothing against AJ's."

"Where would you go?" I'd add whatever he said to my list of places to avoid. Not that I had such a list, but I could start one. He was just too tempting. And some instinct told me getting on Ann Williams bad side wouldn't be smart.

"The Red Bar in Grayton Beach."

Grayton Beach was a small town to the east of here not unlike Emerald Cove. I'd wanted to go to the Red Bar because I'd heard the food was delicious, the bar was eclectic, and their music was always good. It had been destroyed by a fire and had been rebuilt. And while I'd rather not run into Rhett some-where—*now who's being judgy?*—I wasn't going to let him stop me from going to a venue that sounded like that much fun. So much for making a list or trying to avoid Rhett.

"Have you had breakfast?" he asked.

"No time this morning." Was he asking me if I wanted to go out to breakfast, or just being all South-ern and polite? Did I want to go with him or should I make up some great excuse why I couldn't?

"It's the most important meal of the day."

"Okay, Mom."

Rhett laughed and made a call. He glanced at me as the phone rang through his speakers. "Do you like breakfast burritos?"

"Of course." I liked breakfast burritos, or burritos of any kind at any time, for that matter. They were scrumptious. My mouth grew moist as visions of burritos danced in my head. I hoped my stomach wouldn't gurgle. Boone had always teased me about the hunger monster he said lived in my stomach. "Without regular feedings, we all have to hear the hunger monster," he'd say.

"Spicy?" Rhett asked.

"The spicier the better."

A woman with a Spanish accent answered the phone, and Rhett asked for two chorizo burritos with chili verde. "I'll be there in few minutes, Maria."

Rhett drove into the town center and started around the circle. He waved at a couple playing chess at a picnic table under a magnolia tree in the town green. Rhett turned on the street that was the east arm of the starfish, drove for a bit, and parked by a food truck near the beach. "Best Mexican food on the Panhandle. Come on."

I followed Rhett to the truck.

"Rhett," a woman called out.

I presumed she was Maria. Rhett put a hand on my back as we walked to the food truck. His hand was warm and made me shivery. I hoped to heaven he couldn't feel my reaction to his touch. The woman let out a torrent of Spanish, which Rhett responded to in equally as fluent-sounding Spanish with a laugh. I knew some Spanish, but had a hard time keeping up.

I thought I heard Maria say the word "*novia*" and "*amor.*" Was that girlfriend and love? I looked at the sky, my feet, and the sand—anywhere but at Maria or Rhett, because this bypassed embarrassing and went right to humiliating. I wanted to clap my hands over my ears so I didn't have to hear what Rhett had to say.

He responded with "no" and "amiga." We were friends? When did that happen? Not that I didn't want to be his friend, but up to this point, our relationship had consisted of him finding me snoring, then finding me screaming over Elwell, sharing a toast with me, and coming to Boone's house this morning. Oh, and he'd scared the crap out of me when I was eavesdropping. An unusual way to start a friendship.

Rhett interrupted Maria by introducing us. She called to her husband, Arturo, who came to say hello. More rapid-fire Spanish about love and girlfriends. Rhett glanced over at me and smiled. I guessed this was what people assumed when you ate breakfast together in the Panhandle of Florida. Things could be worse. I'd have to remember that for future reference.

Arturo went back to work. After Rhett paid, Maria handed him two cardboard plates with the burritos and handed me two water bottles.

"Come on," Rhett said, and headed toward a picnic table by the beach.

"Wait. I've got to get my car and open the bar. And there's Vivi."

"The bar doesn't open for three hours. And unless you're a criminal defense lawyer, there's nothing you can do right now for Vivi." He tilted his head toward a picnic table with a view of the water. "There's nothing better than something hot and satisfying in the morning."

What? Did he really just say that? *Get a grip.* He's talking about the burritos, not me. Fortunately, he turned and walked toward the table, while I blushed from the thoughts steaming through my head. I hoped the redness had receded by the time I plopped down across from him. I dug into the burrito to avoid looking at Rhett. There was just enough spice to wake me up, but not enough to make me sweat.

"This is perfection," I said. "Thanks for bringing me."

"It is," he said, watching me.

Was he talking about the burrito, the view, or me? Time to get my mind off him. "You don't think Vivi could kill Elwell, do you?" I asked. I hoped she was innocent for Boone's sake. But she might not be. After all, how well did I really know her? I'd heard the argument she'd had with Elwell or someone. Even if it was someone else, it showed she had quite the temper.

Rhett gazed into my eyes—not in a romantic way, but in a why-the-heck-would-you-ask-that way.

"I'm worried about her," I said. "Do you think they have evidence?"

"Of course." His voice was gentle.

"The knife in his neck. It's called a channel knife. Bars have them." I gripped my burrito, felt its heat.

"So that means they're common. There *are* several bars along the beach."

"That's true. And even if it was a knife from the Sea Glass, anyone could steal a knife. Some of the heritage owners come behind the bar to serve themselves or help out if it's busy. The regulars too. The back door is rarely locked and people use it as an entrance." I ate some more of my burrito. "What if someone saw Vivi use a knife and they took it? But why set up Vivi?"

"I've been wondering that too."

I returned to concentrating on my burrito while I spun different scenarios in my head. None of them included Vivi being the murderer.

"I take it you liked it?" Rhett asked ten minutes later as I wadded up my napkin.

"Delicious. Thank you." I drank the rest of my water and stood. "I really need to get going. I could get a ride share to take me so you can get on with your day."

"It'll be faster and cheaper with me."

I fought off another round of blushing. Why did everything he said to me this morning sound like something sexual? My twenty-eight-year-old hormones were in rare form. But his face was pure innocence. Maybe too innocent?

I thanked him once we got to AJ's.

He walked me to my Beetle and waited until I got in.

"Cute," he said.

Was he talking about my car or me? Why did I keep questioning everything he said? *Get a grip.* How many times was I going to tell myself that this morning? "You'll watch for Joaquín while I open the Sea Glass?" I asked.

"I will. Let me know if you need anything."

I nodded and took off. Then I realized I had no way of getting hold of him if I did need something, which was probably for the best.

CHAPTER 14

Joaquín arrived at ten thirty—thank heavens. There was still no sign of Vivi. Joaquín must have talked to Rhett, because he knew about Vivi being hauled off by a deputy.

"I'm so glad to see you, but I'm worried about Vivi," I said to him.

"Don't worry. It will be fine." He turned and started polishing a clean glass.

His words said, "don't worry," but just like Monday, his face said Vivi was in deep trouble. I thought again about Gloria's comment that one of the heritage business owners had killed her husband. But how could I possibly figure out who? They'd all known each other for years. What would trigger one of them to kill Elwell now?

They weren't the only ones on my list. *Oh, for goodness' sake.* I had a list of suspects. I might be losing it. I was no Harriet the Spy. But I had to think about this. And what I was thinking about was Buford. The violent outburst he'd had over cards the other day. It was the only time I'd seen such a display of temper from him, but knowing it lurked there, considering how Elwell was killed, I had to consider him a suspect.

We opened at eleven, as usual. A few minutes later, Ralph Harrison came in the back door, nodding at me as he took a table. I wondered who was driving the Redneck Rollercoaster today. By 11:45 most of the heritage business owners were huddled around one of the tables near the sliding glass doors, drinking and talking. Maybe this would be my chance to learn something, because there still hadn't been any word from Vivi. What could the sheriff's department be doing with her? Were these people here to support her or throw her under the bus?

My determination to eavesdrop was briefly derailed when Wade brought over a big platter of raw oysters from the Briny Pirate and set it on the table for the business owners. Raw oysters repelled me. They looked like something a dolphin would sneeze out. I could barely look at them without getting sick. And as if it wasn't bad enough, all the heritage business owners were very thirsty today. I'd been running Bloody Marys, glasses of water, cranberry and vodkas, plus sodas—that's what they called pop down here—since they had walked in. I kept trying to place their drinks beside them without looking at the big platter of oysters or hearing them be slurped down. Ack. Just ack.

At the same time, I wanted to hear what they were talking about. Vivi was more important than my fear of oysters. I reminded myself of that as I tamped down my nausea by breathing through my mouth so I didn't have to smell their briny scent.

"What happened to make him start wearing that armadillo hat?" Edith Hickle asked. I put an extra spicy Bloody Mary to the right edge of her plate.

"Brain tumor?" one of the owners answered.

"While I wish we could blame it on something medical, I think it was pure orneriness," Ralph said.

"To what end?" asked the owner of the grocery store.

"If we had that figured out, maybe we would know why he was murdered," Leah Hickle said. Leah was Edith's daughter. I'd met her at the memorial for Elwell too. Was the glass-bottom boat docked?

Ann Williams walked in and sat at a table across from the bar with her back to the wall. The heritage business owners acknowledged her but didn't invite her to join them. I went over to see what she wanted.

"A Tom Collins," she said.

I had no idea what that was but wrote it down on the pad that I carried in the little half apron I'd taken to wearing. "Joaquín told me you fix things," I said.

Ann tilted her head to one side. "Yes."

"Rhett pulled the door to Boone's screened porch off the hinges this morning and I need to get it fixed."

She flushed a little. "Sounds like Rhett wanted in really bad," she said, her voice too neutral, and it held a hint of anger.

Oops. I'd forgotten they'd been together the other night. That they were a couple. No wonder she sounded mad. I'd be mad if my boyfriend was yanking the door off someone else's house. "It was so flimsy that the slightest tug did it." That wasn't exactly true, but I didn't want him to get in trouble with Ann. "Vivi asked him to stop by to tell me she needed me to open."

"Oh."

Hopefully, Rhett was off the hook now. "Will you be able to take care of the door?" I asked. "There's no rush."

A little half smile flashed across her face. "Sure. What are they all here for?" Ann asked, nodding toward the heritage owners table.

I didn't want to lie to her after she'd said she'd fix my door, but I didn't feel any need to tell her the truth either. "I thought this was just their gathering place. But I'm new, so what do I know?" I gave a slight shrug to show my indifference. I'm not sure she fell for it.

Ann pulled a paperback out of her purse. I couldn't see the title. She gave me a quick nod.

"I'll get your drink."

An hour later, I'd learned nothing helpful through my attempts at eavesdropping. That's when Vivi slipped in the back just as a group of tourists flocked in the front. She stood behind the bar, looking over the scene. It looked like she gritted her teeth until she spotted the heritage business owners. Then her face softened to a smile. Meanwhile, the tourists took over every remaining table inside and out on the covered deck.

Ann Williams looked them over, put her book in her purse, and left. The two men playing cards in the corner rolled their eyes at the tourists. The heritage business owners hadn't noticed Vivi yet. She looked pale and a bit tired, not that she'd ever admit being tired to anyone—well, at least not to me.

"How are you?" I asked her.

"Joaquín, will you please bring me a glass of sparkling water?" Vivi asked. I didn't think she was going to answer me for a minute, but she turned toward me. "I've had better days."

I was surprised she showed me her vulnerable side. She sounded exhausted. Wade looked up when he heard her voice. He pushed back his chair and hurried over to her. He grasped her arms and studied her face.

"Are you okay?" he asked. Sparks of concern seemed to radiate from his eyes. Vivi leaned into him for the briefest moment before drawing back.

He loves her.

"Of course. I'm fine," Vivi said. "Don't be ridiculous." She flashed a smile at him.

I could tell that Vivi knew Wade loved her, but did she love him? Joaquín handed Vivi her sparkling water. She frowned at me and then tilted her head toward the crowd of people who had just come in. For a minute, I'd forgotten I worked there, entranced as I was with my observations of her and Wade. Had Boone known? That was another thing I'd never have an answer to. I grabbed my pad of paper out of my apron and hurried out from behind the bar.

Joaquín cranked up the music. My body relaxed.

It seemed like the whole place did. I went from group to group, taking orders and getting them back to Joaquín. I filled the easy ones: the beers, chardonnays, and cabernets. Joaquín did the mixed drinks. I delivered them all, still learning the best way to carry a tray full of drinks through a crowd. So far, I hadn't doused anyone, but this was the busiest I'd seen the place. Joaquín was smiling and laughing again, so soon it was one big party. Except for the heritage owners, who huddled, heads close together, talking.

By five, the heritage owners had been gone for over an hour and Vivi had disappeared into her office. Joaquín and I were working nonstop—me like a crazy person and him calmly filling drink orders while flirting with the ladies sitting at the bar. He moved his hips to the music, and even I'd paused more than once to enjoy the view.

A redhead leaned over the bar to him. "Joaquín."

"What can I get you?" he asked.

"An extra-large serving of you," she said. She batted her fake eyelashes at him.

"Oh, honey, do you think you can afford me?"

She laughed. "Maybe?"

"I don't think so, but I can get you another mai tai."

She put on a pouty face, but nodded her head.

Joaquín had a way of deflecting advances without offending anyone. I hoped I could do as well. Because, as the afternoon had worn on, my glare was getting the best of me. At the library, I had used it to stop children in their tracks. It had the same effect here, but probably wasn't the best for customer service or for getting tips. But I did what I had to.

A sunburned, tipsy man reached out to pinch my backside.

"Excuse me," I said as I scooted out of his reach. "I'm not a lamb and this isn't a petting zoo. So don't touch." I lasered a look at him. He withdrew his hand like it had been slapped.

His friends all started laughing, and one said, "Oooh, burn."

He put up his hands in the air. "My apologies."

I looked up to see that Vivi had come out of her office and observed the whole thing. She actually smiled and then put her fist over her mouth like she was covering a laugh.

At nine thirty, Joaquín and I were putting stools on top of tables so we could sweep and mop the floors. Vivi was in the kitchen, emptying and reloading the dishwasher.

"Joaquín, who worked here before I showed up? It doesn't seem possible that it was just you and Vivi."

"On normal days, Vivi is out here working as hard as anyone, but it hasn't been normal around here since Boone died. So you showed up just when we needed someone."

I'd been so caught up in my own life that I'd forgotten how much Boone's death affected Vivi, and Joaquín too. I smiled, but felt embarrassed that I'd been so wrapped up in myself. "He was such a good man." Maybe that was why Boone wanted me here.

He knew Vivi would need help while she grieved if he died.

"He was. Loved his grandmother, worried about her, wanted the best for her."

I hoped I was doing my best. For Vivi. For Boone. If I was going to upend my life, I should make it worth it. I'd been telling myself that all of this had been thrust upon me. But I didn't have to come here or stay. I'd been in Chicago for my entire life. Perhaps a change for a few weeks was what I needed and I didn't know it. Trust Boone to know me better than I knew myself. "You didn't answer my question. Did anyone work here before me?"

Joaquín put another stool on top of the table. "Elwell's daughter."

CHAPTER 15

Elwell's daughter! "Ivy?" I remembered her name from Elwell's obituary. "Why'd she leave?" I asked. I tried to remember who was with Gloria at the memorial service but didn't remember anyone who looked like they could have been her daughter. That was odd, I thought again.

Joaquín ignored me for a couple of seconds, glanced toward the back like he was checking to see where Vivi was. He finally looked up. "Vivi caught her stealing."

Whoa. From what I'd heard and read, Elwell was loaded. Why was his daughter stealing? "Really? I can't imagine Vivi tolerating that. No wonder she fired her."

"Vivi gave her more than one chance. She let her pay the money back. Things were okay for a couple of months, and then it happened again. She tried to blame me. But after the third time, Vivi said no more."

"Did Vivi press charges?" I asked.

Joaquín shook his head. "I thought she should have after the second time. But the heritage owners are a tight-knit group." He paused. "Maybe too close."

What did he mean by that? "But Elwell didn't own one of the heritage businesses, so he wasn't really part of that group."

"They've all known one another since they were in diapers. And their parents knew each other too. Anyway, Vivi wouldn't press charges and just let her go. Didn't fall for the crying, begging, apology routine that last time."

"I'm surprised Elwell hung out here after that. Wasn't he mad?" Or maybe that's why Elwell came in here wearing the armadillo shell. To make Vivi mad, or to interfere with her business. Like I'd thought earlier, it made some people uncomfortable enough to leave.

"Not that you could tell."

"Why do you think she was stealing the money?" Honestly, I was making good money in tips, and Joaquín made even more. A person could make a fairly decent living working here. Although the cost of living was high.

"I'm not sure. Her boyfriend is trouble. Always in trouble."

"Was she using?" I asked. If her boyfriend was trouble and she needed money, drug use could be a common thread.

Joaquín paused again like he was weighing how much to tell me. "Not on the job that I could tell. And I watched her close, because Vivi didn't need those kinds of problems. Maybe recreationally."

We finished cleaning up.

"Let's get out of here," Joaquín said.

"Okay. I need to get some groceries." I didn't mention I'd be stopping by another heritage business to do a little more nosing around.

I walked into Russo's Grocery Store at ten still pondering the fact that Elwell's daughter worked for Vivi until she was caught stealing money. Maybe that was why Elwell and Vivi had been arguing. Although in my opinion he should have been thanking her, not mad at her. Vivi had given Ivy a lot of chances and hadn't pressed charges. Who could be mad at that?

"Hey, you're the little gal who's working for Vivi." The man was one of the regulars at the Sea Glass. He had a big hook nose and a belly that stretched the limits of his shirt.

He stood in the canned food aisle. I walked over to him. "Yes, sir." Wow, that came out more naturally than when I'd said it to Deputy Biffle. Although Boone had "Yes, ma'amed" and "No, sired" everyone he talked to, even when we were in college. So maybe that was why it was getting easier for me to use it. I stuck out my hand. "I'm Chloe Jackson. I need to buy some groceries."

"Kind of figured that, because you came to my grocery store." He shook my hand. "I'm Fred Russo. And you have come to the right place."

That's almost exactly what Ralph had said to the people in front of me when I rode the Redneck Rollercoaster. But Fred had a drawl longer than a ten-foot alligator. Every word seemed to have at least four syllables. "I moved into a place and need to stock up on some food."

"Finding somewhere to live this time of year isn't easy. More tourists coming all the time. Great for business, but tough to find affordable housing."

"That's the truth."

"Where'd you end up?"

I weighed telling him the truth. But I was here for information, so maybe giving some first would soften him up. "Vivi is letting me stay in Boone's cottage." He hid a quick, surprised look as best he could. What the heck was that about? "You seem surprised," I said.

"I am. Never was much good at hiding things. My wife said it was my best quality. Of course, she left me five years ago, so who knows." He shook his head. "I was afraid Vivi was going to make a shrine out of that place. She loved him like a redneck loves his truck. He was the last of Vivi's line. He was supposed to take on the Sea Glass someday."

I knew Boone's mom died when he was a senior in high school. She was an only child, as was he.

Fred shook his head slowly. "It was devastating to Vivi more because she lost her precious boy, but I'm sure what will happen to the Sea Glass weighs on her too. It must mean Vivi's doing okay if she's letting you live there. I'm glad."

"Boone was a dear friend. We met at college orientation and hit it off."

Fred sighed. "Vivi's dream was for him to start a family in that little cottage, then eventually, he could have the big house and Vivi would retire to the cottage. All down the drain now." He glanced down at his feet and then shrugged.

My heart broke a little bit at that thought. My brain was wondering where the big house was and just how big it was.

"How was Vivi doing when you left the Sea Glass?" Fred asked.

"You probably know better than I do how she's doing," I said. "You guys are all so close." I wasn't bold enough to ask outright if he knew why someone would kill Elwell. "Elwell seemed like a nice guy to me."

Fred started shelving cans of black-eyed peas. "He was. He came in here a lot to buy things. Even though he could have saved some money shopping elsewhere. It's hard to compete with the big chain grocery stores. All I can do is provide the highest-quality items I can and encourage people to shop local. You didn't answer my question about how Vivi is doing."

"It's hard to tell, but Vivi was working in the kitchen when I left."

"Sounds like Vivi. Always moving forward."

"I hope she's okay. It worries me that the sheriff's deputies have questioned her a couple of times."

"That's bad business that he was killed out behind the Sea Glass with one of Vivi's channel knives. Her fingerprints were all over it."

Oh no. "It was Vivi's channel knife? How do you know?"

He slapped a hand to the side of his head. "That ex-wife I mentioned? She's a dispatcher and knows what's going on. Please don't pass that on. Me and my big mouth. That's another thing she didn't like."

"I don't have anyone to tell." That wasn't entirely true, but I had to say something to cover all the thoughts I was processing

"Is your ex Delores?"

"Yes, ma'am. Now, what can I help you find?" Fred asked.

Well, that was an abrupt change of subject. Maybe he just wanted me out of here so he could get back to work. Or maybe he regretted telling me about the channel knife. "I'll just wander, if that's okay." The place wasn't that much bigger than the Sea Glass. Not like the big grocery stores in Destin.

"Holler if there's something you're looking for you can't find. Fish market's in the back. Fresh Gulf shrimp's discounted at the end of the day. We'll be closin' up in about twenty minutes."

"Okay, thanks. I'll hurry." Fifteen minutes later, I pushed my cart up to the register. There were three registers and only one was open. I looked around for Fred to say goodbye after my groceries were bagged and I had paid, but I didn't see him. A few minutes later, I was headed back to Boone's house. I couldn't stop thinking that Fred knew about the channel knife. Did he know because Delores had told him or was it because he had killed Elwell?

CHAPTER 16

I unpacked shrimp, garlic, butter, olive oil, pasta, spices, and some other necessities. I'd missed my morning run, so I decided to go now, before I fixed anything to eat. Even though it was dark out, the moon was shining on the sand, so it was light enough to head out. I pulled running clothes from one of my suitcases, which all remained full. Unpacking felt like settling into a life I wasn't sure I wanted. The suitcases represented freedom. Besides, once Vivi got everything straightened away with Elwell's murder and coped with Boone's death, I wouldn't be needed here anymore.

After changing, I crossed the porch and stopped when I realized there was already a new screened door. Wow, Ann worked fast. She'd fixed the old door, and added sturdy new hinges and a new lock. The keys hung inside on the lock. I locked the door behind me and set out on the sand, running away from the Sea Glass for the first time.

It was high tide and I couldn't find any firm sand

to run on, but I pressed on anyway. I passed the area of pine trees and then came to a series of houses. Most looked like they'd been here awhile. An occasional new monstrosity jutted above the others, which were two stories at most. Wide verandas faced the Gulf on most of the houses. Fans whirred on them, and people sat out on the porches even at ten thirty at night.

I hadn't gone far when I turned back. Running in the soft sand took more energy than I had. A trail of silver led across water so flat it looked like you could walk across it to the rising moon. Back at the house, I took a quick shower and started cooking. I liked to cook. I just never had much time to do it. After I got water boiling in a pot and added the pasta, I peeled and deveined the shrimp—the worst part of the whole thing as far as I was concerned. Next came sautéing shrimp in garlic, olive oil, and butter. Little smells better than garlic cooking. When the pasta was done, I drained it, added it to the pan with the shrimp, and tossed it altogether. I sprinkled on some red pepper flakes and chopped a ripe tomato to finish the dish.

I took a plateful out to the porch, along with a glass of ice-cold chardonnay. My pasta was delicious and I dug in with gusto, but I didn't have anyone to share it with. No friends to invite over or to laugh with. I had to admit I was lonely. I missed my weekly trivia nights with my fellow librarians. Our team rocked and we were hard to beat. The thought made me smile.

Going back out on the town held no appeal and I didn't want to sit around feeling sorry for myself, so I video called my parents. I decided not to mention Elwell's murder. Mom's smiling face popped up on my screen.

"Chloe, we were just talking about you. How are you, love?"

"I'm settling in. Where are you two?" Six months ago, my parents had shocked my brothers and me by putting their stuff in storage, renting their house, and setting out in an RV to locations unknown. My parents were the only people I'd told why I was really down here.

"We got to Steamboat Springs, Colorado, just yesterday," my mom said. My father popped into view behind my mom's shoulder. "We plan to stay for at least a month. The air is so refreshing."

"If you can't take the heat down there, come visit for a few days," Dad said. "We plan to go rafting on the Yampa River."

I perked up, picturing the roll and pitch of the raft as it flew down the river. Of course, this time of year most of the snow would have already melted and the river might be calmer. "That sounds like fun."

I'd already visited them once a few months ago and had slept on the table that converted into a bed. A horribly uncomfortable bed. "I'd love to, but work is busy." I didn't want to tell them about the murder or they might pack up and come get me. Or worse, send one of my brothers.

"Do you like it, honey?" Mom asked.

"It's interesting. Drunk people aren't all that different from the toddlers at the library."

My parents laughed. "Where are you staying?" they asked at the same time. The two of them thought so much alike that they often said the same thing in unison. Or the same thing at separate times if you were trying to pull the old if-one-says-no-ask-the-other trick as a kid.

I'd told them that I'd been staying in a hotel the last time we had talked. "Vivi gave me the keys to a cottage Boone stayed in when he was here."

"That was nice of her," my dad said.

"It is. Let me show you around." I walked around the place with the phone out so they could see my new abode. "Wait until you see the view." I went out on the screened porch, opened the door, and walked out, turning a full circle. Even though it was dark the moon was still providing enough light to get the idea. After they oohed and ahhed, I took them into the bedroom I was using.

"You haven't unpacked yet, Chloe," Mom said.

My mom was a bit of a neat freak. She would never live out of a suitcase for ten plus days. "I've been busy. It's next on my list."

"The neighbor just knocked on our door, dear," my dad said. "We're having cocktails with them. Hey, do you have any new drinks we should try?"

"Not yet." Heck, maybe I should try to invent something. That would be fun. "Take care. Love you."

"You too, sweetheart," they said together. My parents were full of terms of endearment.

I stood staring at the closet doors. Up to this point, the thought of seeing Boone's clothes had kept me from even looking inside. But my mom was right, it was time to unpack. I flung the doors open and found nothing. It was empty, with a row of nice wooden hangers dangling on a rod. I hung a few things and then moved to the dresser. It was empty too. Boone hadn't lived here full time—he had lived in Chicago—but if this place was his, I would have expected to find some of his things here. I filled the drawers with my clothes, the combination of sadness and regret wafting around like a spirit as I did. Someone must have cleaned out the cottage before I got the keys.

I pictured Vivi doing it and thought about how sad she must have been. There'd been a week or so between the official notification that Boone's body had been found and when his body was returned to the States. Maybe she'd cleaned the house out then, or maybe after the funeral, when she accepted there was no chance of Boone ever returning. I opened the top drawer of the nightstand next to the bed. It hadn't been cleaned out.

A comb and a pair of Boone's reading glasses remained. He hated wearing the glasses—vanity's name isn't always woman. There were also two paperbacks—a thriller and a cozy mystery. Boone had been an avid reader. We used to trade books all the time. I pulled out the drawer further and spotted an upside-down, framed photograph, which I picked up and flipped over. It was a picture of Boone and me. One I'd never seen before. We were standing by Lake Michigan. My head was thrown back with laughter and Boone was looking at me.

I made a funny, choking noise as I realized the expression on his face was almost identical to the way Wade had looked at Vivi earlier today. Tender. Loving. *He loved me.* I ran a finger over his face. "How could I have been so stupid?" I asked the photo. "You loved me. Not as a friend like you always said, but really loved me."

I'd been engaged for two years, until last year. Boone had never said anything negative about my fiancé, but they had only tolerated each other. Never the friends I had hoped they'd be. I'd gradually realized I had way more fun with Boone than my fiancé, and had broken it off. There had been a reason I'd put off setting a date, planning the wedding. I always told my fiancé I was too busy, but deep down, perhaps I knew how Boone felt. Maybe, given time, I would have fallen for Boone instead of thinking of him as a sidekick. My best buddy. But now we'd never have that chance. I set the photo on the nightstand and fell asleep on top of the covers, looking at Boone.

My phone buzzing with a text alert woke me up at seven. It was from Vivi. This was a first. She sent me the address of a lawyer in Emerald Cove and told me to meet her there at ten. As I threw on my running clothes, I wondered what the heck that was about. Was I in some kind of trouble too? Would I have to testify for or against Vivi? The argument I'd overheard was damning, but how would anyone even know I'd heard it? I certainly hadn't mentioned it to anyone, although it had been weighing on me. Had Vivi told someone that I'd heard? She knew I was in the building at the time. I hit the sand and decided to quit worrying. Ten o'clock would come soon enough.

* * *

This was no ordinary lawyer's office. It was more beach shack than building and didn't seem like it could withstand a decent wind. Surfboards lined the wall behind the table that passed for a desk. A lamp that was a hula girl holding a pineapple-shaped lampshade sat on one corner of the table, a huge conch shell on the other. The gray-headed, shaggy-haired lawyer wore cargo shorts and a button-down shirt printed with sailboats. I recognized him from seeing him at the Sea Glass. He was Buford's card-playing buddy. I hoped I hid my shock.

He stood when I walked in and reached out to shake my hand. "I'm Ed Ashford, and you, of course, are Chloe."

"It's nice to see you again, Mr. Ashford." I wouldn't ever have guessed he was a lawyer from seeing him at the bar.

"Please, call me Ed."

"Okay." I perched on the chair on the left side of the desk. Vivi sat on the chair on the right in pink capris, white, high-heeled sandals, and a shirt with tiny cocktails glasses on it. She'd barely glanced at me when she came in. I still didn't know why I was here.

Ed put on a pair of reading glasses and looked over them at Vivi and me. "So, Boone's will—"

"Boone's will?" I asked.

"Yes," he said. "Why did you think you were here?"

I didn't think I should say. That I thought this was about Vivi being questioned by the deputies. "I wasn't sure."

"You didn't tell her the purpose of the meeting?" Ed looked at Vivi.

She leaned forward. "Can you get on with it, please? I have a business to run."

"Sure. Basically, this leaves Chloe the house you deeded Boone, Vivi, and all its belongings. Plus his boat."

I almost fell off my chair. "What—"

Ed ignored me. He shifted in his chair, looked over his glasses at Vivi, and then back down at his paper. "And Boone has divided his half of the Sea Glass between the two of you."

CHAPTER 17

Vivi shoved out of her chair and looked down at Ed. She turned and stalked out of the room, slamming the door behind her. It rattled the entire shack.

Boone owned half the Sea Glass. That phrase was whirling faster than a new blender through my brain. We'd been so close. How could he not have ever told me this? Especially on the night I agreed to come down here.

"I don't want it. Any of it," I said. "Vivi can have the Sea Glass. I can't imagine what Boone was thinking. She doesn't want me around. I'm just here because of Boone." I poured out the story to this man, a stranger.

"Boone left a letter for you." Ed opened a manila file folder, took out an envelope, and handed it to me. "Read this before you make any decisions."

I looked down at the envelope, a cream-colored vellum. It was heavy, but the weight of what he'd done was worse. I stood. "Okay, I'll read it, and then I'll come back and you can help me figure this out."

"Don't make any rash decisions," he said.
I nodded, not convinced I wouldn't.

At nine that night, Joaquín locked the doors and turned to me. "What's going on with you and Vivi?"

She had spent the day in her office with the door closed. I'd knocked on Vivi's office door more than once during the day. Every time I had, she'd yelled that she was busy. Earlier in the day, Wade had come over for a while. When he left, he had shot a worried glance at me. But it was too busy for me to talk to anyone about what had happened this morning. Vivi left around five with just a quick word to Joaquín, asking him to close the place.

I needed someone to talk to, and Joaquín seemed to be the only one available at the moment. "I'll buy you a drink and tell you what I know."

"What do you want?" he asked.

"Something fruity and happy."

Joaquín laughed. "You want a happy drink? I've never had anyone ask me for a happy drink before."

I watched as he made something with peach schnapps, champagne, and muddled peach. He poured it into a fancy glass and stuck a turquoise paper umbrella in it. "Happy enough?" He got a bottle of Coors Light out of the cooler and popped off the lid. We sat next to each other at the bar.

I took a big drink. "This is delicious."

"Good. Now what's going on?"

I told him about the visit to the lawyer. About Vivi's reaction.

"Whoa. I wasn't expecting to hear that," Joaquín said. "What did the letter say?"

I looked down at my feet for a moment. "I haven't read it yet."

Joaquín arched one of his eyebrows at me.

"I wasn't ready to this morning, and I had to get to work." I took a shuddery breath. "I'm scared to read it."

"Do you want to read it now? I can hang around for a bit longer." He glanced at the clock as he said it.

I knew he got up early to fish, and he had a husband to get home to. "Thank you. But I think I'll wait until I get home. To Boone's." *To my place.* The thought didn't make me happy.

"I get that. I'll text you my number in case you need anything after you read it."

Thank heavens for Joaquín. Without him, I'd truly be alone down here. He was the Scarecrow to my Dorothy. A much better-looking scarecrow. "Thanks, Joaquín. Let's get out of here. I know you get up early." We finished our drinks, Joaquín locked up, and we headed out.

I took a glass of wine onto the screened porch, along with the letter from Boone. I sat in the dark for a few minutes, sipping my wine and listening to the waves. The envelope glowed white in the darkness, like it was pulsating. I finally sighed, flipped on a lamp on the wicker end table, and picked up the envelope. After a few moments, I realized staring at it would accomplish nothing. I flipped it over and ran my finger under the edge, cutting my index finger in the process. Ouch, ouch, ouch. I drew out the stationery. The sheets were folded in half. After taking a deep breath, I forced myself to open the pages and look down. The handwritten letter was dated right before Boone left for Afghanistan.

> *Dear Chloe,*
> *If you are reading this, things didn't go as planned.*

I took a sip of my wine. Set it back down with a shaky hand.

> *I always pictured us gray-haired, sitting on a veranda, watching our grandkids play in the Gulf.*

Could that have been our future? Other than a couple of awkward drunk kisses our freshman year in college, we'd always been buddies. We both dated other people. Although, now that I thought about it, Boone rarely had a relationship that lasted more than a couple of months. I had always teased him about being a playboy, with all his dating around. There'd been one girl a couple of years ago who I thought might have been the one for him. She'd started out being really friendly to me, but the longer they'd dated, the colder she'd become toward me. Now I knew why.

> *Maybe that wouldn't ever have been our lives. Maybe you couldn't love me the way I love you. And if you're reading this, we won't ever know if that dream could have come true. But I've always loved you, Chloe. Since that first day when you got lost at*

orientation. Vivi always told me to marry my best friend, and that's you.

What did Vivi know about Boone and me? Was that the reason she was so cold to me? The reason the picture was left behind in Boone's room when so much else was gone? Maybe she left it there so I'd know what I'd missed out on with Boone. Or maybe she'd accidentally overlooked that drawer.

I'm not sure if you're cursing me or thanking me for giving you a quarter of the bar.

I wasn't sure either. And I still didn't understand why he'd done it.

You probably don't understand why.

I almost laughed. Boone and I had always been so in sync. How could I not have seen us as a possibility? Lord knows I always chased the wrong guys and ended up getting hurt more than I should have.

Vivi is probably going to offer you a lot of money for your quarter of the bar. Maybe more than it's worth. I'm asking you to say no to her. I can't explain it fully, but I think in time you'll come to understand why. Trust me on this one. Please. Obviously, it's the last thing I'll ever ask you to do for me. All my love, Boone

A half sob, half gasp burst out of me with a strange keen to it as I dropped the letter beside me. *Boone.* I clicked off the lamp, leaped up, and went out the back door. I sat on the stoop, feeling about as restless as I ever had. The moon was out in full force. The waves almost flat. I leaped up, grabbed the paddle-board and oar shoved under the porch, and launched myself into the Gulf before the smart side of my twenty-eight-year-old brain told me this was stupid. The water was so shallow here, only calf deep. If I fell in, getting my shorts and T-shirt wet wouldn't matter.

Working my muscles, concentrating on centering myself on the board, kept me from thinking about Boone's letter. I stayed close to shore. Coming out here at night might not be the smartest thing, but staying close in mitigated the risk. I kept at it until I was worn out. Or tuckered out, as a local might say. While I carried the board and oar back up the beach, I spotted someone sitting on the beach halfway between the shoreline and the house. Rhett. Great.

He stood as I approached, and there was no way to avoid him. "What are you doing here?" I asked.

"I was out for a run and saw some idiot out on a paddleboard. Alone. At night." He paused. I kept walking toward my house. "I wanted to make sure the idiot was okay."

I couldn't disagree that it was probably a foolish thing to have done. And I was too tired to argue from an emotional and physical standpoint. I stopped and looked at him. "Thanks. You're right." A breeze ruffled his hair and chilled me enough to make me shiver. "I'm going to head in. Have a good evening."

"Promise me you won't go out alone on the water at night."

"I don't make promises I might not keep." In fact I

think I was off making promises to anyone ever again.

"So, I'm going to have to come out here every night to make sure you're okay?" Rhett didn't make it sound like that was such an onerous task.

Thank heavens it was dark and he couldn't see the blush that came with the every night comment. "I'm sure you have better things to do." Ann, for one. I walked back to the cottage and stowed the paddle-board and oar. Rhett stood where I'd left him for a moment, staring toward the cottage in the moon-light.

"Thanks for worrying about me," I called. I let my-self back onto the porch. Locked the door behind me. "Good night, moon. Good night, Rhett. I will solve this mystery yet." Ah, children's books and rhymes. Loved them. I said it softly so he didn't think I was nuts.

He waved, and then he headed west, back toward the marina. I sat back on the swing and grabbed my glass of wine. Took a healthy drink. Boone's letter glowed on the seat next to me, where I'd dropped it. I forgot all about Rhett and rhymes and children's books.

CHAPTER 18

The Hickle glass-bottom boat did a sunrise tour. It was the perfect morning for a ride. A soft breeze combatted the humidity, and there were just enough clouds to promise a spectacular sunrise. I'd never been on a glass-bottom boat before and could barely contain my excitement. After our captain, Leah Hickle, backed the boat out of its spot in the marina, we headed west. Slowly passing docked boats, including Boone's. Soon we chugged up a bayou I didn't know existed.

Leah had a heart-shaped face with big blue eyes and enviable lashes. She looked like she was in her thirties. Her blond hair pulled back in a ponytail, and she wore a Hickle Glass-Bottom Boat T-shirt. Her family owned the boat and Leah captained it with a deft hand. She'd turn back to look at the twenty passengers who'd boarded with me as she talked about the area. It looked like she could get us to the bay blindfolded. My fellow passengers were a mix of kids and adults. Eyes were rubbed and yawns were catching. But the boat was full even on a Thursday morning.

I took the seat closest to where Leah stood at the wheel. The combination of gas from the engine, live oaks, and humid, salty air wasn't awful. Soft, warm air caressed my face. Live oaks heavy with Spanish moss leaned over above us to form a creepy tunnel.

Cranes and pelicans roosted in the scrub pine below the oaks. Birds called to one another as they woke up.

"You can watch for gators," Leah said, "but it's likely you won't see any. While Southern Florida has millions, we probably only have thousands here on the Panhandle."

Only thousands? One seemed too many to me. I watched for alligators along the too-close banks but didn't see any.

"If you go golfing and your ball lands in the water, don't stick your hand in to get it back." Leah paused. "If you like your hand."

She didn't mention snakes. I hoped we didn't see any. Like Indiana Jones, I hated snakes.

Leah flipped on lights under the boat.

We all stared down. The water here was brown and a bit murky, but I spotted fish darting among the roots of trees. Kids oohed and aahed as fish swam under the glass. I did my share of oohing too. The tree roots looked like bony arms reaching out to grab us.

Leah wasn't as much of a ham as Ralph was on the trolley, but she was knowledgeable. She kept the kids involved, telling them that pirates were rumored to have left treasure and Native Americans had left arrowheads and tools along the bayous.

But the kind of treasure I was seeking was the truth about why Elwell died and who had killed him. Although it was hard to think about that given my day yesterday. I'd barely slept after the twin bombshells Boone had dropped yesterday by leaving me part of the bar and his love letter. He'd given me a lot to think about. My own bombshell had hit around two in the morning. I could be a silent partner in the bar, just rubber-stamping things Vivi wanted to do from afar in Chicago.

"Shout if you see any treasures," Leah said. But this wasn't a ride at an amusement park where fake treasure lined the route. And the calls of the waking birds weren't pumped out on hidden speakers. "There's lots of bayous that stem off this one. Rumors of pirates and moonshiners abound even today."

When we popped out into the bay, Leah sped up. I leaned back against my seat and raised my face and closed my eyes. Maybe it was the boat, fresh air, and being on the water, but I felt lighter this morning. Boone wouldn't want me to mope around. Vivi and I would figure out what to do about the bar. It was hard to feel sorry for myself on a gorgeous morning in such a beautiful place.

Leah cut the engine abruptly. "The sun will pop over the horizon in about a minute."

Rays already shot out into the pink and orange clouds. Phones were out and pictures were snapped. Seconds later, the sun appeared, first a timid slice and then in its blazing glory. All too soon, it was too bright to look at.

"Look," a small boy yelled. He pointed down at the glass.

I gasped as a flash of black beneath the boat caught everyone's attention. Then another and another. We had come across a small pod of dolphins. They danced and played around the boat as everyone reached for their cameras to take videos. I couldn't decide who looked happier—the people on the boat or the dolphins who leaped and dove and smiled. Okay, so they probably weren't really smiling, but it seemed so.

Leah was too busy keeping an eye on everyone to make sure no one went overboard to talk to me. After the dolphins moved on, we chugged slowly back to the marina as Leah told stories about the fishing industry, storms, and early settlers.

"In the forties, during a hurricane, the town of Destin began to flood. In a panic, the residents helped carve the East Pass, letting the water flowing into Choctawhatchee Bay out into the ocean. It forever altered the bay and the landscape of Destin—for better or worse."

Once we were back at the marina, I let everyone off the boat before me. Finally, it was just Leah and me.

"All ashore," Leah said. "Did you have a good time?"

"Those dolphins were amazing. And your stories. The tour was even better than I'd heard." That was a small fib. I hadn't heard anything about the tour. But it was fun.

"How do you like working at the Sea Glass?" Leah asked.

"It's interesting. The beach is beautiful."

"Vivi isn't herself. She's usually charming and funny."

"It's understandable." Was the word out about my part ownership in the bar? I didn't want to come right out and ask. "I'm worried about the Elwell situation and its effect on Vivi. Have you heard anything?" I might as well be blunt. All my trying to eavesdrop at the bar had yielded next to no information.

"Nothing solid. Just the rampant rumors and innuendos."

"What's the rumor mill saying?"

"The three big rumors are: Elwell was gambling, had a brain tumor, or had some kind of deal going on with someone."

The brain tumor seemed the least likely explanation for a murder. Although it might explain his strange behavior, like wearing the armadillo shell as a hat. But it wouldn't explain why someone stabbed him and left him to die by a dumpster. If Elwell did have a brain tumor and had asked a friend to help him on his way, there must be a gentler, more dignified way to do it. The crime seemed planned because someone had taken the time to set Vivi up. Gambling debts seemed the most likely, but the other heritage owners indicated he had money, giving his wife ten million reasons for wanting him dead. And if he had that kind of money, of course he had deals going on.

"Do you know his daughter?" I asked. Elwell's daughter was on my list of suspects. She stole from Vivi, her dad was loaded. It didn't make sense.

"Ivy? I went to school with her."

"Is she in any kind of trouble?" I was thinking about her stealing money from Vivi.

"Probably. We don't really run with the same crowd. But the town's small enough, it's hard not to bump into people. Why are you asking all these questions?"

She had a right to know. "The sheriff seems to have spent a lot of time questioning Vivi."

"I heard that. Everyone's worried." Leah started walking toward the ticket office for the glass-bottom boat. I went with her.

Was everyone worried? Someone—the murderer— was probably grateful. Their plan to set up Vivi was working. "Does Ivy still live in Emerald Cove?"

"She moved to Destin a couple of years ago. But she's around often enough. Especially when she was working at the Sea Glass."

"Do you know where she works now?" I asked.

"The Crow's Nest, over on Okaloosa Island. It's a dive. But don't expect to find out anything from her. She hates Vivi."

All the more reason to talk to her. "Thanks. And thanks for the boat ride this morning. It was great." I put going to the Crow's Nest on my list of things to do. But first I had to get to work and face Vivi.

CHAPTER 19

All my efforts to talk to Vivi had been thwarted. At two o'clock, Ann Williams came in and took a table in the corner opposite Buford and Ed, who were playing cards. I took my order pad and walked over to Ann.

"Thanks for fixing the door. How much do I owe you?"

A smile played around her lush lips. "I'll send you a bill."

"Okay, great. What do you want to drink?"

"Just sparkling water with lemon."

"Do you have to go back to work?" I asked.

"Hopefully not today."

"Everyone deserves some downtime."

As I walked back to the bar, I tried to figure Ann out. She certainly wasn't Midwest or Southern friendly. Maybe she just liked being mysterious. Always with the black clothes and all. She had a New Yorker's attitude, but without the accent. She had some kind of Southern-sounding accent, but I couldn't place it. I shrugged as I fixed her drink—sparkling water I could handle. I glanced at the door to Vivi's office, which had remained closed except for a couple of brief moments that all seemed perfectly timed with me having just picked up a tray of drinks to deliver.

After I delivered the sparkling water to Ann, I went out on the deck to check on the people there. Holy guacamole, it was hot out here. The fans hanging down from the roof over the deck just stirred the hot air. But the view was spectacular and the tables were full.

Since I'd started, I was becoming adept at shifting away quickly to avoid the bottom pinchers and slappers. It was almost like a ballroom dance step. Left, left, right, *right*! I'd managed to do it without dumping drinks on anyone so far. What I couldn't figure out was why anyone thought they could pinch me like my bottom was a baby's cheek.

After Joaquín made the drinks and I delivered them, I knocked on the door to the office. I waited a beat, and then another. Finally, I heard a muffled "Come in." Vivi was staring at her computer, at a spreadsheet. When she saw it was me, she closed the tab. A shot of her and Boone fishing together was her background photo.

"Vivi, we have to talk," I said.

Vivi had on a sundress in bright floral oranges. Her hair was held back with a wide, white headband. She didn't look happy to see me, but she gestured for me to sit down.

"What?" she asked.

"Really, Vivi? What? Don't you think we need to

talk about what happened in the lawyer's office yesterday?"

"There's nothing to talk about. I'll buy you out."

As much as I wanted to scream yes and hug her, I thought of Boone's letter. "No." *Boone, I hope you knew what the heck you were doing.*

Vivi reared back, like I'd threatened to hurt her. And really, my "no" probably did hurt her. She rolled back her desk chair a few inches. If I didn't understand why Boone wanted me to keep a share of the bar, Vivi certainly wouldn't understand it. She took a few deep breaths, composed her face like she was facing a troublesome child. Trust me, I knew that look, having used it on many children at the library.

"I'll pay you double what your portion is worth."

Double? Not that I'd let her pay me more than it was worth, but darn, she must really want me out of here, which, in some perverse way, made me want to keep my share.

A firm knock on the door kept me from answering.

"Vivi Slidell?" a deep male voice said. "This is Deputy Biffle. We need to talk."

Vivi's face paled. I jumped up. "I'll stall him for a couple of minutes. I heard that the channel knife was from here and had your fingerprints on it. Is that true?"

"Yes. It is."

This was bad. Terrible. Dreadful. Pick your synonym. "Call your lawyer. You do have a lawyer, don't you?"

Vivi stiffened. "I do. Thank you for stalling Deputy Biffle."

I opened the door a crack and slipped through, forcing Deputy Biffle to step back. "Vivi will be with you in a minute. She's finishing up a call." He didn't look happy at having to wait.

"Can I get you a Coke or water or something?" I asked him. "We have a great selection of beers on tap if you're off duty." I was hoping he was, and that maybe he was just one of Vivi's vast group of friends. But I guessed her pale face said otherwise, as did his uniform.

"Coke, be nice," he said. "My shift isn't close to over."

Darn. "Why don't you just sit there at the end of the bar while I get it," I suggested.

Deputy Biffle didn't look happy, but he settled on the stool. I filled a tumbler with ice and used the nozzle to fill his glass, taking care to tip the glass so it wouldn't foam too much. I set the glass in front of him, opened a bag of peanuts, dumped some into a small bowl, and gave him those too. He took a few of the peanuts and jiggled them around in his hand before he ate them. Maybe I could find out something about Elwell while he waited for Vivi.

"You must see a lot of interesting things in the line of duty," I said. "I read Florida Man stories all the time." There were online sites that chronicled strange things that happened here. It really did seem like more odd things happened in Florida than other states, but I wasn't sure if there was such a thing as Oklahoma Man, so maybe I just didn't see the news from other states as much.

The deputy chuckled. "Yeah, we read those too.

Makes us feel better about living up here in the Panhandle, where there's less crime." He drank some of his Coke. "But we see enough."

"Anything fun you can tell me?" I asked.

"I pulled over a guy driving a convertible the other day for weaving. Covered in olive oil and only wearing a thong." He pronounced "convertible" slowly: con-v-er-ta-ble. "Smelled like roasting meat."

"Ack," I said. "Drunk?"

"Nope. Claimed he was trying to send a text, but his fingers kept slipping off the keys."

I laughed. "What was with the olive oil?"

"Said it enhanced his tan. Like anyone who lives down here needs help in that department. Sun's damn hot most of the year."

He finished his Coke and glanced at Vivi's still-closed office door. What was she doing in there?

"Any word on Elwell?" I asked. I knew I was going to lose him any minute to Vivi.

He glanced at the door, lowering his eyebrows. He tipped his head toward the office door. "She's got a lot to answer for." He stood, hitched up his equipment belt, and strode over to the office. Just as he was about to knock, Vivi opened the door.

"Come in. I am so sorry for keeping you waiting." She almost fluttered her eyelashes at him, and her drawl was thicker than normal. At the same time, she managed to look like a prim Southern lady. A new look for the Vivi I knew, who was usually in full fierce mode. But maybe that was just with me.

The door closed behind them both. Joaquín came over and stood by my side. "What do you think that's about?"

"The channel knife . . . the one that killed Elwell was from here. It had Vivi's fingerprints on it."

Joaquín muttered in Spanish. "Did Vivi tell you that?"

"She confirmed it but Frank Russo told me first. His ex-wife—"

"Is Delores. The dispatcher."

I looked over at Vivi's office. "You think a glass to the door really helps you hear through it?"

Joaquín shot me a look. We didn't know each other well enough for him to know I was kidding. At least I think I was. I picked up a glass and weighed it in my hand. Rocks glasses had thick bottoms. It didn't seem to me they'd work. A few seconds later, the door opened. Vivi stepped out before Deputy Biffle. She had her hot pink designer purse over her arm and car keys in her hand.

"I'll be back later," she said. Chin up, she led the deputy out the back of the bar.

"Think she's okay?" I asked Joaquín.

"She's a cat. Always lands on her feet." The lines around his eyes belied his words. And I'd seen more than one cat that hadn't landed on their feet. Old wives' tales and all that.

Vivi didn't show back up for the rest of the day. Joaquín changed the upbeat island music to the blues as we cleaned.

"Need a happy drink?" Joaquín asked as we finished up.

"Do I ever, but light on the alcohol. I have some errands to run." I planned to go to the Crow's Nest and look for Elwell's daughter, Ivy, this evening. If I had eyes on her, talked to her, I hoped I could scratch her off my suspect list or go to Deputy Biffle and say, "It's her, she did it, case closed." Then I would take my bows, accept the thanks, and head back to Chicago.

Joaquín made me a drink with strawberries, vodka, and tonic water.

"Hey, where's my umbrella?" I asked.

He laughed and got me a blue one. Joaquín poured a beer for himself.

"Did you have a chance to talk to Vivi about the bar?" Joaquín asked.

"We had just started our discussion when Officer Biffle showed up."

"And?"

"It wasn't going well." I took out the umbrella, closed it, and popped it back open. "Think it's bad luck to open these paper umbrellas inside?"

"I don't believe in bad luck," Joaquín said.

"How come?" I asked.

"I don't believe in luck. I believe in choices that lead to good or bad things."

"You can make all the smart choices you want and bad things still happen."

"That's not luck. It's life."

"You're probably right." We sipped our drinks, contemplating that.

"Did you read the letter from Boone?"

"I did." I couldn't share what the letter had said. It

was too personal to share with Joaquín. Actually it was too personal for me to share with anyone. At least for now. "What's your family like, Joaquín?"

"So you don't want to talk about the letter?" I shook my head. "Okay. My family? Crazy. Loud. Loves a party."

"Do they live here?" I asked.

"My mom does. One sister. The rest of my siblings are scattered around."

"How many siblings do you have?"

"I'm the youngest of six. Three boys and three girls. Girl, boy, girl, boy, girl, boy. My dad died when I was twelve, which my mom says was a good thing."

My eyebrows drew together for a moment. "She does? Why?"

Joaquín took a long drink of his beer. "Because she said I would have killed him or him me."

I couldn't have been more confused. The Joaquín I knew was lighthearted, lovely, and caring. He didn't seem to have a mean bone in his very toned body. Then it slowly dawned on me. "Because you're gay?"

"Yes." He shoved away his beer. "I'm a Latino male who grew up in a devout Catholic family and I'm as gay as a rainbow. It probably would have killed my dad. Especially now that I'm married."

"I can't believe I haven't met your husband yet." Maybe he liked to keep his work life separate from his personal life. "Do I get to meet him?"

"I would love for you too. I'm just never sure how people will react."

I couldn't begin to imagine how hard that must be. "And how is your family about the situation?"

"They've all come around. My mom feels bad that she said I'd have killed my father. And everyone loves Michael."

I patted his arm.

"Let's get out of here," Joaquín said. "You have errands to run and I have a husband to get home to."

If he knew what I was up to, he probably wouldn't be so calm.

CHAPTER 20

Ten minutes later, I drove west on 98. Traffic in Destin wasn't too bad at nine thirty at night. The beachgoers must have finished dinner and returned to their rentals, and the party animals weren't yet out. I took the Destin Bridge over the East Pass. Only a few boats remained at Crab Island. The Crow's Nest was on the west end of Okaloosa Island. The east end was less developed because of the Coast Guard station and the land owned by Eglin Air Force Base. A little sand blew across the divided, four-lane highway. It looked like blowing snow, and I instinctively slowed down until I remembered I wasn't in Chicago anymore.

I sped along until the speed limits lowered and I came to rows of restaurants, bars, and shops. Just before the Brooks Bridge, which went over the intercoastal waterway to Fort Walton Beach, I took a right. I drove past some restaurants and a park to a darker, seedier-looking area. The Crow's Nest was right next to a strip joint. Lovely. I took a quick glance in the mirror after I parked. My eyes looked a bit weary, but I'd do. A couple of Harleys were parked along with trucks jacked up on huge tires.

The bar's windows had a dark tint with neon signs advertising a variety of beers. There was no way to look in and get an idea of what I was facing. I did a quick online search on my phone, but the Crow's Nest didn't even have a website. No more stalling. I forced myself out of the car, walked to the front door, and pushed open the heavy steel door. A few tables were scattered about, a pool table sat in the far corner. Barstools with backs lined the bar. A couple of booths were positioned near the restrooms. People sat as far away from one another as possible.

My flip-flops made little sucking noises as I walked to the bar across the sticky concrete floor. I slipped onto one of the barstools, my feet dangling, and positioned myself near the taps and register. That's where the action would be, if there was any. I left two barstools between me and two cowboys. They wore leather-tooled boots, neatly pressed jeans, long-sleeved, button-down shirts, cowboy hats, and big buckles that made them look like they were on the rodeo circuit. Or maybe they just bought them on Amazon. They stared openly, and I realized I'd been staring at them and hastily looked forward at the line of bottles of booze. The labels were faded on some bottles and torn off on others. That was odd, but this whole place reeked of misery. The two cowboys looked as out of place as I probably did.

A woman with bleached, weathered hair slapped down a napkin in front of me. Thick black eyeliner smeared her upper eyelids. "What'll you have?" she asked. Her voice had more gravel in it than Kathleen Turner's in *Body Heat*. This woman looked about the same age as Leah, but more worn down, kind of like this whole place.

The counter of the bar was cloudy with various stains. The taps had a little rust around the edges. "A bottle of Coors Light would be great. Thanks." That should be safe enough.

"Wanna glass?"

"Nope. The bottle's fine." I didn't trust that anyone had done a good job of washing out the glasses. A hard rock song that I couldn't identify played through tinny-sounding speakers hung by suspiciously worn-looking wires. Bras in a range of colors and sizes hung from the rafters. Classy.

The woman noticed me noticing them as she handed me my beer. "If you want to add yours, you get a free drink."

"I'm good. Thanks."

She laughed. "That's what they all say when they come in. But obviously, they don't all feel that way before they leave."

I laughed too. "Touché. Worked here long?"

"Little over a month."

"How do you like it?" I took a sip of my beer for show. It tasted funny. Skunk beer.

"Not bad. The last place I worked, the woman had a stick where the sun don't shine."

Sounded like Vivi. This might be Ivy.

"Sounds like my boss."

She gave me the once-over. "Yeah? Where do you work?"

"The Sea Glass in Emerald Cove."

She swept another look across me. "Poor you."

"You know the place?"

"Yeah. It's where I used to work. The witch accused me of stealing and tossed me out. Then she killed my dad. I'm going to see to it she fries."

Woah. She had a lot of hostility going on. I wondered why she was so convinced Vivi killed him. "Elwell was your father? I'm so sorry."

"Thank you." Her voice sounded shaky, but there was no glisten of tears to go with it. "I heard some new girl found him. That you?"

"Yeah. No one deserves to die like that." Now what should I say? "He seemed like a nice man. You know how it is working in a bar." A little crazy, with that whole armadillo shell thing going on.

Ivy gave a small nod. "Elwell had his moments, but he could be a mean sumbitch too. It's why my mom moved out a few months ago."

Interesting she called her father Elwell instead of some form of "father." "Was he having health issues? I know sometimes that changes a person."

"Yeah, his health was at risk. My mom just about killed him when she caught him with the pool girl."

Elwell had been cheating on Gloria? Maybe she did kill him.

"That's just a figure of speech, of course. She was mad, but she still loved him. They were getting ready to get back together."

"That's so sad." I shook my head. "Do you know anyone else who had it in for him? If it wasn't Vivi. I hope it wasn't because I need a job." *Liar.* "If Vivi is arrested, I don't know what I'll do."

Ivy narrowed her eyes and tilted her head back for a moment. "What's it to you?"

I'd always been too direct, but if I wanted people around here to answer my questions, I was going to have to give them a reason to do it. "He was good to me. And I found him." I closed my eyes briefly as the image of Elwell behind the dumpster appeared like an unwanted specter. "I can't help wondering what happened. And why. I want justice for Elwell, no matter who did it."

Now a tear glistened, or maybe some mascara had flaked off into her eye. "Lots of people were jealous of his success. Those snooty heritage business owners. They think they run Emerald Cove, but change is coming."

I took another sip of my beer, hoping she'd continue. I set it down and picked at the label.

"They've stopped any real development for years. My dad was helping improve the area. He was gonna pass some laws so they could get more tourism."

Emerald Cove seemed chock full of tourists from what I could tell. The old Florida-style cottages with their wood frames, deep overhangs, lots of windows, and sleeping porches were a huge draw. Each with a unique picket fence only added to the charm that drew people there. Not to mention the beach. It was always on the list of top beaches put out annually.

"How so?"

She gave a quick glance up and down the bar before leaning in. "He had an insider on the town council. New zoning laws allowing for high-rises."

I shuddered to think of high-rises ruining the beaches in Emerald Cove. How could one person on the town council make a change on his own?

"Who was Elwell talking to on the town council?" Not that I'd know them, but maybe I'd heard of them in the bar.

Ivy narrowed her eyes at me again. She muttered something about helping another customer and moved to the other end of the bar. She leaned an elbow on the bar and talked to a man, but kept her eye on me. I really needed to work on my investigative technique so people would be more open.

"You're as pretty as a magnolia that just blossomed."

I turned to look at the cowboys. The one closest to me leaned in. "Or a just-born foal."

"That is possibly the weirdest compliment I've ever had." I turned my back to them and pretended to take a couple more sips of my beer. When Ivy didn't come back my way, I decided it was time to go. I put down the money for my beer plus a five as a tip before heading out.

As I started my car, I again pictured high-rises lining the beach where I ran. That would ruin Emerald Cove. I sure hoped Ivy was wrong. But if she wasn't, that seemed like a motive for murder. It made me wonder about the councilman who was pushing for change. It seemed like he or she would be in danger too if that was the reason Elwell was killed.

I hadn't gone very far when I realized a big pickup truck was following me. The lights glared in my

rearview and side mirrors. It had turned out of the
bar not long after I did. It was a straight shot from the
bar to the light at 98. There I'd taken a left to head back
across Okaloosa Island to Destin, and so had the truck.
Of course, anyone wanting to go to Destin would have
to go the exact same way, so maybe I was being para-
noid. You didn't grow up in a city like Chicago with
two older brothers and concerned parents without
multiple lectures about safety. So I was usually aware
of who was around me in my car or on public transportation.

After we passed bars, restaurants, the Gulfarium—
billed as a marine adventure park—and hit the
more-deserted stretch, the pickup sped up. I hoped
it was going to pass on the left, but instead, it almost
crawled up my bumper. My Beetle had never seemed
smaller. Well, maybe the night I'd slept in it. What
the heck was this guy doing? I hated tailgaters.

I knew I couldn't outrun such a big vehicle, so I
slowed down a bit at a time, hoping they'd get bored
enough that they'd find someone their own size to
pick on. Instead of going around, they stuck with me.
Backing off a little. Just enough that I thought I saw
two cowboy hats silhouetted in the cab of the truck.

Was that the guys from the bar? Why would those
two follow me? Had Ivy sent them after me? Maybe
one of them was the boyfriend Leah had mentioned.
Or was it my big mouth telling them their pickup
line was weird? I wiped a damp palm on my shorts
and tried to relax my grip on the steering wheel.

When we hit the bridge on the East Pass, they
came up beside me. Their truck was so high and my

car so low that I couldn't see who was in the passenger seat. As I lifted my foot to hit the brakes, they swung over toward me. Oh no. I swerved right, coming perilously close to the guardrail. Glimpsed the deep water below. The truck edged closer.

CHAPTER 21

Back off. What was wrong with these guys? I was either going to be squished or forced off the bridge. Or both. I scanned my rearview mirror. No one was directly behind me, although I could see lights in the distance. I slammed on my brakes. The pickup shot forward, grazing the rails of the bridge before swinging back into the left lane and accelerating off.

I sat for a moment almost hyperventilating, working my fingers loose from the grip I'd had on the steering wheel. I could see cars approaching in my rearview mirror. I wanted to stay here for a while, getting up my nerve to drive. But I was an accident waiting to happen.

I slowly sped up as the cars behind me drew closer. *Ivy.* If she thought Vivi killed her dad, she had no reason to send someone after me. But she had told me about the plans for developing Emerald Cove. Maybe no one was supposed to know, and she realized her mistake. Even as the thought chilled me, it also made me more determined to find out what was going on.

A few minutes later, I passed the parking lots at McGuire's Irish Pub on the left and the Emerald Grande on the right. They were packed. Now 98 was full of traffic. It made me feel better. Safer. Though each time I saw a pickup—and there were lots of them—panic started to creep through me. But pickups were popular in this area. If the South ever rose again, they'd do it in monster trucks.

Through this part of Destin, 98 was a four-lane road, but not divided like it was to the east and west. Businesses, from glass companies to souvenir shops to restaurants, lined the roads. The harbor, with its famed fishing fleet, was to my right. Lights twinkled off the water, and groups of people roamed around. I leaned back against the seat. I hadn't even realized I'd scooted up during the chase. If it was one. Maybe it was just a couple of jerks who liked scaring other drivers and nothing to do with me. My car had out-of-state plates. Some natives didn't like all the tourists who invaded this time of year. I relaxed a little but kept a watchful eye out as I drove by AJ's.

After passing Big Kahuna's, a popular water park, I noticed a truck behind me again. My heart pounded harder than the bass of the rock music at the Crow's Nest. My grip tightened on the steering wheel again. At least there was plenty of traffic here. And that traffic gave me an opportunity for some evasive maneuvers. I wanted to see if this was just some random truck, or if my "friends" from the bar were back. They could have easily parked in a lot in Destin and waited for me to pass. The bad part of having a vintage Beetle was, it stood out.

If I'd learned anything driving in Chicago, it was

how to cut someone off and how to weave in and out of traffic lanes. I didn't know Destin well enough yet to go off on side roads. Which ones dead ended or led to quiet, dark street was a mystery to me. Sticking to 98, with its businesses and traffic seemed smartest. A light in front of me changed to yellow. I accelerated through it, as did the truck behind me. Sugar.

I cut over in front of the minivan in the left lane, silently apologizing as I did. The truck sucked in behind the minivan. I dodged back over to the right lane in front of a sedan and back again two cars farther up. Screw whoever was on the bridge. I wasn't going to let them scare me. I'd use the skills I had to keep me safe.

Amazingly, not one person honked at me. I hoped they weren't all on their phones, reporting an erratic driver with Illinois plates. Or maybe I did hope a sheriff's deputy would show up, because I was more than a little freaked out. I didn't remember seeing a sheriff station or fire department around here. Stopping at any other business seemed risky. My companions could just lie in wait for me to come out.

Eventually, I lost them, or thought I lost them, or they weren't after me in the first place. The truck on the bridge could just have been someone texting. Distracted drivers were the worst. I drove around the circle in Emerald Cove, catching my breath. The shop windows were dark. Even the diner was closed. No trucks. No anyone. No kids hanging out in the town circle, although why hang there when there were miles of beaches to spend time on?

A few minutes later, I pulled into Boone's house. So dark. So quiet, except for bugs and frogs and the *whoo* of an owl. So strange for a city girl like me. Once inside, I poured a glass of wine and went out on the screened porch. After settling on the porch swing, I took a few deep breaths. The salt air was calming. As was the wine. Had I really poked a bear, so to speak? When?

I'd asked a lot of questions the last few days. Tried to overhear a lot of conversations in the bar. I'd been too obvious. My trips to the three heritage businesses—the trolley, the grocery store, and the boat— seemed casual enough, at least to me. Maybe not so much if you were a murderer and thought someone was nosing around. Someone killed Elwell and maybe just tried to kill me. I should pack up and head home.

But with Vivi going off with Deputy Biffle again today and Ivy's promise to see her fry, I couldn't do that. I couldn't leave Vivi to fend for herself. Especially not when I was living in Boone's house. I may not have been *in* love with Boone, but I loved him, and he'd been counting on me. I couldn't let him down after what I'd heard tonight.

The beach was deserted. The moon covered by clouds. Off in the distance, far out over the ocean, lightning streaked cloud to Gulf. I was too far away to hear any rumbles of thunder, but the light show was spectacular. It reinforced the situation I found myself in. Something was going on, but it wasn't close enough for me to figure out. I finished my wine. There was nothing further I could do tonight. But I didn't leave the slider open to listen to the Gulf. I made sure it, and everything else, was locked up tight.

* * *

Friday morning brought a pouring rain. The beach-goers would be unhappy, but the shop owners would be delighted, as their stores would fill with restless tourists. I showed up at the Sea Glass early, antsy because I hadn't done an evening run last night or one this morning. Joaquín was already there.

"Where's Vivi?" I asked.

"She said she'd be in later." Joaquín looked a little worried again.

"Is that unusual for her?" I was still too new to know. At least she wasn't in jail.

"Yes. Until you found Elwell murdered, she always opened. She knew with the marine warnings out this morning that I wouldn't be out fishing, so she could come in late."

"Someone followed me last night." I blurted it out. I hadn't meant to, but it obviously scared me more than I wanted to admit. "They tried to run me off the road on the Destin Bridge."

"What?" Joaquín raised his eyebrows at me. "Does this have anything to do with your errand last night? I pictured you picking up milk or getting gas. What were you up to?"

Can. Worms. Opened. "I went to the Crow's Nest to check out Ivy."

"The Crow's Nest?" If Joaquín's voice went any higher, he could audition for soprano at the Lyric Opera of Chicago. "The Ivy who used to work here?" He muttered something in Spanish that sounded like *ay, chihuahua*. Maybe I needed to learn more Spanish.

"Girl, have you lost your ever-lovin' mind?"

"I don't think so." I stood a little straighter. "Vivi's

in trouble. She's been questioned by the sheriff's department. I can either sit around waiting for things to fall apart or I can try to help."

"Why are you doing this?" Joaquín asked.

"Because of Boone. Before he left for Afghanistan, he made me promise to come help out here if anything ever happened to him." I did some rapid blinking to fight back tears. "In my family, we don't renege on promises. No matter what, I can't let Boone down."

Joaquín came over and rubbed my left arm. "Chloe. Honey. You don't have to keep a promise to a dead man."

I threw myself against Joaquín's chest, and he wrapped his strong arms around me. "Yes. I. Do. And if part of that is making sure Vivi stays out of jail, I'll do it."

"You can't put aside your personal safety," Joaquín said.

I stepped back away from him and ran a hand through my short brown hair. "I'll be careful. But obviously, I've done something. Struck a nerve, hit a chord, stirred up a wasp's nest. Pick your cliché."

"I don't like the thought of you staying at Boone's house. It's too isolated. Why don't you come stay with Michael and me for a few nights? The boat isn't huge, but the dining table collapses to make a bed."

"Or you could come stay in the big house with me."

Joaquín and I jumped at the sound of Vivi's voice. Vivi stood by the kitchen door. Keys dangling from one hand and a red designer purse from the other. When did she come in, and how much had she overheard? Her expression was different from usual as she looked at me. Part concern, part her usual imperious look, and part anger. Anger at me or the situation—I wasn't sure.

Vivi's offer was a shocker. I couldn't imagine taking her up on it, no matter how scared I was. "No, thank you. I'm fine at Boone's. I like being there. It makes me feel close to him." I fought back tears again. I missed him. "Besides, Ann fixed the back door and put on a better lock."

"Ann Williams?" Vivi asked.

"Yes. Joaquín told me she's a handyman/woman, or whatever you call someone."

"Joaquín?" I heard a hint of mirth in Vivi's voice. Joaquín looked mystified.

"I told her to send the bill to me," I added.

"I told you she fixes things," Joaquín said.

"Exactly," I answered. "And very efficiently too. The toilet was running the other day, and she fixed that too."

"You asked her to fix the toilet?" Joaquín said.

"She was in here reading, and it was running, so yes." I paused. "Oh, she might have been on a break and wouldn't want to be interrupted. I should have thought of that. Does she have a card, so I can call in the future when something's broken?"

"I'll give it to you," Joaquín said, looking at Vivi.

Vivi made a bit of a choking sound. "I'll add the toilet repair to her bill."

Vivi must have Ann on some kind of retainer to fix things when they broke. I looked out front. The rain had stopped, and some bikini-clad girls were peering in the still-locked doors. "I'll let them in," I said.

"Wait, just a second. Let's sit down tonight after we close and see if we can figure out what you said or did that got you in trouble," Vivi said.

Joaquín and I agreed. Vivi must have overheard most of my conversation with Joaquín about why I was really here. She offered to let me stay with her. Maybe Vivi didn't hate me after all.

CHAPTER 22

Joaquín took a break at two. A well-deserved one, considering how busy we'd been. But Joaquín's breaks made me nervous. I still had no idea how to make most drinks.

A college-age/surfer-dude/frat-boy type swaggered up to the bar. *Please, let him want a beer.*

"I'd like a mojito." Oh no. That was one of those drinks that might seem simple to a customer but seemed complicated to me.

"I need to see your ID." I pointed to a sign that said everyone under forty would be carded.

The guy gave me an exaggerated sigh and dug out his ID. He just made it. He'd been legal for a whole month. Little did this guy know that sheriff's deputies posing as underaged drinkers came in on occasion, according to Joaquín, to see if we were carding people. Joaquín had once seen a bartender in New York City handcuffed and paraded down a street. I didn't want to risk it and carded almost everyone.

I went to the corner of the bar and turned my back to the frat boy so I could look up the recipe. I read through a few and chose the one that sounded the easiest. A mojito only had five ingredients: fresh lime juice, superfine sugar, fresh mint, white rum, and club soda. I found a Collins glass and added the sugar and the lime juice, stirring until it dissolved. Next, I ran the mint around the rim of the glass. Ack. The next step was muddling. What was it with drinks and muddling? I found the stainless-steel muddler I'd seen Joaquín use. He said it was more sanitary than wood ones, although bartenders argued over which was better. The recipe called for twelve mint leaves. Why twelve? What would happen if I only put in eleven, or if I accidently put in thirteen? Would the world end? Would the drink be ruined?

I muddled the mint with the lime juice/sugar mixture. After that, I added the ice, rum, and club soda. This recipe suggested a stirring time of fifteen seconds. Again with the specifics. I couldn't quite see how exactly fifteen seconds would impact the flavor, but I counted one Mississippi, two Mississippi as I stirred. Vivi had insisted we add a piece of sugarcane as garnish along with mint. All of it left my hands sticky, but the mojito looked perfect.

I finally finished and took the drink over to my surfer dude. He took a sip.

"It doesn't taste like the one I had on my last cruise," he said.

I shrugged. Making two cocktails taste exactly the same was almost impossible. From the recipes I'd read, some used simple syrup instead of dissolving sugar in lime juice. Some used Rose's lime instead of real lime juice. There were hundreds of kinds of rum from cheap to rare. It seemed like it was almost impossible to duplicate drinks from another bar. It's why complaints like this drove bartenders crazy, or so I'd recently learned.

The guy picked up the drink, paid, and walked off without leaving a tip. But I didn't have time to worry about it because a line of impatient, couldn't-wait-for-me-to-get-to-their-table drinkers had formed. Fortunately, I had a lot of beer, wine, and rum and Coke drinkers. All of those I could handle myself without problems. By the time Joaquín returned, the line was taken care of and I was feeling pretty good about myself.

I took a break and went for a walk along the waterline. The rain had cleared and left the air heavy and damp. Sunburned kids were building sandcastles while tired-looking parents were eyeing the people lying on lounge chairs under umbrellas with envy. I'd never been one for lying out in the sun. Heck, my skin was so pale, I could probably lay on the sand and blend right in. I liked being by the water or on the water but not just sitting or lying there. I walked along the water to the inlet and then headed up to walk back along the marina.

As I did, I spotted Rhett walking toward me. He was walking with his head down and obviously had something on his mind by the way he was frowning. I stuck to the far side of the walkway, not wanting to bother him, wondering if he could hear my heartbeat rattling harder than the "L" rattled windows in Chicago. *Down, girl.*

"Chloe," he said, looking up as he neared.

"Hey." Odd. I didn't use "hey" as a greeting in Chicago. I'd always been a "hi" or "hello" kind of gal. But people down here said "hey" a lot.

"I see you haven't drowned yourself."

If he only knew. I smiled. "No yet." We looked at each other—awkwardly, in my opinion.

"Chloe—"

"I've got to get back to work."

"How's Vivi?" he called as I set off.

I whirled around. Had he heard something? "Fine as far as I know. Have you heard anything?" He'd been pretty chummy with the dispatcher Delores the day I found Elwell. He might have information that was helpful. I did a wide-eyed thing that had always been effective on men.

"Why don't you have dinner with me and I can fill you in?"

The wide eyes worked every time. "I have to work."

"No dinner break?"

I hadn't really been taking one. I'd been bringing something to eat on the fly. The place was busy. "Tourist season." Plus, there was the whole feud thing between the Slidells and the Barnetts. It seemed like Vivi had just warmed up to me a bit and I didn't want to lose momentum.

He nodded like he understood. It made me wonder what he did for a living. Joaquín might know.

"Another time?" he asked.

"Can you fill me in now?" I had a few more minutes before I should get back.

"Lots of eyes and ears out here. Voices carry on the water."

Now I was curious what he knew. "Okay, Boone's place at ten thirty tonight."

"See you then."

"Okay." Then I hurried back to the Sea Glass.

I sprinted through closing so Vivi, Joaquín, and I could chat, and then I could get home to talk to Rhett. Joaquín had his usual beer. I had something he'd whipped up with blueberries and basil. Vivi pursed her lips when she saw the pink paper umbrella. But couldn't everyone use a little something to make them happy? Vivi sat with her usual sparkling water. It reminded me again that the night of the argument, she'd had a bottle of bourbon sitting in front of her. How much of it had she drunk? Could she even remember what had happened that night?

We all sat down at the table usually reserved for the heritage business owners and looked awkwardly at one another.

"I need to apologize to you both for lying to you about my car being broken down. I was following Boone's wishes and didn't know what else to do."

Vivi put her manicured hand on top of mine for a brief moment. "I understand. I also would have done anything Boone asked me to. He was my heart."

I nodded and looked up, trying to use gravity to keep the tears I felt forming from leaking out. Good grief I was full of tears today.

Joaquín cleared his throat. "So, just what have you been up to?"

CHAPTER 23

"I took a ride on the Redneck Rollercoaster, bought groceries at Russo's, took the sunrise cruise on the glass-bottom boat, and went to the Crow's Nest last night. I just talked to people. Asked a few questions. So really, not much."

Joaquín and Vivi exchanged a look that I couldn't quite interpret.

"You call that not much?" Joaquín asked. "My mother would say your snooping schedule is fuller than a tick that's been on a hound for a week."

My feathers felt a little ruffled. "I was pretending to be a tourist enjoying a day off. Why would anyone think anything else? Oh, did I mention I rented a Jet Ski and saw Gloria with some man's hand on her thigh over at Crab Island?"

Joaquín muttered something in Spanish that ended with *ay, caramba*. I'd been the cause of most of his muttering lately.

"Did you mention Elwell while you were *pretending*?" Joaquín asked.

I thought back. "Ralph told me that Elwell pissed off the wrong people, but didn't say more than that. Do you know what he was talking about, Vivi?"

Vivi lifted a shoulder and dropped it. Wow. These heritage business owners were like some secret society the way they protected one another. But it seemed like Elwell was on the periphery. Maybe Elwell's family hadn't been here as long. I thought back. Buford had said they'd been friends since kindergarten, so Elwell's family had been here over sixty years at the very least. But if they didn't own a business, he was always on the fringe of the group.

"What else did you talk about?" Joaquín asked.

I wondered why Joaquín was asking all the questions. Did he and Vivi plan some kind of good cop/bad cop routine? "Why I'd shown up here." They both knew now why I had. "I gave him my standard car story."

"Where did you go next?" Joaquín asked.

"I stopped at the grocery store on my way home the other night to get some supplies."

"Anything happen while you were there?" Joaquin leaned his forearms on the table.

I wiped a little condensation off the side of my glass. "No. I picked up some food and got a great deal on some shrimp that was left over from the morning's run."

"What about on the glass-bottom boat? Anyone paying extra attention to you there?" Joaquín asked.

"I took the sunrise cruise. It was mostly families with little kids. It didn't look like anyone local."

"Leah didn't say anything unusual on the tour?" Joaquín chugged some of his beer. He was probably as eager to get home as I was.

"No. After we docked, we talked about Elwell and Ivy." I paused. "She mentioned some rumors swirling around that Elwell was gambling, had a brain tumor, or had some kind of deal going on with someone."

Joaquín and Vivi exchanged another of their looks.

"Why do you two keep doing that? What aren't you telling me?"

"Nothing," Vivi said.

Yeah, right. It seemed like Vivi and Joaquín knew something that Vivi didn't want shared. This was so frustrating. They both knew I was trying to help. Why were they keeping me in the dark? Joaquín was loyal to her. He'd been working here for more than ten years. I'd try to find out from him later.

"So then I went to the Crow's Nest and talked to Ivy." Ivy had talked more than Ralph, Frank, and Leah combined, but was any of it truthful? "She claims Elwell had a deal going with one of the town council people here in Emerald Cove. That they were working on getting high-rises approved. Ivy seemed convinced it was going to pass, but one person can't ram a law through on their own, so her confidence seems unwarranted. Right?"

Vivi paled.

"They can't, can they?" I asked.

"No," Joaquín said. "But a couple of the newer members think it's time for change."

"But that would be awful," I blurted out. "It's gorgeous here. There are plenty of high-rises in Destin if people are interested." And from what I'd seen of Destin, people were interested. Parking lots were packed. The tax revenues must be incredible. I could see how that could appeal to some people in Emerald Cove. More people, more money, more revenue for the town, more revenue for developers.

"Vivi, is it true? Is there a vote coming up that could change the face of Emerald Cove?" I asked.

Vivi did a slow nod. "Things are changing. People don't see what a gem this place is, as it is. Money talks, as they say."

"I saw in Elwell's obituary that he was a land developer. And from what Ivy told me, it sounds like he was involved." Was he some kind of middleman and someone decided to cut him out? "So who's behind the money?" I asked.

"I wish I knew," she said.

I'd spilled enough without getting much in return. That stopped now. "Who were you arguing with the night Elwell was murdered?"

Joaquín raised his eyebrows.

"You were gone by then, Joaquín. I was cleaning, but Vivi and a man were going at it by the back door."

"It was Elwell. I've told Deputy Biffle. I'm surprised you didn't." Vivi looked at me.

No wonder she'd been questioned so often. "I couldn't. I knew you couldn't have murdered Elwell. Not because you're not capable. I mean, look at your toned arms. You could kick my butt and probably anyone else's." I blew out a breath of air. "What I mean is, you wouldn't stab Elwell and walk away. You're not that kind of person." I hoped.

Her eyes widened. "I'm glad you have so much faith in me."

"It's because of Boone. Do you know who else has been questioned?"

"All the heritage business owners. They've talked to the employees at Elwell's dealership."

"Did they find anything there, because I got a weird feeling in that place. A hint of desperation."

"They're taking a closer look at the books, but so far, they haven't found anything felonious."

"You seem to know a lot about what's going on."

"If you've lived here as long as I have, there are lots of people who are willing to tell you things." Vivi stood. "Thank you for sharing what you've found." She picked up her drink and disappeared into the kitchen with it. A few moments later, we heard the back door click shut.

I looked at Joaquín. "She's hiding something."

He drummed his fingers on top of the table. "You may be right."

"What was with all the looks you and Vivi kept exchanging?" I thought for a minute about what I'd said. "Does Vivi have a gambling problem?" Was that why Boone wanted me here? Why he'd given me a share of the bar? To keep it safe?

"Not does. *Did.* It was a long time ago. Before I worked here."

I hoped Vivi hadn't fallen off the wagon and done something stupid. But it might explain why she didn't want me around. I was a connection to Boone. She wouldn't want to let him down and maybe, somehow, that extended to me.

A few minutes later, as I climbed into my car, my phone buzzed that I had a text message. It was a number I didn't recognize.

This is Rhett. I had to work and won't be able to make it. My apologies. I'll catch you later.

I didn't bother responding to his text, but I did wonder how he'd gotten my number. Only a few people had it, one being Vivi. I couldn't imagine that was where he got it. Maybe Joaquín had given it to him. I hoped Rhett didn't mean he'd be around later tonight. I huffed about what kind of work one did at ten o'clock at night. Probably work called Ann Williams. It annoyed me that I was so annoyed.

On the off chance someone was following me, I drove around the circle in Emerald Cove a couple of times. Vivi's behavior made me more worried, not less. The diner's neon light winked at me, and I remembered the coupon I had for a milkshake. Finding a place to park was easy this time of night and, a minute later, I pulled open the door to the diner.

A couple of people sat at the counter. A few of the aqua-colored vinyl booths were filled. Ralph Harrison sat in a big corner booth all by himself. The remains of a dinner was pushed off to one side, a cup of coffee in front of him. He spotted me and waved me over.

"Join me," he said.

I worried he was going to grill me again, but, hey, maybe I could turn the tables. "Sure. Thanks. I'm here for that milkshake you gave me the coupon for." I sat down and scooted into the booth. A waitress with big, brassy hair, unusually pale skin for a Floridian, and bright red lips, who looked to be about the same age as the other heritage business owners came over. She stood by Ralph, and he looped an arm around her waist.

"This is my wife, Delores. And this is Chloe."

My mouth opened while my brain tried to work through things. Fred Russo had been married to the dispatcher Delores. Here was another Delores. It must be a popular name down here.

"Hi, honey. We spoke the other day on the phone. I'm so sorry you had to find Elwell. Not a very good introduction to Emerald Cove."

Did I suddenly have lockjaw because I seemed to have lost my ability to speak as I looked from Ralph to Delores and thought about Fred. "You're the dispatcher?"

"And I own this place." She waved a hand around. "What can I get you?"

"You were married to Fred?" I looked back and forth between Ralph and Delores. "I'm sorry. It's none of my business. A chocolate shake, please."

"How about a couple of pieces of your pecan pie for us too, please, darlin'?" Ralph asked.

"You bet." She kissed the top of Ralph's head and sashayed off.

In my head, I was doing calculations. Fred said he'd been divorced for five years, so these two couldn't have been married for long.

"My first wife, the mother of my two children, went boating with friends one day twelve years ago and never came back."

"You don't have to tell me this."

Ralph bobbed a quick nod. "Coast Guard searched, most of Emerald Cove searched, even half the fleet over in Destin. No sign of the boat was ever found."

"I'm sorry."

Delores came back over with a chocolate shake in

a tall glass and the two pieces of pie. The pie was twice the height of any I'd ever seen. "That's my special, double-high pecan pie." She handed me a straw, a long spoon, and a fork. "Napkins are right there." Delores pointed to a chrome dispenser by the salt and pepper shakers. She grinned at Ralph and left us.

I took a sip. After a couple of tries, I grabbed the spoon. This was the thickest shake I'd ever seen, but its icy goodness made my mouth sing with happiness. I tried the pie and sighed out loud with satisfaction while Ralph smiled his approval. Between the shake and the pie, I wondered if I would ever be able to sleep off the sugar high.

"She's something," he said, looking past me. "We were high school sweethearts, but neither set of our parents approved, so there was a lot of sneaking around. I left for the Air Force and she ended up marrying Fred." Ralph ate some of his pie. "After they divorced, we reconnected. Happiest I've ever been."

"Delores works as a dispatcher and you both own businesses." I kept eating while Ralph talked. "You're busy people."

"It's how it is for the locals. Profit margins are low. The cost of living keeps rising with the influx of newcomers. It's a love-hate relationship. This town was always the one for teachers, laborers, fisherman, artists, just common folk. We're trying to keep it that way, but it's harder every year."

Ralph sure was in an expansive mood tonight. A way of life was at stake. How had Elwell played into that? For that matter did Ralph really want to keep the town for "common folk" or did he wish he and Delores didn't have to work so hard?

"People keep saying Elwell made the wrong people angry. Who are they talking about?"

Ralph pushed some pie crust crumbs around on his plate. "Elwell always was a hothead. It'd probably be easier to list who he didn't make angry. Because far as I can tell, people he angered starts with his own family, passes on through the heritage business owners, and beyond. Not very helpful."

"Why'd he make you angry?" I asked.

"Closing time," Delores called out.

Ralph stood. "Better get going. I don't want Delores to be unhappy."

More like he didn't want to answer that question.

It was close to midnight when I got home. Rhett wasn't parked in the drive—I wasn't sure what he'd meant when he said he'd catch me later. I went through the house to the back, but he wasn't out there either. I wasn't going to wait up any longer. The sugar high had worn off and I was crashing. After I got in bed, night sounds settled around me— the soft whir of the air conditioner, a couple of sleepy-sounding birds, what might be a tree frog, at least I hoped it was. For all I knew, it was a feral hog or panther or alligator. Did alligators even make noises? I pulled up the sheet under my chin. Wildlife is terrifying. I'm a city girl through and through. I liked my wildlife encounters to occur in bars.

It was so dark and so quiet out here. It was something that would take some getting used to. I had lived in the heart of Chicago, not far from Wrigley Field. I was used to traffic, people, and the roar of the "L"—the elevated train that was one mode of public transportation in Chicago.

I didn't trust the quiet.

CHAPTER 24

I dreamed I was camping. The bonfire grew larger and larger. It snapped and popped like a wild alligator over a piece of meat. Maybe they do make noises. Instead of the woodsy scent I was used to from my youth, it smelled of gasoline. I jerked upright, awakened from a nightmare. My room was dark except for a glow outside the bedroom window. Flames flickered and danced outside behind the curtain. I yanked the curtain aside and saw burning wood piled up near the side of the house.

Holy crap. The inside wall was warm, smoke started to seep through cracks around the window. I grabbed my phone, called 911, and calmly gave them the address of Boone's house. I yanked on shorts and a T-shirt, coughing, as more smoke came in through the screened porch and started to fill the house.

I hustled into the living room, looked out the front windows, and didn't see flames. I felt the front door, which was cool, so I ran outside just as the smoke detector started to wail. Better late than never. Sparks drifted in the air. At least it wasn't windy out. I turned the outside faucet on full blast and uncoiled the hose running to the side where the fire was. I depressed the nozzle and water shot out toward the flames, but the fire was bigger than the stream of water could handle.

The frame of the concrete block house was safe from the flames, but the wooden windows, roof, and porch weren't. So I turned the hose first on the windows, soaking them, and then the eaves under the roof. The flames started crawling across the ground. I soaked as much of the roof as I could. I couldn't reach the screened porch from here. Sirens sounded as the fire tried to creep up the side of the house and grab the roof. Sparks danced toward the scrub oak and brush, but, thankfully, the recent rain helped slow the fire's progress.

A whoosh of flame sent me running back to the front corner of the house. The smell of gasoline finally woke me to the fact that this wasn't an accident. That's when I noticed the other piles of wood. One more on this side of the house, one near the front door. Neither of them had been started, for some reason.

The piles of wood were set up like teepees. As if a group of Scouts had come by. But this wasn't the work of anyone good. Little flames licked around the bottom of another of the wooden teepees as embers from the pile by my bedroom window jumped over. It was perilously close to my Beetle. I hosed it off and ran back into the house to grab my keys so I could move my car.

The smoke hit me like a wall when I went in. I

dropped to my knees and crawled toward where I thought my purse was by the couch. My eyes burned. It was so dark and smoky. I felt my way around, only opening my eyes when I absolutely had to. Maybe I should just give up and get out of there. But my hand touched the couch. I coughed some more as I snagged my purse. I heard a fire truck roar up and people shouting instructions to one another as I started to crawl back toward the door, dragging my purse behind me. A fireman burst through the door, breathing mask in place, and swept a powerful flashlight around until it landed on me.

The fireman scooped me over his shoulder like I was a beach towel, carried me outside, and dropped me off at an ambulance. I called a thank-you as he headed around the side of the house. Flashing red lights reflected off the front windows of the house. I waved off the EMTs. Told them I was fine. However, the minute I started coughing, they insisted that they take my blood pressure and heart rate. Both were slightly elevated, but that was to be expected. I watched as water shot out of the tankers, squelching the fire in a hurry.

I hoped there wasn't too much damage. It wasn't like I had a lot of valuables in there. Boone's letter and the picture of us were the most precious things. My clothes could be replaced. The furniture was nothing special. I wasn't sentimental enough to get teary over Boone's old furniture. I'd found out long ago that life was what was precious. A fireman tromped over to me and raised his mask. Ralph.

"You trying to make s'mores and things got out of hand?" he asked.

My mind was a whirl of emotions—anger and anxiety—but I managed a laugh. Grateful to Ralph for trying to defuse the tension. "I didn't know you were a fireman."

"We have a small paid staff and a large contingent of volunteers. I'm a volunteer. You have any idea what went on out here?"

"No. The wood wasn't here when I came home."

"Did you come straight home after you left the diner?"

"I did. I don't even know what time it is now."

"Just after one."

"I can't believe I slept so soundly." Someone had snuck around out there, piling up the wood, dousing it with gasoline. I wondered why they didn't light all the piles. Did something scare them off? My snoring?

"It's the Gulf. Darn relaxing under most circumstances."

"Or Delores's pie."

A sheriff's car trundled down the drive. Lights, no sirens. The county was big; hard telling where they'd come from to get here. Another car, a sedan, followed it. I turned at a noise in my house.

"We're opening all the windows and running some big fans to help dissipate the smoke," Ralph said. "There's no fire or water in the house. You'll probably need to call a professional to clean the place. Smoke settles in furniture like gravy on biscuits. Seeps into every nook and cranny. You have somewhere else you can sleep tonight?"

I looked at my Beetle. Thought about Boone's boat. Either would do. If I could sleep. "Yes. I do."

"Have any idea who would do this?"

I thought about the two cowboys. But I also thought about Gloria saying one of the heritage business owners had killed Elwell. Why was Ralph asking me these questions? Shouldn't it be someone from the sheriff's department, or an arson investigator? I didn't owe him an answer. If the cowboys wanted to kill me, they could have set the back porch on fire, or tossed a Molotov cocktail through a window. Or run me off the road. Or just shot me. Death could come in many ways. This seemed like a back off message instead of an actual attempt to kill me. Unfortunately, whoever did this didn't realize it gave me more to ask.

Ralph watched me. I hadn't answered his question. "I don't have any idea."

"What part of Illinois are you from?"

I was kind of surprised he didn't know. I figured all the heritage owners knew my story. "Chicago."

"Anything bad follow you down here? Were you running from something?"

"No to both. That's not why I came."

"Why did you really come?"

"For Boone." He didn't need to know more than that.

Another fireman came up. Well, firewoman. "I found this tossed on the other side of the pile." She dangled what was left of a plastic gas container. Singed and melted in spots. The nozzle drooping.

"The arson investigator just got here. Give it to her. Maybe they'll get lucky and find some evidence on it."

She walked toward a deputy and a woman who must have arrived in the sedan.

Ralph looked at me. "Don't get your hopes up about them finding anything on it."

"I won't."

"The deputy and arson investigator are going to want a statement."

"Didn't I just give it to you?" Not that I'd said much.

"Come on. They'll need to hear it all too."

An hour later, the deputy and arson investigator had left. There wasn't much to investigate unless they thought I did this for some crazed reason. The last crew was bringing fans out of my house and rolling up hoses. Even after they'd put out the fire it still reeked of gasoline out here. Nothing like the pleasant woodsy smell I remembered from camping trips after a fire was put out. I walked around the edge of the house, checking out the scorched wall, and almost plowed into a fireman.

"Sorry." I took a step back. Peered up in the darkness. "Rhett?"

"Could you sound more astonished?" he asked. "I told you I had to work tonight."

"You're a fireman?" I wasn't about to admit that I thought his "work" had something to do with Ann Williams. But it explained why, the day I'd found Elwell, he'd called a number and known the dispatcher was Delores.

"One of the volunteers."

"Oh. Well, thank you for putting out fires."

He unsnapped the front of his heavy yellow coat.

His face was smoke-stained and streaked with sweat. "Never go back into a smoke-filled house."

"That was you who carried me out?"

"Yes. Smoke kills people faster than fire."

"Thank you for coming in after me." Not that I thought I couldn't have made it out on my own. "It wasn't that bad." *Who was I kidding? It had been terrifying. Even worse than almost getting knocked off the bridge.* "I wanted to move my car."

"Losing your car is a lot better than losing your life."

"Got it." I was annoyed at the lecture. I wasn't stupid. Though I'd obviously made myself a target. I turned away.

"Let's talk tomorrow."

I was still curious to find out what he'd wanted to talk to me about earlier today. "Okay."

I finished my circle around the house. All in all, except for a scorched wall, the house looked fine. When I got back to the front, Rhett and Ralph were gone. Another fireman told me it was okay to go in. I packed a few toiletries and clothes, locked the house, and left with the last of the firemen. Now where to go?

CHAPTER 25

"Rise and shine," a voice said. "I brought breakfast burritos."

Rhett. He'd found me sleeping on Boone's boat. Again. Although now it was my boat—I couldn't get used to that thought. I was surprised I'd managed to go to sleep, the way my brain had swirled and eddied last night. Picturing the fire, still smelling the smoke. Maybe the slight rocking motion of the boat had helped. "You found me. Was it the snoring?" I asked.

He laughed. "Sure was. It's kind of cute in a frightening way." No one had ever said my snoring was cute in any way. He loosened more of the tarp and joined me as I sat up. I wiped the back of my hand across my mouth and tried to rearrange my hair by combing my fingers through it. I smelled like a smoker at a barbecue place. And there was Rhett looking so delicious. Smelling so delicious. He handed me the sack, which I peeked in. Yum. Two burritos were tucked in there. Rhett sat down beside me. He placed a cardboard carrier with two cups of coffee on the floor.

"I'll trade you a coffee for a burrito," he said.

"Deal. What time is it?" The sun was shining.

"Eight, sleepyhead."

The fire was out by one forty-five this morning, the fans pulled by two thirty. It had been after three when I got here. "You have too much energy for someone who didn't get much sleep. No rest for the wicked?"

"The righteous don't need any." He smiled and took a bite of his burrito.

I sipped my coffee and dug into my food. "Maria is a goddess when it comes to cooking." I'd wanted another burrito ever since I'd eaten my first the other day. But I hadn't taken the time to go back.

"She is. How are you doing this morning?"

"No permanent harm. I'd like to say no foul, but what happened at the house was a foul. A bad one." And I was scared. First finding Elwell, then the truck almost running me off the road, and now a fire. A dolphin swam by the boat, its back arching out of the water, reminding me that life always combined the ugly bits with some beauty.

"Any idea who did it?" he asked.

I shrugged, my mouth full of burrito. After I swallowed, I spoke again. "What were you going to tell me about Vivi last night?"

"So, you aren't going to answer my question?"

"You go first. Age before beauty," I quipped.

"Ouch. That hurts." Rhett grinned.

Like he didn't know he was beautiful. I really didn't know how old he was.

"I'm not sure it matters."

"You seemed concerned yesterday, so why not just tell me?" A breeze rustled through my hair. It reminded me of the first time I'd met him, right here. Of my finding Elwell and of him telling me we didn't need to tell the deputy he found me sleeping right here on Boone's boat. Why would he think that needed to be kept secret? Was it really to protect me from blame for Elwell's death?

And why had I gone along with his suggestion that I'd just been out for a run. My humiliation at having no place to stay had overcome my common sense to tell the truth. That, and the worry that I'd be suspect number one if they knew I'd slept out here. It's always easier to blame the new person than think someone you knew well could do something so horrible. I watched Rhett out of the corner of my eye. He seemed decent enough. Maybe I'd been wrong to distrust him.

"Someone is out to get Vivi," he said.

This wasn't news to me. But not just Vivi, me too. But to what end? What would setting up Vivi for Elwell's murder and getting rid of me do for someone? *The bar!* Was that it? The land it sat on had to be valuable. I wasn't so sure about the business. It made me wonder about Wade and the Briny Pirate. Had he had any threats against him? I didn't want to share any of that with Rhett. I still didn't know him well enough. I wasn't sure I knew anyone here well enough to talk through this.

"That seems fairly obvious." I didn't mean to sound so sarcastic. I guess I was pinning a lot of hopes on

Rhett knowing something that would be helpful. Now it was my turn to ask the questions. "Do you know who?" He was a local. If anyone should have an idea about what was going on, it would be someone who'd lived here a long time. Unless these people were all *too* close to one another.

"I don't."

"No guesses?"

"I'm not a guessing kind of guy."

"So that's all you wanted to say?" I sounded more confident than I felt. I still worried about Vivi's argument that I'd overheard at the Sea Glass. I didn't want to believe Vivi had anything to do with Elwell's death, but even after my talk with Vivi and Joaquin I had doubts.

Rhett gazed across the harbor. "You know our families have a feud going back years."

"I'm not part of Vivi's family. There's no 'our' when it comes to me."

"But you're working for Vivi. Standing up for Vivi. So the feud extends to you."

"Do you want to explain that feud to me?" It was a little off topic. At least I thought it was. All I knew was that Vivi had stolen Elwell from his grandmother, but surely there must be more to it than that.

"No. You can ask my grandmother or Vivi. I've tried to stay out of it. Boone was a friend. A year younger than me in school, but our school wasn't large, so we knew each other. Played sports together. After he went off to college, he'd come home full of stories about a girl named Chloe."

I shifted on the hot seat of the boat. "Oh."

"When I found you on Boone's boat that morning and realized who you were, I did what I knew Boone would have wanted me to. And keeping that one small thing from the police was worth it."

"That's what the secrets toast was about?"

Rhett nodded. "It's probably obstruction of justice."

"It is." He reached over and brushed a crumb off my cheek. Left his hand there a moment longer than necessary. *Don't look into those dark green eyes. Remember the feud.* Vivi might have softened toward me yesterday, but we still had the bar ownership to work out. And probably a lot of other things too.

"Rhett." I turned to see Ann Williams standing there in black shorts, with a black shirt edged with a bit of red. The hot breeze lifted her hair and she looked like Wonder Woman or a warrior princess standing there. "We need to get a move on."

For a brief moment, I wondered what kind of move she wanted to get on with Rhett.

Rhett leaped up and jumped off the boat. "Sorry. I lost track of time."

Talk about someone jumping when called. "Ann," I said, "there was a fire out at Boone's last night, and the house is smoky."

"Is everyone okay?" she asked.

"Yes. The fire was outside, but the inside smells like a campfire. Do you do that kind of cleanup or know someone who does?"

Ann glanced at Rhett. "I'll take care of it for you."

"Thanks," I said. I took an extra key off the ring Joaquín had given me and handed it to her.

Rhett gave me a quick look, like he wanted to say

something and decided not to before they headed west toward his boat.

"Thanks for the burrito and coffee," I called after them. Rhett raised a hand in response. I cleaned up the stuff from our breakfast and finished my coffee before snapping the tarp into place. I still had questions for Rhett Barnett, but they would have to wait.

CHAPTER 26

Before heading back home for a shower, I walked behind the Briny Pirate and Sea Glass, around to the other side of the harbor, looking for the Emerald Cove Fishing Charters. It was another of the heritage businesses. I'd shoved aside my doubts about going. If the fire had been a message, if I caved to my fears, I'd be done.

I found a small kiosk, but it was empty. As were the two boat slips across from it. That figured; it was prime fishing time. From what I'd observed since I'd arrived, most fishing boats came back between ten and noon, but I'd be at work by then. Maybe I could take a break and head back over here later.

I grabbed a brochure and read through the options for going out fishing. Emerald Cove Fishing was owned by Jed Farwell. They had two large boats: an older wooden one and a new fiberglass boat. Each boat held up to one hundred eighty people, but limited the number to eighty so people could fish comfortably. Both boats had galleys and cooks onboard. Trips lasted for four, six, or ten hours. *Ten hours?* Yikes. They went out six to fifteen miles, depending on the length of the trip.

They offered three types of trips—party, group, and private charters. Costs ran from sixty to one hundred dollars per person. To me, a party boat meant people drinking and dancing, but in the fishing world it meant a large number of people all going on the same boat. It was cheapest to go on a party boat, around sixty dollars. Chartering the boat for a small group ran from one to four thousand dollars. Wow. You had to be serious about fishing to do that.

There was a bulletin board with pictures on the side of the kiosk. Lots of happy people holding up fish after they returned from their trips. A few shots on the boat with lines cast over the edge. I looked closer at a shot of a group of people being greeted by the captain as they boarded. There was Elwell with the armadillo shell on his head. So he wasn't just wearing it to the Sea Glass. A little boy was pointing up at him. His mom leaned away from Elwell. I'd seen similar reactions to him at the Sea Glass. It made me wonder if Elwell showed up at the other heritage businesses with the armadillo on his head too. What was his endgame? It didn't seem like anything good.

It was nine a.m. when I hit the end of the long drive to Boone's house. I could already smell burned wood. It made me shudder to think what could have happened. I tossed a load of wash in on the quick-wash setting. Every piece of clothing I owned smelled like smoke. Fortunately, everything I'd brought down here with me was machine washable. I'd left all my dry-clean-only coats and dresses behind in my apartment. Rachel may have packed them by now.

After a quick run, I showered and put on a little makeup to counter my tired-looking eyes. I put the clothes I'd just washed in the dryer so I'd have something to wear to work. Then I grabbed an apple and took it outside. The tang of gas and the sharp smell of burned wood belied the beautiful blue sky and inviting emerald water.

I walked around the piles of wood, looking for something to tell me who did this and why. An ID would be nice. A confession note. A cowboy hat. Anything I could point to, so the deputies could make an arrest and I could relax a little. But the only thing I saw were some little green lizards with red, bubble-like things that bulged out from under their chins at random intervals. They refused to talk about what they'd seen.

Fifteen minutes later, as I pulled out of the drive, I passed a pink truck that said, "Stink Away—Odor Removal Service." I waved at the woman driver as she went by. She turned down the drive to Boone's house. I wondered if Ann owned the company along with her handywoman business or if she contracted with them. That was fast service. Ann was good at her job, and I'd have to thank her next time I saw her.

I drove over to the glass-bottom boat, hoping I'd catch Leah Hickle between trips. "Leah," I called when I spotted her walking between the kiosk and the boat. I was in luck. She turned and waited for me. "It's quiet out here this morning."

"Someone posted a bunch of bad online reviews saying we didn't have proper life jackets, or enough of them. And that our boat had failed its Coast Guard inspection. Another one said we were endangering the wildlife in the bay. None of it's true, and the reviews will come down eventually, but it probably explains why, in the height of tourist season, I have a boat with only five people signed up for the next trip."

"Oh, no. I'm sorry. How long have the reviews been up?"

"Over the past week or so. I ignored the first few. There's always someone unhappy. But we've never had any effect our business like this." Her face reddened as she talked about it.

It sounded like some were posted before Elwell died and some after.

"I heard you had your own problems at Boone's house last night."

"How did you hear that?"

Leah laughed. "You are going to have to get used to small-town living. That, and my husband's a volunteer fireman."

"I'm trying to adjust," I said with a laugh. "I went out and saw Ivy two nights ago."

"At the Crow's Nest?"

"Yes," I said.

"You're brave."

"Or foolish. She isn't too happy with Vivi. And

there were a couple of cowboys in the bar that I think were eavesdropping on our conversation."

"One might be Ivy's boyfriend. He used to ride the rodeo circuit but got kicked out for unethical behavior. But he still dresses like he's part of the community."

I didn't want to know what that unethical behavior was. Unless it was gambling. Elwell was rumored to be a gambler. But would Ivy's boyfriend kill her dad and keep dating her? "There are rodeos around here?"

"There's one on the beach every spring called Bulls on the Beach. And some up north. Inland is a whole different world than the beach cities. You don't have to go very far north to see it. Bonifay—it's about sixty miles from here—has a huge rodeo every fall."

Sixty miles outside of Chicago was a different world too, so I understood what she was saying. "Interesting."

"There's always a push-pull between the beach and the inland areas. Our taxes provide most of the revenue for the entire county."

"Did Elwell ever come by here with his armadillo shell hat on?"

"Yeah, he took several rides at various times in the past few weeks."

"How'd the other people take that?" I asked.

"Stayed as far away as possible, which isn't easy on a crowded boat when you are supposed to stay in your seat."

"Are there any other glass-bottom boats around?" I asked.

"Not in Emerald Cove, but a couple in Destin."

"Leah," a woman's voice screeched from the kiosk. "You gonna take these good folks for a tour or stand around talking all day?"

"Oops. Gotta run. Last thing we need is more bad reviews."

At noon, I took a break and stopped by the Briny Pirate. Elwell had gone to at least four out of the six heritage businesses with the armadillo shell on this head. By now I was fairly certain he was out to hurt the heritage businesses. Other than the glass-bottom boat, it didn't seem like his efforts had that big of an impact. Certainly not enough for any of them to close. Just enough for him to be annoying. Was that reason enough to kill him?

"Is Wade around?" I asked a waitress.

"In the back," she said, pointing. "It's fine if you head back there."

Wade had a bandanna tied around his gray hair and wore a white chef's coat. He was stirring something in a big pot. The air was spiced with hot sauce.

"Wade?" I asked.

"Hey, Chloe. How are you, honey?"

Awww, he called me honey. Maybe he called everyone that but it warmed me anyway. "Okay. That smells delicious."

"Gumbo. Want a bowl?"

It had been a few hours since I'd eaten the breakfast burrito. "Sure. I'd love some."

Wade dished up two bowls. "Let's take this out to

the picnic table in the back." He loaded a tray with the two bowls, a few packs of oyster crackers, extra hot pepper sauce, two cans of Coke, and utensils. I held the door open and helped sort everything out once he'd placed the tray on the table. Seagulls soared around as fishing boats came in. The water sparkled. The picnic table was in a shady spot under a small pergola. If it hadn't been for Elwell's murder and Vivi's and my troubles, it would be a perfect day.

Wade added a couple of dashes of hot sauce to his and held up the bottle. "Want some?"

"Sure," I said, and added a couple of dashes to mine. I gave it a good stir and tasted it. "Ummm, Wade. This is melt-in-your-mouth yummy." It had the right amount of seafood-to-sausage ratio. Just enough heat to make me happy. We ate for a few minutes.

"I'm guessing you didn't come over here just to get some free gumbo."

"I'll pay," I said. I didn't want him to think I was a mooch.

"Not what I was talkin' about. You must want to ask me something."

He said ask, not tell. I guessed he knew about my poking around, asking questions. That probably wasn't good. I nodded, because my mouth was full. "It's about Elwell." Wade didn't look surprised. "Did he come here wearing his armadillo shell?"

"Yep. Started a couple of weeks ago."

"Did you ask him why he was wearing it?"

"Sure did. Mumbled some nonsense about 'the gub'ment.'"

"So you didn't buy that?"

"Not at t'all. Fact is, I told him he wasn't welcome in the Briny Pirate until he quit wearing that darn thing. Customers didn't like it. I didn't either."

There was a definite pattern emerging here. The question was why?

"Has anyone threatened you or the business?"

Wade shook his head before I got the words out.

"Has anyone wanted to buy your business recently?"

"All the time. Anyone who owns property along here gets offers. On bad days, some are darn tempting. But I'm not going to sell."

"Chloe."

I glanced over to see Vivi heading toward us. She wore silver sandals, navy skinny jeans, and a spotless white shirt. Wade's face did the equivalent of a happy dance.

"Why didn't you call me last night and tell me about the fire? I had to hear about it this morning. That was irresponsible. I have a right to know."

Emotionally, she had a right to know, even though the house was mine now. "I don't have your number."

Vivi opened and closed her mouth. She recited two numbers, which I typed into my phone. I figured one was her home and one was her cell.

"Shouldn't you ask her if she's okay?" Wade asked gently.

"I can see she is." She gestured up and down at me.

"Don't you think it might have been a tad bit traumatizing?" Wade asked.

I ate some more gumbo to keep from saying anything. I'd let the two of them verbally duke it out, although I was disappointed my détente with Vivi seemed so strained.

Vivi put her silver designer purse on the picnic table and sat down next to Wade. They were arm to arm. "You're right as usual, Wade." She looked at me. "He's the angel to my devil."

That sounded a lot like Boone and me. A little ripple of hurt went through me.

"Are you okay?" Vivi asked. "The fire chief told me that you hosed down the house and probably saved it. So thank you."

I perked up a bit. "I'm fine. Glad there wasn't any real damage." To lose another piece of Boone would have been devastating for Vivi. For me too.

"Did you hear anything?" Vivi asked.

"No. The flicker from the flames and smoke woke me up. By the time I got outside, whoever set the fire was long gone."

"Hopefully, the fire or sheriff's department will come up with some answers," Vivi said.

I stood up. "Can I carry all this back inside, Wade? I have to get to work. My break is over and my boss is a real stickler for all things work-related."

Wade laughed, and something even flickered across Vivi's face that might have passed for a smile.

"From what I understand," Vivi said, "we'll need some kind of professional cleanup crew to get the smoke smell out."

"We." It was nice to hear Vivi talking about me as part of her team. "I've already taken care of it. Well, I asked Ann Williams to. Stink Away was showing up just as I left. I dropped by to do a load of wash this morning."

"Ann Williams?" Wade asked.

"Yes. She must have a lot of connections," I said. "And she sure is efficient."

Wade's eyes crinkled up in what looked like amusement. What in the heck was so funny about Ann's efficiency? What was up with Ann?

CHAPTER 27

After I made sure all our customers were happy, I took my phone and read through the reviews for the other heritage businesses. All of them, including the Sea Glass, had had a series of bad reviews posted in the last week, with an uptick in the last forty-eight hours. According to the reviews, the Sea Glass watered down its drinks and used cheap ingredients. One mentioned a bad mojito. Hmmm. If it was the one I'd made, the reviewer might have had a valid point. But the rest of them couldn't be further from the truth.

The fishing boat was accused of giving away people's fish, of stacking people shoulder to shoulder so it was hard to fish, and canceling trips with no notice. The grocery store had complaints of people being shorted shrimp, getting sick from it, and that it wasn't real Gulf shrimp.

The glass-bottom boat had reviews that said the glass was too dirty to see through and that the reviewer didn't see any dolphins. How could they complain about that? It wasn't called a dolphin tour. The dolphins were just a bonus. Someone was disappointed that the Redneck Rollercoaster wasn't really a roller coaster, and that it had been hot the day they went. In July. In Florida. I shook my head. Other reviewers said it was too crowded and they couldn't understand a word being said on the tour. Wade's restaurant was called filthy, his fish dry, and his gumbo flavorless, among other things. I knew that was a lie.

I put down my phone when a few customers drifted in. Apparently, they weren't the type to read reviews. Joaquín came in and saved me from attempting to make mixed drinks. After I served the customers, I wrote my own positive reviews of all the businesses. Then I reported all the negative ones to the website, pointing out the timing of the reviews. I hoped they'd take at least some of them down.

Vivi called me into her office at three, which made my heart pitter-pat more than it did when I saw Rhett. She gestured for me to sit down, so I did. There was a beautiful new painting behind her desk of the Gulf at sunrise or sunset.

Vivi cleared her throat and handed me two checks. "The first one is for your first two weeks' wages."

It was quite generous. Vivi paid above minimum wage. Add tips to that, and a person could actually eke out a living. "Thank you. I know you don't really want me here, so I wasn't sure I'd get paid."

"It's what Boone would have wanted."

I looked down at the second check. "What?" The check had more zeros on it than any check I'd ever seen. "I don't understand."

"It's for your part of the bar. Doubled, like I offered the other day, with a generous bonus thrown in."

Oh, the things I could do with that kind of money. I pictured vacations in Europe. A condo all paid off in Chicago. Clothes and shoes that weren't purchased at a thrift shop. A whole life was flashing before my eyes. But no. I couldn't. I ripped it in half and then half again. Placed it back on the desk. Vivi's face turned bright red.

I stood up. "It's what Boone would have wanted." I walked out and got back to work, wondering what would happen next.

At one thirty, one of the guys I'd danced with at AJ's the other night walked in.

"If it isn't cute Chloe. The mystery woman." His dark eyes, close-cropped, curly hair, and bright smile perked me up after the scene with Vivi. He looked a bit like Trevor Noah.

Joaquín looked back and forth between us.

"Hi—" Oh boy, I couldn't remember his name.

"Hunter," he said, his smile dimpling his dark-skinned cheeks.

I blushed. "Hunter. Can I get you something to drink?"

"I'm devastated that you didn't remember my name."

"Sorry. So many men, so little time. A drink?"

Hunter laughed. "Sure. What's on tap?"

I ran through the beers, and he chose a pale ale. I poured it and handed it to him. Hunter settled on the barstool directly in front of me.

"You are a difficult woman to find," Hunter said.

"You were trying to find me?" That was flattering. And a bit creepy.

"You said you worked at a bar in Emerald Cove. I've been working my way through them."

I laughed. "All four of them? Such a hardship."

"Some of the restaurants have bars too." He said it in a mock hurt voice.

"Oh, you poor thing." Hunter was in the Marines. Doing a temporary assignment of some kind with the special forces at Hurlburt over in Fort Walton Beach. It wasn't anything he could talk about.

"Some of my friends and I are going wakeboarding in an hour. Want to come along?"

I loved wakeboarding. Wakeboards were short boards with foot bindings that were towed behind a speedboat. Flying across the water, looping up and over the wake the boat created. Gliding back and forth, catching air. I sighed. "Work."

"It's slow," Joaquín said. "Why don't you take off? You could use some fun."

"But you'll be here all alone." Vivi had left not long after I'd torn up the check. I'd yet to tell Joaquín about that whole incident.

"I've done it many times. I can handle it."

I turned to Hunter. "It looks like I can come." And boy, did I need an escape.

CHAPTER 28

At five I pulled back into the driveway to Boone's house. Sunburned. Windblown. Exhilarated and exhausted. Hunter and his friends had been fun. All of them trying to outdo one another on the boards. There'd been lots of tumbles and more laughs. I'd only fallen once and was going to have a heck of a bruise on my left thigh, but it was worth it.

An old station wagon with a surfboard lashed on top was parked to the side of the house. Ed Ashford, the lawyer, sat on the front porch, forearms resting on his thighs. He stood when I got out of the car. I noticed new floodlights had been installed at the corners of the house. There was also a sign for Farley's Security by the porch.

I gestured toward the sign. "Did you have anything to do with the new lights and security system?"

"Nope."

Why was he here, then? It didn't take long for me to come up with a reason. "Let me guess. Vivi came to see you."

"Yes, she did. Quite fired up too."

I unlocked the door. "Come on in." The house smelled lemony fresh. No one would guess the place could have burned down last night. Another thing to thank Ann for. "Can I get you something to drink?"

"Tea?" he asked.

"I don't have any sweet tea. I've only been in the South a couple of weeks. Do you want unsweetened?"

"No, thanks."

"I have beer, wine, and water."

"Water it is, then."

I found the operating instructions for the security system on the counter next to the refrigerator. I'd have to read them later. For now, I poured two glasses of water. "Let's sit out on the screened porch."

"Sure can't tell there was a fire here last night," Ed said as we crossed the room.

"Does everyone in town know about the fire?" I asked.

"Of course they do. It was the talk of the diner this mornin'. People speculating all kinds of reasons as to why it happened."

"Anything useful?"

"'Course not."

There was still a bit of smoke smell hanging in the air outside. I sat on the porch swing, and he picked a rocking chair.

"Was it bad inside?" Ed asked.

"It was. Ann William's company is amazing. They must have worked here all day."

He looked puzzled but nodded.

"But you probably aren't here to talk about that."

"You're right. Vivi came slamming into my office

this morning. Sounds like you turned down a lot of money."

"More than I've ever seen."

"It must have been difficult."

"It was."

"She's going to offer you even more. So be prepared."

"Oh, no. I only have so much willpower."

Ed smiled. "I just wanted to give you a heads-up. I wouldn't be a very good lawyer if I didn't advise you to consider her offer. It would set you up for a long time."

"Can she really afford to offer me more? Without putting herself in jeopardy?"

"She can. Is that going to change your mind?"

I thought that over for a minute. Thought of Boone. "No."

He laughed.

"What?" I asked.

"I don't think I've ever heard anyone put more disappointment into the word 'no.'"

"Would you tell her I won't accept any offer? No matter what."

"I can, but Vivi's stubborn."

"So am I." We sipped our water and stared out at the Gulf. The clouds were pinking to the west. The sunset would be spectacular. "Have you heard anything about Elwell's death?"

"Bless your heart. The rumors about you are true."

It was the first time someone had given me the old bless-your-heart routine since I'd arrived. I'd heard what people said it really meant, but I wasn't so sure.

"Rumors? About me?" As far as I could tell, Emerald Cove thrived on rumors and innuendo. Unfortunately, so far almost everyone but Leah and Ivy had doctoral degrees in how to say something without saying anything.

"That you're poking into Elwell's death and the heritage businesses."

Oh, great. "I'm new in town. I've been visiting as many of the area attractions as possible. I've been to AJ's on the harbor in Destin. Rented a Jet Ski and visited Crab Island. I just got back from wakeboarding with friends." Friends might be a stretch, but it sounded good. "Along with doing the touristy things here in Emerald Cove. Can you report that to the rumor mill for me?" I hoped he'd buy this line of thinking. If it got spread around, maybe the car-swiping fire starter would back off.

"No need to get huffy."

"I'm young. Does everyone expect me to stay home reading?" I loved to read, but I was starting to feel a righteous indignation building up, even though Ed and the rumor-mill people were spot-on with what I'd been up to.

"And what about Elwell?"

"I found him. Of course I'm curious about what happened to him." I paused. "And I'm worried for Vivi. The deputies have questioned her a couple of times."

"Three, to be exact."

"Are you representing her?"

"No. I don't do criminal law."

"But you know who is?" I asked.

"I know who should be."

"Who?"

"Rhett Barnett."

"Rhett's a *lawyer*?" And here I'd thought he was some kind of ne'er-do-well playboy, not a criminal defense lawyer. He must keep really strange office hours.

"Was a lawyer. He quit a year ago."

"Why?" I asked.

"You'd have to ask him about that."

"I can't. The feud and all that." I almost rolled my eyes at myself. Hadn't I just decided this morning that I wasn't going to get pulled into it? I was all over the place, wanting to please Vivi and, well, wanting Rhett. Not that I'd tell him that.

Ed made a snorting noise.

"What's the feud about anyway?" I asked, not really expecting any kind of answer.

"A man and a piece of land. Perceived insults."

Intriguing. I'd heard the part about the man before if Ed was talking about Elwell. "Tell me more."

He paused. "Back in the sixties, Rhett's family wanted to buy land that Vivi's family owned to develop. A deal was in the works until Vivi came home from college and convinced her family to donate the land to be preserved."

"I'm glad she had the foresight to do that. What about the man?"

Ed rubbed a hand over his face. "Elwell."

That fit with the picture I'd seen at the Sea Glass and what I'd been told.

"Vivi stole Elwell before prom their senior year of high school and then dumped him in the fall. It was bad all around. I think Vivi just dated him out of spite. She's changed a lot since back then, but some-things in a small town don't go away."

It didn't seem like that had anything to do with El-well's murder. Since Ed was here, I might as well try to find something more out. "Buford has a bad tem-per. It was scary when he accused you of cheating and grabbed you by the collar. It seems like whoever killed Elwell was angry about something."

Ed stared out at the Gulf. Drank some water. Wiped a hand across his mouth. I waited and kept my mouth shut.

"He does have a temper. The thought crossed my mind too."

"At Elwell's memorial, it sounded like Buford har-bored a grudge against Elwell because he got all the glory on the football team. Then he made that com-ment about Elwell being the shark and everyone else the minnows. Do you know what that was about?"

Ed nodded slowly. "Buford is a hard worker. Owns a roofing company but was never as successful as El-well. Elwell tossed business his way whenever he could, but it was never enough for Buford. If some-one else got a job on one of Elwell's projects, Buford would go ballistic."

I wasn't surprised to hear any of that. "Will you tell me if what I've heard about Elwell is true?"

"I will if I know it."

I ran through what I'd heard—gambling, medical issue, some kind of real estate deal.

"Any of those are possible."

"But are any of them true?"

He crossed a leg, knee extended out. "I think he might have been trying to get some zoning passed. The old guard around here is dead set against it. But new folks, they see dollar signs."

"What do you think?"

Ed gestured toward the Gulf. "I come from a long line of surfers. We don't like to share."

"Do you think Elwell could have been blackmailing someone? To get them to bend to his will?" I'm not sure where that idea popped into my head from.

He stood. "That's entirely possible. Stay safe."

"I'm doing my best." But that wasn't going to prevent me from heading out again.

CHAPTER 29

Fred Russo greeted me when I walked into the almost-empty grocery store. "Everyone must still be watching the sunset," I said.

"Or writing bad online reviews."

"I countered with a good one."

"Saw it. Thanks. Looking for anything special?" he asked.

"Need some salad fixings. And I'd take more shrimp. It was really good."

"Gulf's finest. How much do you want? I'll get it for you while you pick out what you want for your salad."

"A pound sounds good. I can cook it all tonight and have some leftover for tomorrow."

Fred nodded, and we went our separate ways. I found some gorgeous heirloom tomatoes, fresh Bibb lettuce, red peppers, carrots, and some Brussel sprouts that I could shave thin and add to the salad. I went down the row for salad dressing and saw that Russo had its own brand. I grabbed a balsamic vinaigrette, and then I found some Russo hot and spicy cocktail sauce. I added it to the cart too.

I headed toward the back but heard two men arguing and stopped. One was obviously Russo with his slow drawl. The other voice was rapid-fire. Definitely not a native.

"Don't give me any grief about this," the outsider said.

"I don't know what you expect me to do," Fred said.

"Deliver. That's all I ask."

I looked up and could see both of them in a large, round mirror up in the corner of the store. But the mirror distorted them enough that I couldn't tell what the other man looked like. He was a bit shorter than Fred and had a big, round bald spot that he tried to cover by slicking his hair back over it. Fred glanced at the mirror and spotted me. He said something I couldn't hear to the other man. He didn't look at the mirror. Instead, he went around the fish counter and out the back.

I walked over to the counter, not quite sure what to say. The counter had some red snapper, grouper, oysters, and shrimp all on ice. Local foods.

Fred smiled at me as he weighed out my shrimp. "Sorry about that. Suppliers. None of them are ever happy."

I nodded. Fred handed me the shrimp. "I'll give you the end-of-the-day discount."

"You don't have to do that."

"You're almost family." He handed me the package and followed me to the front of the store. "Let me ring you up."

After my food was bagged, I headed out to my car. Something wasn't right. If the outsider Fred was arguing with was a supplier, why was he telling Fred he'd better deliver?

After dinner, I pulled out my laptop. I typed in "Ann Williams" and "Emerald Cove, Florida." Nothing came up. How does a businesswoman not have a website? I typed in "Stink Away," and a website plus some news articles popped up. I read the news articles first, which dated back five years to when they opened the business. They not only cleaned up after fires but also floods and crime scenes. I hoped there wasn't much call for the last around here. One article mentioned they joined the Chamber of Commerce. Another talked about how they donated to the local Scout troop. Nothing interesting, and no mention of Ann.

I went to their "About" page. It mentioned how the couple had started and expanded their business, but again, no mention of Ann. It was too small a company to have a board. Maybe she was some kind of silent partner. Whatever it was, it intrigued me. I tried doing another search, spelling "Ann" a couple of different ways. Still nothing. Maybe she was one of those people who ran their business by referrals only. But with all the funny looks on people's faces when I talked about her, I knew something was up. Figuring out what might be fun.

Next, I went to the City of Emerald Cove's home page. There were four councilmen and a mayor. She voted to break ties. Both Ralph and Fred were on the town council. I read through the bios of all the council members. Ralph was a sixth-generation resident, Fred a fifth. Two of the members were first generation. One from Atlanta and one from Nashville. Both had extensive real estate and business ownership backgrounds.

The mayor was third generation. I read several speeches where she talked about managed growth. Just how managed was she talking? Managed as in no growth, or managed as in let's grow this place. It was hard to tell. She seemed like a typical obfuscating politician. The two businesspeople seemed to use the same talking points she did. Ralph and Fred were more along the lines of no growth. It seemed to me if Fred, Ralph, or the other councilman voted with the businesspeople, things could be set to change drastically in Emerald Cove. But why would they do it? And did any of this have anything to do with Elwell?

I shut my computer. Between hardly any sleep last night and the wakeboarding this afternoon, I was done in. I read through the instructions for the security system, set the alarm, and went to bed.

I woke up refreshed and pulled on my running gear. Just before I went out the door, I remembered I had to turn off the alarm. Whew, that was a close one. I wasn't sure exactly what the response would be if it did go off. I guessed I needed to do some more reading because I didn't want to find out by accident.

I jogged across the soft sand, thighs a little sore from the wakeboarding. A heck of a bruise had bloomed on my thigh. My shorts covered some of it. I headed east, away from the Sea Glass. I wanted to run by the houses I'd seen the other night and was curious to see if one of those houses might belong to Vivi.

A half an hour later, I was sweaty but no wiser. There were no neon signs on any of the houses that said, "Vivi lives here." I should have just done a search on her before I set out. In fact, that's what I'd do when I got back. At the end of the row of houses, I turned back to the west. I slowed down to a walk and looked for shells. I found a tiny hinged one that was purple inside. I kept walking and found half of one that looked like an angel wing. Surely it must be lucky. A little bit farther on, I spotted a small piece of sea glass and picked it up too. My neck was getting sore, so I quit looking and jogged back home.

I put the shells on the dresser. I couldn't call it "my dresser" yet. Thirty minutes later, I'd showered, made some scrambled eggs, and sat in front of my computer. I searched for Vivi and was surprised to see how much information popped up about her. She'd been a longtime member of the Chamber of Commerce and was Businesswoman of the Year several years in a row. I ate my eggs as I searched. Years earlier, she was on the pageant circuit, as was Rhett's grandmother. Was that also part of their feud? Or at least contributed to it?

I found Vivi's address and searched for it online. Wow! Vivi owned the big, yellow, Florida-style house just on the other side of the nature preserve. No wonder she called it the "big house." Upper and lower verandas faced the beach, and a long, broad one ran across the front too. It was my favorite of the houses. I had run by it this morning. I'm not sure how knowing this helped me. I thought again about Elwell and Vivi. I had to do something so I searched on social media and came up with a plan.

It wasn't that hard to track down Elwell's wife, Gloria. She loved her social media and posted almost every move she made. All her posts were public too. Dumb move for her, but great for me. So, if Gloria stuck to her routine, at nine this morning, she would drop her dogs—two Pomeranians—at the groomer's and then cross the street for coffee while she waited for them.

At 8:55, I was seated at her favorite table right by the window, where everyone walking by could admire her. The barista looked nervous when he saw me sit there with my iced—not sweet—tea, but he didn't have the guts to tell me to move. It made me wonder how Gloria was going to react when she saw me sitting here. Through the window, I watched Gloria drop off the dogs and sashay over to the coffee shop.

Her order, a large, iced caramel something or other, was waiting when she walked in. It was comical to see the shock on her face when she finally noticed me sitting in her spot. Patrons at other tables nudged one another as she made her way over. I smiled pleasantly at her.

Instead of my usual shorts and T-shirt, I wore a belted sundress with a full skirt. Vintage sixties, from the wardrobe I'd inherited from my grandmother along with the Beetle. The woman had been a style icon long before that was a thing. Red, strappy heels completed my outfit. I wore more makeup than usual, and my hair was slicked back away from my face and tucked behind my ears. It made my face look more heart-shaped and my chin more pronounced. While a wig or hair dye would be the way to go, this was the best I could do on short notice.

Gloria had seen me once at the memorial service at the Sea Glass. She hadn't paid any attention to me then, so I was hoping she wouldn't recognize this new, improved version of me. My dad would say I was up to shenanigans. He'd be right.

"Would you mind moving? This is my regular table." Gloria smiled pleasantly at me.

"I would." I smiled pleasantly back at her, but emphasized my nasal, flat Midwestern tone to let her know I wasn't from around there.

Her face changed from pleasant back to shocked. I think she was about to say, "Do you know who I am?" And I didn't want to answer that question.

"Why don't you join me?" I said, gesturing to the chair across from me. The one she had posted selfies in. A cushy number upholstered in purple. To my surprise, she sat down without a fight. I'd played out how this could go in my head numerous times. Easy acquiescence wasn't one of the scenarios I'd counted on. Now to get her to talk. I figured focusing on her was the only way to go.

"Where do you get your nails done?" I asked. "They are stunning. Mine are in desperate need." I splayed my fingers. My nails were unpolished, but I'd learned quickly that working in a bar was a waste of a good manicure. Too many opportunities for chipping and breaking.

"Over on the other side of the circle." She smiled sweetly at me. "I could do you a favor." She glanced down at my hands. "And arrange an appointment for you right now."

Ah, so she'd have the table to herself. Very original. "I couldn't possibly impose like that. Plus, I need to finish my tea before I get on with my day." I lowered my voice and leaned in a bit. "You just don't want to be around me when I haven't had my caffeine."

Her face said she didn't want to be around me at all, but her inbred Southern hospitality fought with that. I fired my next salvo. "You look familiar." I tilted my head to one side. "Are you Southerngrl on Instagram?"

Her face pinked a bit. "I am."

"I follow you!" I hoped she wouldn't look later and notice I'd just followed her this morning. "Oh. Do you have your sweet Pomeranians with you?" I looked around hopefully. They did look like sweet dogs, and it was obvious she loved them. There were way more pictures of them than Ivy and Elwell on her account.

"They are at the groomers right now."

I looked suitably disappointed. This was all well and good, but I'd yet to find out a single thing about Elwell or Ivy. "What about your lovely family? I recall seeing photos of a beautiful daughter and a handsome man in your life."

Gloria arranged her face in an expression I could only call "tragic loss." And in reality, it was. Murder was never anything else. But I wasn't sure Gloria would understand that. She'd cried and pronounced her love for Elwell at his memorial service, but she'd been sloshed at the time. And not too long after, I'd seen her on the pontoon with a man's hand on her thigh. Gloria had seemed to enjoy that. But maybe you could love someone and not miss them all at the same time if the person you loved was hurting you too. Life and people were complicated.

"My precious Elwell was killed, heinously, last week."

"I'm so sorry." I really was. "I hope they've found his killer so he or she can be brought to justice."

She shook her head, and for a moment, she really did look sad. "Not yet." Her voice was low. "They've had someone in for questioning several times. An old girlfriend. People seem to think she must have done it, but I don't know if I agree."

I had to be careful here. It was like trying to walk across lily pads on the coastal lakes without getting my feet wet. Impossible. "It must be very scary for you." That also was true. If the killer went after Elwell, could Gloria herself be at risk? That made me wonder if Elwell's murder stemmed from a family issue and nothing more. If it was a crime of passion or opportunity, it might not have anything to do with Vivi or the Sea Glass. That idea made me hopeful for about three seconds. As much as I'd like it to be true, with everything else going on, and the information about the channel knife being Vivi's, I didn't believe it.

"It is scary. Especially—not to speak ill of the dead— but something changed in Elwell a few months ago."

"That must have been awful for you." I had to

keep the focus on her while I tried to get any information she might have. I'd actually learned something from my previous snooping attempts. "What changed?" I hope this question wouldn't make her wake up and realize she was talking to a stranger. But if working in a bar had taught me anything, it was that people talked to strangers all the time, and told them personal things they usually didn't want to hear. Maybe instead of running around questioning people, I should be doing heavy pours to loosen lips.

"Elwell was always an open-book, life-of-the-party kind of guy. Then he just kind of shut down. Stayed in his study with the door closed, talking on the phone. Would go out in the middle of the night without saying where he was going or why."

It sounded like Elwell was having an affair. Ivy said he'd been caught with the pool girl. If his own wife wouldn't tolerate him wearing the armadillo shell, would a lover? "At least you have your beautiful daughter." Ivy did look pretty in some of the photos Gloria had posted on social media. A far cry from the Ivy I'd met at the Crow's Nest.

"She should be on the pageant circuit. I'm sure she'd be Ms. Florida by now."

"Ms. Florida?" I asked. The pageant world was a mystery to me. Although when I was little, my grandma and I had curled up on the couch together with a big bowl of popcorn to watch them. We always wanted Miss Illinois to win.

"It's a pageant for women twenty-six and above. Ivy was runner-up for Miss Emerald Cove."

"That's not surprising."

"But lately she's had job and boyfriend woes." She

actually turned up her nose. "Ivy is too good for a cowboy. But we all make choices in life that we have to live with. And Ivy is making hers."

I made a sympathetic noise. The boyfriend *was* trouble and what girl needed that? But unless the boyfriend was the murderer, we were getting off the track I wanted us to stay on.

"Oh, dear. That on top of your poor husband. How are you doing?"

She looked up from her nails, which she'd been admiring. Shark's-blood red with a dash of sparkle nail polish, and filed to dangerous-looking points. Considering the damage they looked like they could do, I hoped I hadn't laid it on too thick. Fortunately, I really was interested in her. For all I knew, she killed Elwell and did it behind the Sea Glass to set up Vivi.

I'd have to see what I could dig up about the two of them. Vivi was a bit older than Gloria. Some of that sincere interest must have shown in my face because she didn't get up and leave or shut up.

"The problem is, there are too many suspects," Gloria said. "You can't be as successful as Elwell and not make a few enemies along the way."

I widened my eyes as an expression of sympathy, but kept my mouth shut.

"I believe it is one of those heritage," she used finger quotes when she said heritage, "business owners who want to keep running this town. They think they are better than anyone who might have grown up inland."

I guessed that was where Gloria grew up and it went along with what Leah had said.

"They think we're all hillbillies. And don't like it when people rise above them."

Another interesting layer of dynamics at play. Maybe one that could have contributed to Elwell's death. "That's just unfair."

"And their ancestors certainly didn't have a problem with the moonshine my ancestors made that kept all of them in business. That glass-bottom boat wasn't always carting tourists around, you know. Probably still isn't."

I sat back in surprise. At last, something more concrete.

Gloria looked at her very expensive diamond-encrusted watch. "I've got to go get my babies."

"Take care of yourself," I said, meaning every word.

"Thank you for listening to me. Some days it seems like no one does."

I glanced down at my own watch. *Oh no.*

CHAPTER 30

I was late for work. Although no one had ever really given me a schedule. I always arrived no later than ten thirty, which gave me time to do the prep work. I slammed out of the coffee shop, ran to my car, and sped over to the Sea Glass. I raced, as fast as I could on heels, from the parking lot to the Sea Glass. On the way, I passed a startled-looking Rhett. He did a double take as I went past.

"Looking good, Chloe. As always," Rhett called out as I entered the back of the bar.

Joaquín also looked twice before recognizing me.

"For a moment, I thought Vivi had hired some hot new *mamacita* and had given you the boot." He fake-fanned himself.

"Ha. Ha. Such a disappointment to be stuck with me." I started cutting lemons and limes like I did every day. When I had a chance, I'd change into the regular clothes I'd brought with me. I was counting on the fact that if Gloria came back to the Sea Glass—which I doubted she would—I would look different enough that she wouldn't recognize me. She probably wasn't interested in the people serving her anyway.

"I like your hair like that," Joaquín said as he inventoried the liquor lining the back shelves. "And those shoes."

I turned a heel back and forth so we could both admire them. "I like them too, but an hour working in these things and you'd have to call an ambulance."

"What were you up to this morning to be all dressed up like that?"

"Trying to save Vivi."

"And did you?" Joaquín asked.

"Maybe I'm one step closer." I hoped I was anyway. The problem was, I didn't know who to ask about all the questions Gloria had raised for me. Or how to follow a glass-bottom boat when it was off duty. However, maybe a first step would be seeing if the boat did indeed go out at night.

It was midnight, and I was sleepy. I was dressed all in black in my best imitation of what Ann Williams wore, I lay on my stomach on the front deck of Boone's boat with a pair of binoculars close by. If only they were night vision. Maybe my wakeboarding pal, Hunter, could get some for me. Although he'd want to know why I wanted them. If I was going to start a career in espionage, maybe ordering from Amazon would be a better idea.

The glass-bottom boat was docked on the other side of the marina. Far enough away that it was hard to see, especially in the dark, when clouds blocked the light from the moon. It was good cover for me, though. Birds had gone to roost—if that's what birds actually did at night. Boats were in their slips, and most people seemed to be asleep. I heard the occasional laugh or ice clinking in glasses. It reminded me again of how noises carried on water and how quiet I had to be.

Every time I heard a boat start up, I grabbed the binoculars and scanned the water. Two fishing boats had left, but the glass-bottom boat had stayed put so far. I was tired. Surveillance was indeed boring. Just like every real-life private investigator I'd ever read about said it was. I should have brought a book to read. But that was impractical. If I read an e-book, the glow would give me away. If I read a regular book, I'd need some kind of light, which would also expose me.

At least it wasn't cold out here. I'd taken the tarp off the boat so I didn't have to sweat under it. Although, any time the slightest breeze hit, I shivered a little. Another engine rumbled to life. I grabbed the binoculars in time to watch the glass-bottom boat back out and head down the marina. Just as I'd suspected. *Thank you, Gloria.* I hadn't seen anything on their schedule about midnight tours on cloudy nights. But boats made enough noise that any regular trips—or irregular ones, for that matter—would be one of those secrets everyone knew about.

How was I going to follow the glass-bottom boat without being spotted? Boone's boat rocked just then, and not from the wake of the glass-bottom boat. The back dipped and the front rose. Someone must have come on board. I flipped onto my back and saw a shape silhouetted in the weak light from the marina lights. I sat up.

What had I been thinking? There was a murderer on the loose, not to mention I'd been chased, side-swiped, and almost turned into a crispy critter. I might as well have "idiot" stamped on my forehead. I could track the person's progress toward me by the way the boat rocked. How the silhouette moved. They took a slow step forward and I scooted forward, closer to the front of the boat, where the two benches met in a deep V. It was like we were playing the world's slowest game of keep-away.

How did anyone know where I was? I edged closer to the front of the boat. Not that there was anywhere to hide now. I could always go overboard if need be. In the summer, the water was like a warm bath, and I was an excellent swimmer thanks to all the lessons my parents made me take. As long as I managed not to hit my head on the boat or dock if I had to jump, I could just swim away.

The shadow came around the console. I stood up, ready to jump if I needed to.

"What are you doing out here?"

Rhett. I plopped back down onto the deck, exhaling a huge breath. Grateful it was him and not the boogeyman. "Stargazing." We both looked up at the cloudy sky. Drat. That excuse didn't hold up. "I heard there was a meteor shower tonight and was hoping the clouds would clear." That sounded good. "How did you know I was here?"

Rhett came and sat beside me. "Honey, you stand out like a tick on snow."

I looked down at Boone's shiny white boat and my

dark clothes. Next time I'd have to find an outfit that blended in better. And I probably should be worried that I was thinking there would be a next time.

"Plus the tarp was off and your car's in the parking lot."

With all that, it didn't take a genius to figure out where I was. Next time I'd take more precautions. And there I was again with the "next time." I glanced over my shoulder toward the glass-bottom boat, but I couldn't see it any longer. The slight chug of the motor made it sound like it was going north toward the bay, not south toward the Gulf.

"I see you have binoculars. Better to see the meteors with?"

I didn't think I had Rhett fooled for a minute. He'd probably seen me with the binoculars focused on the glass-bottom boat. "Of course." I yawned. Whether he bought it or no, this was my cover story and I was sticking to it. "Boone always told me how magical the stars were out here."

"And you didn't think about just walking out the door of the cabin and sitting out there?" Rhett must have been a great lawyer.

"I bore easily."

"I'll have to keep that in mind."

Was that another sexual innuendo? He was so close. So hot. It was too dark to see his expression, but I leaned toward him for a moment until I came to my senses. "Doesn't look like the clouds are going to dissipate, so I'll just get going. Have a good evening." I sat on the edge of the boat, swung my legs over the side, and dropped to the dock. "Will you snap the tarp back into place when you leave?"

Rhett stood on the boat with his hands on his hips as I walked off. Enough thinking about Rhett. I'd have to come up with a plan to track the glass-bottom boat some other night. Kayak? Paddleboard? Both were probably too slow. Boone's boat? Too obvious. But a Jet Ski? That just might work. Or I could just ask Leah why the boat went out so late.

Just as I was about to unlock my car, another idea hit me. I reversed course, hoping to find some answers about who killed Elwell.

CHAPTER 31

Two Bobs was the newest bar on the strip of build-ings that ran behind the marina. I hadn't run into Rhett as I backtracked and passed Boone's boat. Well, I guessed he wasn't following me, which was a relief. I think. Two Bobs was closest to the inlet that led from the marina to the Gulf. According to Joaquín, it had opened about six months ago after the owner had torn down an old concrete building. Its replacement was shiny and new. As I walked to-ward it, I could see people dancing on the rooftop deck, which was decorated with pretty twinkling lights.

Unlike the Sea Glass, there were entrances from the marina and the Gulf side. They also had a couple of reserved slips on the marina where boats could dock. I wondered if the Sea Glass could be reconfig-ured so people could come through the back too. Then I reconsidered. Some of the regulars already came in that way. More people tramping through the small kitchen didn't seem wise. It made me think of

Elwell. How easy it would have been for someone to grab a channel knife out of the kitchen and stab Elwell with it. We really needed to start keeping that back door locked.

I arrived at Two Bobs around twelve forty. It had decks on the front and back of the bar. The one facing the marina was packed. I walked up the two steps and went into the bar. It was sleek, with an industrial feel. Nothing beachy about it, except for the crowds of sunburned people and the fruity drinks. The bar was along the east side and had those frozen drink machines Vivi abhorred.

But the place was hopping and had a fun vibe. It was hard to argue with that. I worked my way through the crowd and walked out to the Gulf side. That deck was packed too. There was a row of barstools—fifties throwbacks in chrome with bright-red vinyl seats—that faced the Gulf. A ledge in front of them, so patrons could set down their drinks. A smattering of small tables filled the rest of the space. Every stool had a butt on it, and the tables were full too. I wondered if the Sea Glass stayed open later if it would attract these kinds of crowds too.

I went back inside and skirted around the crowd to a staircase that went up to the rooftop deck. The banister and balusters were shiny chrome too. As I climbed, the layout started revealing itself. Small, round tables sat at the outer edge of a dance floor. Music was piped through speakers. I could only see people's feet from this position. I spotted two sets of cowboy boots at one of the tables, and it scared the bejesus out of me.

I stopped and let some people go around me

while I figured out what to do. Certainly the two men from the Crow's Nest weren't the only people wearing cowboy boots around here. I went up another step. With the two sets of cowboy boots was a wedge-heeled sandal with a beautifully manicured foot. I couldn't see beyond the ankle in my current position, but the ankle had a flag tattoo—red border, yellow rectangle, green rectangle, and a small starburst in the middle. Ann Williams. I flattened myself against the wall because I didn't want the cowboys to spot me, if they were the ones from the Crow's Nest. My curiosity got the better of me. I crept up two more steps for a better view.

Ann spotted me right away. So much for being stealthy. She leaned into the cowboys, but directed their attention to the other side of the bar. It *was* the two men from the Crow's Nest. I hurried back down the steps. What was Ann Williams doing with them? It didn't seem like it would be anything good. And why did she have them look the other way? So they wouldn't see me, or so I wouldn't recognize them?

While keeping a close eye on the staircase, I squeezed into a small space at the bar and ordered a frozen margarita. It came straight from the machine into a plastic cup. I gave the bartender, a weary-looking girl, a good tip, which earned me a thank-you and a smile. I tasted the margarita. It was way too sweet and fairly strong. Look at me, a couple of weeks working in a bar and suddenly I was an expert, or at the very least a margarita snob.

I must have made a face because the bartender

laughed. She leaned over to me. "If you want a good margarita, go to the Sea Glass down the beach."

My eyes widened in surprise.

"Bad thing is, they're closed right now, so you're stuck with that." She pointed at my drink.

"I heard there was a murder down there."

"Yeah, Elwell Pugh. It's crazy."

"Is he the guy who wore that armadillo shell as a hat?" I asked. That's what I'd come here to find out.

"He never did in here. But I heard about him wearing it around town. Kind of nuts, right?"

Nuts or a strategy. "Did he come in a lot?" I asked.

"Depends on your definition of a lot." She lifted a shoulder at me as she left to help another patron.

Monday morning, I parked my car and walked around the far side of the harbor to where the glass-bottom boat sat. Leah wasn't around, but a wizened man hunched on a stool in the booth. He looked familiar, but I hadn't ever seen him in the bar. Probably a good thing, because I might have to lie. I finally realized he was in the brochure about the glass-bottom boat. He was Leah's grandfather.

"Mornin'," the man said cheerfully, drawing out the word to "m-ore-nin." He was as tan as a light roast coffee bean. "What can I do for ya?"

He had the same bright-blue eyes as Leah. "I'm interested in a nighttime tour. Do you do anything like that?" I knew the brochure made no mention of such a tour.

"How late at night?" he asked, leaning forward and giving me a squint eye.

"Say around midnight?" I might as well go for it.

He leaned back, putting some distance between us. An assessing look entered his eyes, and I felt like I was losing him.

"I thought it would be fun for my boyfriend and me to do a late-night tour. A moonlight tour. A midnight tour sounds romantic to me. He's fascinated with the wildlife here, but doesn't like to be out in the sun."

"Kind of an odd place to vacation if you don't like to be out in the sun."

"Tell me about it. But he agreed to come here for me. I swear, I must have been a sun worshipper in a previous life." I leaned in. "I want to do something nice for him in return." I summoned up the sincere look I used on kids at the library.

"Well, I might be able to work something out for you. Name's Oscar."

He pulled out a pipe and started chewing on the stem. All he needed was a rakish hat and huge forearms and he'd be Popeye's older brother. I had a feeling Leah had no idea people could arrange a late-night tour.

"You meet me here at midnight and we'll see what we can do."

"Great," I said. Now all I had to do was drum up a boyfriend the old man wouldn't recognize.

CHAPTER 32

Midnight came slower than Christmas morning for a five-year-old. I'd called my wakeboarding friend Hunter and told him I had an extra ticket I didn't want to go to waste. Hunter couldn't make it, but sent Mark, one of the guys who'd gone wakeboarding with us. I met him in the lot by the Sea Glass as we'd arranged earlier in the day.

"Hi, Mark," I said when he got out of his car.

"So, a late-night glass-bottom boat tour, huh?" Mark was tall, with a large Adam's apple and a deep voice. His hair was military-precision short. "How are we going to see anything in the dark?"

"I'm not sure. It just sounded like fun." Now for the awkward part. "Would you, uh, mind acting like you're my boyfriend? It's the only way I could arrange the tour."

Mark grinned. "I think I can handle that." He slung an arm loosely around my shoulder. "Let's go, babycakes."

Ugh. I reminded myself this was to help Vivi. "Okay."

Minutes later, just before midnight, we stood in front of the kiosk. It was as dark as the inside of a coal mine. Drat. Had Oscar forgotten? A whistle sounded from the direction of the glass-bottom boat, and we headed over.

"Getta move on," Oscar said. "Places to go."

"But we haven't paid yet," I said.

"Hop on. I have to make a quick stop during the tour." Oscar held out his hand. I took it and stepped on, worried about what the stop entailed. Mark stepped on behind me.

"I'll give you a discount because of the stop." Oscar fired up the engines before I could ask any more questions. I noticed a tarp thrown over something that looked like boxes in the middle of the boat. I glanced at Mark. He'd settled on one of the bench seats and patted the spot beside him. I certainly didn't want to involve him in anything untoward. I slumped onto the bench next to him.

As we left the harbor and turned toward the bay, the night folded blanketlike around us. No more high-pressure sodium streetlights with their orangey glow to light our way. The water streaming below our feet through the glass was darker than squid ink. Oscar hadn't turned on the boat's lights, and I was worried about how he could see where we were going. We headed the same way Leah had taken the boat the day of my sunrise tour, but at a slower pace. The engines throbbed through the boat. I kept staring at the tarp because I wanted to see what was under there. Mark threw an arm around my shoulders and drew me closer to him. Frankly, I appreciated his body warmth. Either the breeze created by the boat or my nerves made me colder than normal. Probably my nerves. Mark leaned in and kissed my cheek.

Oscar grinned over at us. "How long have you two been dating?"

"Four years," I said at the same time as Mark said, "Six months."

"That's right, sweetie, it's four years *and* six months." I looked at Oscar. The clouds were drifting off and the moon started to provide a modest amount of light. "He's such a romantic, he could probably tell you almost to the hour when we started dating."

As another cloud came over, Mark dangled his hand over my chest, and I slapped it away. "What the hockey puck do you think you're doing?" I whispered. Librarians are good at whispering and crafting euphemisms.

"Just trying to help you out."

"Any more help like that and you're going overboard. I want to see what's under that tarp. Distract Oscar for me." I stood up and walked casually over to where the tarp was. I kept my back to it so I didn't look interested. Oscar slowed the boat more and turned east on another bayou. This one was even more narrow. Trees with Spanish moss crowded the sides of the boat. I started worrying about running aground, but Oscar drove with a steady hand.

I sat down and leaned my arms against the side of the boat. Now I was facing the tarp. I stretched out so my feet were almost touching it. My tailbone was on the edge of the seat, and I hoped I didn't fall off.

Mark moved over to stand beside Oscar. We turned into another bayou. This one was more open because it was lined with marsh grass instead of trees on one side.

"Ever see any gators out here?" Mark asked Oscar.

"All the damn time," Oscar said. "'Specially on nights like this. It's feeding time for them."

Ack! I drew my arms in away from the side of the boat. As Oscar pointed and told Mark he thought he'd spotted a large male, I lifted the tarp with my foot. It was a white cardboard box stamped "whiskey." Oh, boy. Emerald Cove, we have a problem. I dropped the tarp back into place. Oscar took another turn. Any light disappeared, branches and roots scrapped the boat's sides. Mark came back over and sat by me. He put his arm around me again, his lips near my ear.

"Any luck?" Mark asked.

"Yes."

"Want to tell me what's going on?"

"Maybe you don't want to know."

"Ignorance isn't bliss," he said. "Oscar is involved in something or he wouldn't be out here at night."

Fudge. "I'm sorry. I shouldn't have dragged you into this. Whatever this is." Probably smuggling. Great. Just perfect.

"I'm a big boy." He grinned.

Not what I needed to hear just now. "The boxes under the tarp are labeled 'whiskey.'" He let out a long breath. Surely Oscar wouldn't want us to know he was involved with smugglers. It didn't bode well for the end of this journey.

"Almost there," Oscar said. "Now, if you two could just do me a favor and slide underneath the benches and be real still for a few minutes, I'd appreciate it."

There was no threat in his voice, but after exchanging alarmed looks, we scrambled to do as Oscar asked, even though it was beyond weird. Oscar had to know we'd realized something fishy was going on. I lay on the right and Mark on the left. My nose was about a foot from the tarp. I hoped there weren't any spiders or other crawly things under here. A couple of minutes later, Oscar shut off the engine. The boat drifted a few feet before bumping into something.

"Grab the rope and tie her up," Oscar said. The boat rocked as someone came on. Cowboy boots came into sight. Not good at all. The boat rocked a second time, and tennis shoes came into view. That's when I spotted the flag tattoo on the ankle.

CHAPTER 33

I bit my lip so I didn't make any noise or yell something like, "I knew you were shady with that handy-woman routine."

The boat dipped again, and another pair of cowboy boots came into my view. The same ones I'd seen on the cowboy last night at Two Bobs. Oscar and the other two worked quickly. Minutes later, the boxes had been removed. Oscar maneuvered the boat around and motored back the way we had come. A few minutes later, Oscar told us to come on out.

"Sorry to make you crawl under there, but my friends don't like strangers."

I wasn't a stranger to any of them, but it wasn't something Oscar needed to know. And thank heavens neither of them had spotted Mark and me. They obviously trusted Oscar. As we chugged back to the harbor, Oscar told us stories of the good old days, before the North discovered the Panhandle and its beautiful beaches.

"How much do I owe you?" I asked Oscar once we docked. A gust of wind blew my hair. Oscar looked at the sky. "Better get a move on. A storm's brewin'."

Oscar, Mark, and I headed to the kiosk. Mark held my hand.

"You don't owe me nothin'," Oscar said.

"That's quite the discount." The wind picked up. The boats docked in the marina started to rock.

"I enjoyed your company. Gets lonely out there."

It made me wonder how often Oscar was making runs. "What's your family think about you going out by yourself?"

"You know what they say," Oscar said.

"What?" I asked.

"Need to know. That's the basis I work on. Have a good evening," he told us.

As soon as Oscar was out of sight, I tried to pull my hand away from Mark, but he hung on. "We can drop the pretense now," I said. "Thanks for going along."

"Interesting evening. But I think we can make it more interesting." He yanked me to him and kissed me.

I pulled my head back and tried to push him away. "Stop." I said it in my best librarian voice. Loud. Firm. The one that stopped the orneriest patron from doing whatever it was they were doing that they shouldn't be.

But he didn't and was bending in for another kiss.

"Let her go," Rhett yelled.

I could hear him running toward us. I stomped on Mark's instep. As he yowled in pain, I shoved him. He landed in the harbor with a huge splash. I looked down to make sure he was okay. He was treading water, sputtering, staring up at me with a stunned look. I shook a finger at him. "No means no. You jerk."

Rhett arrived by my side. I turned to him. "I don't need saving."

Rhett put up his hands. "I never said you did."

"Then why are you here?"

"Being worried about someone doesn't mean you think they need to be saved. I just got off duty."

He did smell smoky, and there was a smudge of ash on his cheek that, against all common sense, I wanted to wipe off. Instead, I pointed toward Mark. "You might want to help him out." I didn't wait to see what happened and set off toward my car.

"What's wrong with her?" Mark asked.

"Not a damn thing," Rhett answered.

I smiled in spite of myself.

Memories are powerful. Tonight, I couldn't shake mine. The Gulf was in a fury. Its usual calm gone. Every bolt of lightning made me jump. The windows shook with each rumble of thunder. I hunkered down in my bed curled into a small ball, trying to fight the flashback that returned on nights like this.

The massive waves on Lake Michigan had gotten bigger and bigger that night all those years ago. The strobe-light lightning surrounding us. My friend and I clinging to each other in the rocking rowboat we should never have taken out. It hurt to breathe, just as it had when I was ten. The boat had flipped over. I tried to hold on to my friend's hand. Never forgot the sensation of her cold hand slipping out of mine. The last touch of our fingertips. The look in her eyes as she disappeared into the water. I'd floundered in the water that night eighteen years ago until I somehow washed back up onshore. My friend wasn't found until two days later, drowned.

CHAPTER 34

Tuesday morning, I had a huge dilemma, and it wasn't just that I didn't want to go for a run. I was tired from my late-night adventure, the storm, and memories it brought. I'd kept trying to figure out what I'd seen last night when I should have been sleeping. I dragged on my running clothes and shoes anyway. Hit the sand and headed east, away from the Sea Glass. The air was warm, the pelicans dove for breakfast, and sanderlings ran back and forth from the waves. The Gulf made a soft, sucking sound as it shifted the sand from one spot to another. So peaceful.

Should I tell Leah what her grandfather was up to or not? I didn't know her that well, but she seemed nice and honest, and her grandfather could be headed for trouble. The cowboys were dangerous, and I wasn't sure if Ann Williams was or not. But what if Leah knew and was part of what was going on?

Maybe I should talk to Joaquín about all this. I trusted him, even though I didn't know him that well.

What did Rhett know about the whole thing, and why the heck did he keep popping up in my life? Was it more than a small-town thing?

I'd figured out that he stayed on his boat sometimes, or maybe he lived on it, so it was natural that we'd see each other in passing. Quite a few people were starting to look familiar to me as I went about my everyday routine and on my runs—fishermen, other runners, shell seekers. I could hardly accuse him of being out at odd hours when I was the one who was out at odd hours. At least he had an excuse. Firemen didn't necessarily have regular schedules like some of us did.

After I made the turn and headed back toward Boone's house, I eventually came even with Vivi's house. She stood out on her porch with a cup of coffee in her hand. The tide was low, so we were almost half a football field apart. I veered toward her. We needed to talk about the bar. About halfway through the soft sand, I had to slow and change my stride. My legs worked a thousand times harder. Vivi and I made eye contact. Vivi turned, went into her house, and closed the door. Slammed it actually. Great. And I'd really thought we'd made progress. She was one heck of an ornery woman.

I got back home with no answers to any of my questions. So I showered, finger combed my hair, and brushed on mascara and eyeshadow. In the time I'd been here, my face was already getting a bit of color. A soft sprinkling of freckles dotted my nose. I needed to up my sun protection routine.

* * *

Confronting Vivi was uppermost on my mind when I walked into the Sea Glass. Her office door was closed, and I hadn't seen her car in the parking lot.

"Where's Vivi?" I asked Joaquín. She could only avoid me for so long.

"Back in for questioning."

Now I felt guilty for being angry with her.

"They don't seem to have any other suspects but her," Joaquín said. He leaned a hip against the side of the bar.

"I have other suspects. Why don't they?"

Joaquín bolted up. "You do? I'm making you a cup of coffee and you are spilling it, girl."

"I'd rather have a happy drink." I clasped my hands in front of my chest and looked at him hopefully.

He shook a finger at me. "Oh, no. We are not starting the day like that. I'll make you coffee like my *abuelita*—grandmother—did. So strong you'll think you're Atlas. Then you are going to sit over there and tell me what's going on in that tired-looking head of yours."

I didn't think I looked that bad. "Coffee it is."

Instead of making me coffee, he picked up his phone. "Michael. I need you to get over to the Sea Glass." He hung up and looked at me. "Are you just going to stand there looking like a piece of seagrass or are you going to do something while I get started on your coffee?"

I took the hint and started taking barstools off tables. "I'm looking forward to meeting Michael, but why did you call him?"

"He's great at puzzles. Former Navy intelligence. And three heads are better than just yours."

"My, aren't we sassy this morning."

"Yes, we are," Joaquín said.

Ten minutes later, Michael had walked over from their boat, and the three of us sat at one of the round tables, cups of steaming coffee in front of us. Michael had graying hair, slicked back from his face, and see-into-your-soul blue eyes. He was tall and broad. I wondered what getting around on a Navy ship with their tight quarters had been like for him. We exchanged the usual nice-to-meet-you, heard-so-much-about-you greetings. Although I hadn't really heard that much about Michael, and I now wondered what he'd heard about me.

"As I told you on the phone, Chloe has suspects." Joaquín tipped his head toward me.

They both looked over their coffee cups at me. I twisted a ring around and around on my finger. It was my favorite ring, one Boone had given me for my birthday our senior year in college. The aquamarine stone matched the color of the Gulf today.

"Go ahead," Joaquín said. "We're just here to brainstorm."

I took a deep breath. "I've been digging into El-well's behavior. Gloria left because something was going on."

"What did Gloria say?" Michael asked.

"Elwell had been closing himself in his office, talking on the phone in there, and leaving in the middle of the night." I paused. "It sounded suspicious. Then he started wearing that ridiculous armadillo shell. She mentioned that too."

"You think that had something to do with his murder?" Michael asked. "The shell wasn't why he was murdered but could be a reason for his murder?"

"Exactly." Maybe I wasn't so far off. I smiled at Michael and he smiled back. The kind of smile that gave me hope. "He'd been wearing it to all of the heritage businesses. And as far as I can tell, it freaked the patrons out. But he didn't wear it when he frequented Two Bobs."

Joaquín muttered something in Spanish. "He'd been pretending to be Vivi's friend—all the heritage business owners' friend—while sabotaging their businesses. As you hear down here in the South, 'he had it comin'.'"

"I don't think a murder victim ever really has it coming, but I can see folks making a case for that." I paused. "There's also been a spate of bad reviews of the heritage businesses recently. But they didn't stop after Elwell died."

"Hang on," Michael said, "let me look up reviews of Two Bobs to see if there's a pattern that matches the heritage businesses."

Joaquín and I sipped our coffee while Michael tapped on his phone.

"There aren't many negative reviews. In fact, if anything, there's been a spate of positive ones the past few weeks. Some include things like 'drinks are so much better than the Sea Glass's.'"

"Well, that's just a lie. I tried a margarita there and it tasted like sugar. Joaquín's drinks are way better."

"Of course they are. But if Elwell was leaving or arranged for the bad reviews, they should have stopped after the murder," Joaquín said.

"Not if more than one person was involved," Michael said.

We smiled at each other. "Exactly," I said. "Do you two know who owns Two Bobs?"

"Two guys named Bob?" Michael said.

Joaquín whacked him on the arm as I groaned. All three of us picked up our phones and started searching. The "About" section on the Two Bobs web page was vague. It talked about when it opened and all their fun activities.

"There's not much information on their web page," I said.

"A business permit was filed for Two Bobs," Joaquín said. "It shows Two Bobs LLC as the owners. But when I searched Two Bobs LLC, there isn't any information about who it belongs to, and the address is a PO box in Panama City. It could belong to anyone."

"A shell company?" Michael said.

"Could be. Let's put that aside for now and talk about the other players. Fred Russo is on my list," I said.

"The grocery store owner is on your list?" Joaquín asked. He sounded dismayed. "We love shopping there."

"I do too, but I was there the other night and he was arguing with a man. The man told him he'd better deliver. Later, Fred told me the man was one of his suppliers."

"Obviously a lie," Michael said. "Suppliers are the ones who deliver."

"That's what I thought," I said. "I don't know what's going on with him."

"But it doesn't sound good," Joaquín said.

"You would think the deputies would be looking at Gloria and Ivy, if they are the ones who will inherit all Elwell's assets." I looked down into my coffee cup for a moment. "Ivy seems especially suspicious. Setting up Vivi could be for revenge for firing her."

"But kill her own dad? Why?" Michael asked.

"To quote one of the heritage owners, 'she had ten million reasons,' or at least part of that. And to top that off, Ivy has a cowboy boyfriend who is trouble."

"Tell Michael that part," Joaquín said.

"I went to the Crow's Nest and talked to Ivy. And I'm pretty sure her boyfriend was there, listening to our conversation. Ivy wasn't happy with me at the end. I guess I seemed too nosy about what her dad had been up to. Gloria and Leah both told me the boyfriend was trouble."

"Your going to the Crow's Next made the cowboy and his friend try to run you off the road and set the fire," Joaquín said.

"Did the fire investigator figure out who started the fire?" Michael asked.

"Not that I know of. I don't have any proof they did it. Just a bunch of suspicions," I said.

Michael frowned at that. "What else?"

CHAPTER 35

"Ivy told me that Elwell had something going with someone on the town council to get zoning laws changed so high-rises could be built."

Michael and Joaquín shuddered at that.

"What if one of the town council members is pretending to be anti-high-rise but isn't?" I said. "The third anti-vote would have to be either Ralph or Fred." I really didn't want it to be big, cuddly Ralph.

"Two of them are heritage owners," Michael said, pointing out the obvious.

"Fred seems the most likely," Joaquín said. "Taking into consideration what you overheard in his store."

"Couldn't Ralph be just as likely, or the other council member?"

"Why?" Michael asked.

"More tourists, more revenue," I said.

"But this area has always been about something more than revenue to the heritage business owners." Michael downed the rest of his coffee. "I guess one of those three council members might be in financial trouble and needs cash. That could give a lot of people a reason to change their vote."

"More coffee?" Joaquín asked.

"Someone can drink more than one cup of this stuff?" I asked. I was already feeling jittery and I was only halfway through the cup.

"You just need some Latino blood," Joaquín said. "Is that it for the suspects?"

I shook my head. "Buford has a bad temper and a long-running love/hate relationship with Elwell." I filled them in on what Ed had told me the other night.

"We need to figure out a way to whittle down this list," Joaquín said.

"One more. Ann Williams, the handywoman."

Michael burst out laughing. "Handywoman?"

"Yes. She fixes things."

Michael looked over at Joaquín and grinned.

"Okay. That's it. What's with everyone and all the looks when I mention Ann being a handywoman? Are you all so old-fashioned you don't think a woman can handle it?" After all, this was the South. Maybe they still thought like it was the Stone Age. I hated that kind of thinking.

They both burst out laughing.

Joaquín finally got himself under control after wiping a tear away from his eye. "I never said she was a handywoman. I said she fixes things."

I looked back and forth between them. "She. Fixes. Things?" They nodded encouragingly, and suddenly I felt like an idiot as the truth crashed down on my wee brain. "She fixes things like people's problems, not their broken toilets?" They nodded again. I clapped my hands to my face for a moment. "Oh. My. Heavens. Why didn't someone say something when I was asking her to fix my door and other things?" I gulped down some coffee. "And why didn't she just tell me no?" I'd gone from embarrassed to humiliated in two seconds.

"She knows everyone," Joaquín said.

"Ann's a nice person. You're new here. She probably just wanted to help you out." Michael reached over and patted my hand. "It's okay."

It wasn't. How could I ever face her again? But then, how could I have known? I'd never met a "fixer" before. Who'd expect one in this small town? It's something you'd expect in a big city like Chicago or Boston, where there were plenty of goings on. "That explains why I couldn't find her business listed on social media."

"And of course, Williams is her mother's last name, not her father's," Michael said.

"Michael—" Joaquín said with a warning tone.

Michael looked at Joaquín. "It seems like y'all have been keeping a lot of secrets from Chloe."

Joaquín huffed. "She's new. Northern. How did we know if we could trust her?" Joaquín turned to me. "No offense, Chloe, but you did just show up out of the blue."

"Northern? Really? You're prejudice against Northerners now?" Michael asked. "We of all people shouldn't judge."

"I'm sorry, Chloe. It's more the new thing, not the Northern thing."

"Understood," I said. But I felt a little disappointed.

"Her actual last name is Lafitte but she doesn't use it," Joaquín said. He cast a sharp look at Michael that I interpreted to mean *see, I'm being upfront now.*

Lafitte. Lafitte. "As in the pirate Jean Lafitte?" I asked.

"He wasn't just a pirate," Michael said hastily.

"He was a hero during the War of 1812," Joaquín added. "And please don't tell anyone. Ann is—sensitive."

She was about as sensitive as a sadistic dentist. Joaquín stood up when someone banged on the Gulfside sliding-glass doors. Customers were here already. "I have a headache," he said as he walked over to open up.

I looked at Michael. "Let me know if you make sense of any of this. Because none of it explains why Elwell was killed, or why he was killed here."

"I will."

We exchanged phone numbers and hugged our goodbyes. Eleven o'clock and I hadn't sliced one lime yet.

Vivi called, said she had a headache and wasn't coming in. Lots of headaches going around, but you couldn't blame the weather. If the water was an emerald today, the sky dazzled with a showy blue topaz. The bar was busy, the tourists were happy, and the regulars, except for Buford and Ed, were nowhere to be found. Joaquín swiveled his hips in time to the music as he always did, but with a bit less enthusiasm than usual. There'd been no time for follow-up about our discussion. No time to talk about anything but drink orders—things like two beers, two tequila shots, one daiquiri, and order up. I wished one of those orders was for me.

At four, I got a text from Michael saying to come home with Joaquín and he'd make us all a late dinner. It sounded like heaven, and maybe he'd figured something out. The rest of the day went faster than our blender whirred. People had cleared out around eight thirty, so we were able to clean up and lock the doors just after nine. Joaquín and I were too tired to talk as he traipsed down the dock toward his boat.

"This is your fishing boat?" I asked Joaquín as we stepped into the air-conditioned cabin of the boat. It was outfitted with teak and leather-cushioned furniture. Very grand to go fishing on.

"No. The fishing boat is the one in the next slip." Michael came forward to greet us with a fruity drink with an umbrella in it. It looked happy. I took the drink. Michael had a beer for himself and sparkling water for Joaquín.

"Cheers," we said.

I took a sip, and my taste buds danced with the mango and peach flavors. "Delicious."

"Michael is a genius when it comes to mixed drinks," Joaquín said as we settled at the dining room table, which was across from the small but well-appointed kitchen. "We tried living on the fishing boat, but it was too small."

"And I had to get up at the crack of dawn every morning." Michael looked at Joaquín.

"It smells delicious in here," I said.

"Caesar salad, steak with three sauces because I didn't know which you'd like, and flan for dessert,"

Michael said. "And no shop or suspect talk until dinner is over."

Forty-five minutes later, I'd tried all three sauces on different bites of steak and truly couldn't say if the Béarnaise, red wine, or garlic butter sauce was better. Each one was delicious in its own way. Michael had also baked French bread that was crusty on the outside and soft inside. I didn't think I had room for flan, but once he set a piece in front of me, I devoured it.

"That was spectacular. If you ever decide to leave Joaquín, I have an extra bedroom."

Michael laughed. "Not going to happen."

I insisted on clearing the table and washing the dishes. It was ten thirty by the time I finished.

"An after-dinner liqueur?" Joaquín asked.

"Not for me. I wouldn't be able to stay awake, and I'd have to unbutton my shorts."

Joaquín, who hadn't had a predinner drink or any of the cabernet with dinner, poured himself a Chambord, a black raspberry–flavored liqueur, into a tiny, expensive-looking liqueur glass. We went back into the living room.

"So, getting back to the main event, do you have any other suspects?" Michael asked in a way that made me think he had one.

"Just Rhett Barnett."

"Why him?" Joaquín asked.

"He's always around," I said. "I know that sounds odd because he has a boat here too. But I've run into him a lot at odd hours." I thought for a moment about him saying nothing was wrong with me last night. I repressed the smile that wanted to go with that thought. "He's a fireman, so he knows how to set a fire. There's some long-running feud between his family and Vivi's." I looked back and forth between them in hopes they would confirm what Ed had told me. Nothing. "And he was out on the dock the morning I found Elwell."

"He was?" Joaquín asked. "What was he doing there?"

"He was probably staying on his boat." I explained how I'd met Rhett. The snoring. Heat creeped up my face. Michael made a little hiccup sound. Joaquín made a *meep* noise. Then all three of us burst out laughing, and laughed until we could hardly breath.

"Now I'm definitely not going to be your roommate," Michael said.

"Poor me." It felt good to laugh so hard. "And I was sure it would work out between us."

"Seriously, though," Joaquín said, "you think he could be involved?"

"He's very chummy with Ann Williams. I keep seeing them together. It's one of those she-says-jump and he says how-high situations. It made me wonder about both of them. But you two probably know him better than I do."

"Not really," Joaquín said. "He moved back about a year ago. My two jobs keep me busy, and it's not like he hangs out at the Sea Glass."

"Where'd he move back from?" I asked.

"Birmingham. He practiced law there," Joaquín said.

I'd known he was a lawyer, but not where he practiced. "From what I know of him, he seems like a good guy," Michael said. "Doesn't rule him out, though. But why Ann?"

"I've seen her with those cowboys a couple of times. And they are definitely up to no good." Fixers must have to blur some ethical lines. Good. Evil. Right. Wrong. Murky shades in between all of them.

Joaquín yawned, so I stood up and said my good-byes. I let them think I was heading home, but instead, I was going to track down Ann Lafitte.

CHAPTER 36

I walked west from Joaquín and Michael's boat until I reached Two Bobs. I hoped Ann was there, with or without the cowboys. Well, preferably without, but I needed to talk to her. She wasn't on the back deck, so I went on in. The place was packed again. I studied the big chalkboard they had up listing their drinks and prices.

The prices were a few dollars less than the drinks at the Sea Glass. I thought our prices were reasonable, especially compared to what I was used to paying in Chicago. Maybe the cheap drinks were why this place was always so crowded. I noticed that the beer prices were the same or higher than the Sea Glass, which fit right into my theory.

I ordered another margarita, this time on the rocks instead of a frozen one from the machine. Maybe they skimped on the amount of alcohol they put in their drinks and that was why they were less. When the bartender handed me mine, I took a sip. Nope. There was plenty of alcohol in this; my eyes al-

most watered. It was so different from the frozen one
I'd had here the first time I came.

I thought about the day I'd made the mojito for
the college guy. How he'd complained it didn't taste
like the one he'd had somewhere else. Vivi, like any
bar owner, had a range of qualities of alcohol, from
the cheapest used for well drinks to the super pre-
mium that people requested by brand. If Two Bobs
was using smuggled alcohol instead of purchasing
like everyone else had to, their profits would be
through the roof even if they charged less. I didn't
plan to drink anymore of it, but it made an excellent
prop as I wandered around looking for Ann.

I found her out on the front deck, her back against
the wall and a glass of beer in front of her. She didn't
seem all that surprised to see me. I sat on the stool
across from her and set my drink on the table. "Why
didn't you tell me you aren't a handywoman? Why
take care of all of that stuff for me?"

Ann lifted a shoulder and dropped it. "You're new
and needed help. I don't exactly advertise what I
really do, especially not to newcomers."

I got that. "Thanks for taking care of all that for
me. I'd like to pay you."

"Not necessary."

I took a sip of my margarita. "Drink prices are
cheap here." It was time to talk about why I was really
here.

Ann nodded, but didn't say anything.

"And I think you know why. I was with Oscar last
night on his midnight run."

"Stupid old man." A flick of distress passed across

Ann's face. "Oscar's a problem I'm going to have to take care of."

Now I was distressed and didn't try to hide the fact. "What do you mean 'take care of'?" I should have handled this differently. I should have gone to the sheriff's department. If Ann was working with the cowboys, I knew how they tried to take care of problems. But it wasn't too late to do that. I stood up.

"Sit, please," Ann said. She looked like she was going to smile, or maybe it was the dim lighting. "I mean I'm going to call Leah and tell her what Oscar is up to."

"Smuggling whiskey?"

Ann hesitated. "Vivi was suspicious something like that was going on and asked me to look into it."

"Why didn't she call the authorities?"

"You don't get it yet. How close these people are. They go back generations and would rather chop off an arm than hurt one of their friends, even if one is hurting them." She took a sip of the beer in front of her.

"It looked to me like you were an active participant in the smuggling."

"You aren't wrong, but it was the only way I could find out who was doing what."

"So, do you know?"

For the first time she looked hesitant. "Not enough. I'm still working on who the higher-ups are."

"Why don't you go to the authorities?"

"Because I don't know who's corrupt and who isn't. But I will soon, if you stay out of it. I'm good at what I do. Just give me a bit more time. Please."

I remembered a case in Chicago when the Secret Service had helped investigate and convict liquor store operators. "The Secret Service worked a case like this in Illinois. There must be some agency you can go to for help if you don't trust the locals."

"It might not be just the locals. Millions of dollars can be made by not paying taxes on alcohol. If it comes from Mexico or Cuba or someone making their own."

I thought of all the swamps and woods around here. There were plenty of places to hide a still.

"I'm keeping someone I trust in the loop, so if something happens to me, they will share what I've found out so far," Ann said.

This must be really serious if Ann was worried something could happen to her. "Rhett?" Ann's face was so neutral, it could have been Switzerland. We stared at each other for several moments.

"Yes."

"And you two are dating?"

Ann burst out laughing. I'd rarely seen her smile. Much less laugh. "No. But I can see why you might think that. We've ended up sneaking around a lot. Someone else has captured his attention."

"Oh," I said. Figures. I couldn't imagine any warm-blooded, straight woman who wouldn't want him.

"I'm talking about you."

"*Oh!*" I didn't want to talk about this with Ann, even though she claimed she wasn't interested in him. "What about Oscar? Keeping him safe?"

Ann drooped a little. "I was shocked to see him out there last night. He must be reliving his youth."

"What?" I decided I needed a drink of the margarita after all and took a healthy swig. This time my eyes did water.

"Back in the sixties, when business was slow, Oscar would run bales of marijuana up to Alabama for distribution farther north. Somehow, he never got caught, but plenty of people around here knew about it." She took another swig of her beer. "I'll make sure Leah knows he's been out on the boat late at night. And you should be more careful. These people don't want to be messed with."

"Does Elwell's death have anything to do with this?"

"I don't think so. I haven't seen or heard of any connections."

"Why should I trust you?"

"Because I answered your questions."

Everything she said had a ring of truth to it. But I'd be following up with Vivi anyway. Even if Vivi vouched for Ann, I still might not be convinced. Who was to say Ann wasn't really working with the bad guys, double-crossing Vivi? You don't become known as a "fixer" if you weren't willing to cross some lines.

An hour later, I sat out on the screened porch, unable to sleep. My mind was buzzing with conversations from today. I focused in on a thought that had been rolling around the edges since I'd come out here. What if Boone died because someone wanted the bar? It was an excruciating thought. It was ludicrous to think that someone from here could kill someone halfway across the world. But I could see the logic—if one could call it that—in it, as horrible as it was.

There were four active military bases in a one-hundred-mile-stretch between Pensacola and Panama City. It meant thousands of active-duty military personnel and numerous contractors were in the area at all times. Murder was in the realm of possibility; Boone had been killed by a sniper.

The wind picked up, and thunder began its low rumble across the sky. The air temperature dropped, and I shivered. If it was true that someone killed Boone a world away, then it seemed like Vivi was in terrible danger too. All this time, I'd thought her only fear was being charged with murder. But maybe staying alive was the true concern.

If I was really honest with myself, maybe it was a big concern for me too. The sideswipe and the fire might have been more than someone trying to scare me. They might have been failed attempts on my life. I should have realized this earlier. I guess I had been in denial because I couldn't figure out why someone would want to kill me. But I wasn't in denial anymore.

If someone took Boone out, they would have thought Vivi was their sole remaining obstacle. Until I came along. Maybe someone wasn't after me for what I'd learned, but for what I'd inherited. And Vivi too. Maybe they thought Boone's death would break Vivi and she'd sell the bar. I needed to ask Vivi if she's had any recent offers to buy the Sea Glass. If she had and she'd refused, they—whoever they were— might have changed tactics. If that didn't work, killing Elwell behind the bar and making her a prime suspect might do the trick.

But who knew that I was now part owner of the bar? I'd only told Joaquín, and I was guessing Vivi hadn't told anyone or I would have heard about it.

That left the lawyer. Our lawyer.

CHAPTER 37

Ed. Who I'd sat out on this very porch with a couple of nights ago, discussing who might have killed Elwell. I thought I was so clever talking to him, when all the while he was finding out what I knew and what I planned to do next. *Vivi!* Ed could get to her under any number of pretenses if he thought his plan was falling apart. I could picture him telling her I'd decided to sell my share of the bar. Could he come over to talk to her about it? Or maybe he'd just drop by, like he had here the other night.

I called Vivi's landline. No answer. Bits of anxiety rushed and swirled around me, pelting at me like blowing sand. I shoved on flip-flops and raced out to my car as I called Joaquín. *Overreacting. That's what you're doing. She's out with friends. Or sound asleep.* I leaped into the car. It didn't start. No lights. No noise like it wanted to start. I'd just driven it home without any problem.

I got Joaquín's voice mail. Told him to call Vivi. Told him my worry about the lawyer. As I got out of the car, I heard a branch snap on the other side of the car. It hit me that the brand-new floodlights weren't on. Lightning flashed and illuminated two grinning cowboys. I bolted.

"Dang it. Now we've got to chase her. If you weren't scared of fire, this would be over."

I dashed around the side of the house through the scrub brush and soft sand. I heard them grunting behind me like two wild pigs as I kicked off my flip-flops. At least I didn't have cowboy boots on. Something pierced my foot, but I kept on running, even though it stung. I'd learned when I was ten to keep going or you died. Those were my two choices now.

"You might have escaped us in your car on the bridge, but not tonight," one of them yelled.

"You can run, girl, but you'll only die trying," the other yelled.

Their laughter followed me as I sped down to the surf to find the hard sand. I raced eastward toward Vivi's house. Maybe it wasn't too late. Maybe I was fast enough to outrun these guys. Shouts rang out behind me.

The Gulf was riled up. Waves crashed. Lightning flashed again, closer this time. Made it easy for the cowboys to spot me. The waves and lightning took me back to my ten-year-old self for a moment, and I slowed. Lake Michigan had been riled up with waves bigger than these. I tried to look forward, not focus on the waves on the Gulf or the waves of my past. The air choked me and I couldn't breathe.

I risked a glance back now. I had to stay in the present. To fight. I could see one cowboy was struggling about twenty yards behind me. His cowboy boots and

jeans slowing him down, making him flounder in the
sand. Like I'd floundered in the water eighteen years
ago. Where was the other cowboy?

I forced myself on and ran as fast as I could, passing the stand of pines up the beach, weighing my options. Continue on the hard sand where I was faster,
or cut up to Vivi's house, which I could see now?
Vivi's dark house. *Please, be sleeping.* But if they were
after me tonight, they were probably after her.
Maybe their boss—Ann? The lawyer?—was at Vivi's
now. Someone Vivi trusted and would invite in without question. Now I was coming up with conspiracy
theories—at least I hoped that's what they were. But
the men chasing me said otherwise.

I fished my cell phone out of my back pocket without breaking stride. Dialed 911 and gave them Vivi's
address. Told them there was a possible intruder and
a medical emergency. I would have told them anything if I thought it would make them get there
faster.

I started to angle up toward Vivi's house when I
heard the whine of an engine. I looked back as a dune
buggy with the other cowboy in it flew over a dune. It
bucked and rocked. I hoped it would flip over, but it
righted itself and headed straight for me. I didn't know
if I could make it to Vivi's house before it caught up
with me. But I would die trying if I had to.

The driver must have decided it would be easy to
catch me, because he detoured to pick up his partner. *Keep going,* I told myself. Stride, stride, glance
back. Both the cowboys were in the dune buggy now.
Whooping and hollering like I was the calf they were
going to rope at the rodeo. Like this was some game.

I propelled myself forward and made it to the steps that led to the long, wooden sidewalk that went over the dunes to Vivi's house. I could run faster here, but my foot hurt more each time it slammed down on the splintered wood. I forced myself to ignore the pain. I wasn't sure what I was running toward, but I knew what I was running from.

I made it to Vivi's back porch. Her back door was wide open. That wasn't good. It was still dark in the house, and I wasn't about to flip on any lights. I closed the door gently and flipped the lock. The lightning flashes picked up, which helped me move through the house without tripping over anything, but also had me cringing. I didn't want to call out to her or cry out accidentally because of the storm. Once I reached the front door, I unlocked it quietly. Hoping it would let the deputies in faster. Hoping it wouldn't help the cowboys.

I stopped and listened, which wasn't easy to do as the thunder rumbled closer and the wind lashed out. A scraping sound came from upstairs. A moan. I couldn't stand there and do nothing. There was a large, black umbrella with a curved wooden handle and a long, pointy end in a stand by the front door. It wasn't much as weapons went, but it was better than nothing. That's what they'd said in the self-defense-for-librarians class I'd taken—use whatever you can. I started up the steps, staying toward the edge, hoping they wouldn't creak. Hoping the thunder would cover any sounds I made. At the top, I stopped and listened again, pressed against the wall before stepping into the hall.

"Got it," a male voice said. "I'll take care of her,

but get your asses up here. Bust a window if you have to. I can't do everything."

Ed Ashford. I figured what he was going to "take care of" was me. That the cowboys must have called him to let him know I was in the house. I glanced back toward the front door, wishing I could run outside and just keep going until I was back home in Chicago. *Not possible. Focus.*

I poked my head out to look down the hall just as Ed turned to come down the steps. We stared at each other for a millisecond. Then I hooked the umbrella handle around the back of Ed's knee and yanked. His knee gave out. I pulled him toward me, then let go of the umbrella. Watched him tumble down the steps. Yelling and cursing until he smacked down on the floor. He lay at the bottom unmoving. Now silent.

I looked down at him, shocked that what I'd done had worked. Shivered at the image of his surprised eyes as he flew past me, the sound of the thumps as he somersaulted down the stairs.

"Vivi?" I yelled. Where the heck were the deputies? This town wasn't that big.

"Take a left. Third room on the right." That was followed by some swearing.

Vivi sounded as mad as a drunk customer who'd gotten cut off. And it was one of the best sounds I'd ever heard. I hobbled toward her. Finally feeling how hurt my foot was. Trying to move quietly because I knew the cowboys were still out there. As I reached Vivi, who was tied to a chair in her bedroom, I heard sirens.

* * *

Thirty minutes later, Michael sat beside me on Vivi's living room couch while an EMT examined my foot. Joaquín sat next to Vivi on another couch, facing us. She'd leaned her head against the back of the couch, her face pale. Ed had been hauled off in handcuffs, and the cowboys were caught out on the beach.

"Ed told me he killed Elwell. Set me up for it by taking a channel knife he saw me use." Vivi sat up. "He hired those two thugs to go after Chloe."

"At least this time, the third time, wasn't a charm," I said.

"That bastard was going to chum the water around his boat and toss me in and leave me to the sharks."

There was a group shudder as that sunk in. What a terrible way to die. How diabolical for Ed to have thought about killing Vivi that way. It would have seemed like a tragic accident. But Vivi and I had survived. I knew overcoming this night and its aftermath would be easier than overcoming my friend's death when I was ten.

Back then, my dad had gently encouraged me, along with a therapist, to get back in the water. To not let water hold any power over me. I'd taken that advice. Probably to the extreme. Always wanting to conquer some new water sport to prove I wasn't afraid. Running, trying to stay strong, so I could survive. I'd learned that it was okay to survive. Not easy, but okay. It had helped me through Boone's death too. Maybe that's why Boone wanted me here. Maybe that was what he wanted me to help Vivi with. Survival.

I looked over at Vivi, spitting mad, strong, determined. Maybe I was wrong. Maybe Boone wanted Vivi to help me.

"It's hard to believe Ed sat in the bar day after day, knowing he'd framed Vivi. That he'd killed Elwell," I said.

Rhett stood near the front door, arms crossed over his chest. He'd shown up after the deputies, along with most of the volunteer fire department and the EMTs. When Rhett saw me limping, he'd carried me over to the couch so an EMT could look at my foot. Most of the other firefighters had left, but Rhett had declined to go with them.

"Ouch," I said. I tried to draw my foot away, but the EMT held firm.

"You need stitches," she said.

"I'm sure it will be fine." Vivi's wood floors had dots of blood on them where I'd traipsed around the house.

Everyone started to protest.

Michael stood up. "I'll take her to the hospital. Joaquín, you stay with Vivi."

I hobbled over to Vivi and took her hand. "I can stay."

"No," she said, "get your foot looked after. Thank you for coming. I've misjudged you, and yet you stayed." She tightened her grip for a minute, then released my hand.

I had stayed, but I knew I wouldn't for much longer.

CHAPTER 38

Wednesday morning at eleven, there was a sign on the Sea Glass's sliding glass doors saying there was a private event. My foot was stitched, bandaged, and sore, so I'd missed my morning run. The storm had blown through and the beach was packed with people enjoying the weather. In here, it wasn't as festive. There was no island music playing over the speakers. The heritage business owners were all here, as was Ann Williams.

Last night at the hospital, I'd told Michael my terrible fear that Ed Ashford had Boone killed. He'd pulled me aside this morning. Michael had found out, through his old Navy connections, that Ed didn't have anything to do with Boone's death. The military had found videos taken by insurgents the day Boone was killed. One of them had done it. As sad as it was, I was glad, because it would have been difficult for all of us, but especially for Vivi, to handle if Boone had been killed over someone wanting the bar. Michael had also managed to trace the IP address of the bad reviews posted after Elwell was killed to Ed.

Vivi and I had a long, hard talk about Ann, the bar, Boone, and my 25 percent ownership. It was interrupted when everyone showed up.

Fred Russo's head hung down so low, it almost touched the table.

"What is going on with you, Fred?" Vivi asked. She put a hand on his arm, and he lifted his head.

"Y'all may never speak to me again."

"Better to just get it out there," Wade said.

He sat on the other side of Vivi. Their arms were touching like they leaned on each other for support. Maybe the events of last night had changed things between them for the better. I hoped Wade's love wouldn't be unrequited.

"Elwell found out I'd been passing off farmed shrimp from overseas as Gulf shrimp. Farmed shrimp that was grown in polluted waters," Fred said. "It saved me a bundle of money, but I shouldn't have done it."

I thought about the dinner I'd cooked the other night. Inferior shrimp from polluted waters. Ick.

"So he was blackmailing you?" Ralph's voice boomed across the bar. "To vote for the new zoning regulations."

"Ed and Elwell had a lot of resentment built up against all of you, and dollar signs in their eyes. I saw the designs they had drawn up for this stretch of beach. They already owned Two Bobs."

"Why didn't you just tell someone?" Vivi asked. "It would be embarrassing, but not the end of the world."

"Because not long after Elwell started blackmailing me, someone started threatening my family. I was scared."

"Who?" I asked.

"Might have been Elwell for all I know, just to keep me quiet."

"Did the threats stop after Elwell died?" Vivi asked.

Fred look out at the Gulf with pursed lips. "No."

"So it might have been Ed, just to keep you in line," Vivi said. "Hopefully, the sheriff will find out."

"Who was the man in the store last time I was there buying shrimp? The one who said you'd better deliver. The one you said was a supplier?" I asked.

"That was one of the prodevelopment councilman. He wanted to make sure I was going to deliver my vote. He knew I was vacillating." He looked around the group. "In the end, no matter what, I wouldn't have betrayed you. Betrayed Emerald Cove and all it is."

I wasn't sure that was true, but everyone else nodded. "Why did they resent the heritage owners?" I asked.

"It didn't really make sense," Fred said. "Your ancestors all started businesses and y'all worked hard to keep them going, but they thought y'all were entitled. When in reality, they were the ones who were. Wanted to snatch away what you've built without putting much work into it."

Ralph leaned forward. "I heard from Delores that the councilman was picked up for questioning this morning. Probably won't be long before he's arrested and charged when they hear Fred's testimony."

"Elwell must have been wearing that armadillo

shell to our businesses to drive customers away." Vivi frowned. "Then he and Ed could get us to sell."

"Seems like a long shot," Ralph said.

"It seems like Ed had a two-pronged attack," Vivi said. "Blackmail Fred so he'd give them the last vote they needed to change the zoning laws. And try to ruin our businesses so they could buy them cheap before the vote next month."

"After the vote, the value would skyrocket," Leah said. Oscar sat by her side. We had exchanged some long looks. Now he knew I wasn't just some tourist.

"And they'd have some prime real estate to build their monster high-rises on," Vivi said. She was still pale, which wasn't surprising, considering what she'd been through the past couple of weeks.

"But why kill Elwell?" asked Ralph.

"I talked to someone who said Elwell was going off the rails. Ed couldn't trust him to stay silent," Ann said.

Ann had come to my house this morning. I'd been sitting on the screened porch with my foot propped up, reading. She'd told me she'd contacted a Secret Service agent she knew after she'd thought about our conversation. What had started out as a small favor had turned into something bigger than she'd expected. "I won't know who did it until we read it in the newspaper." She had sounded a little frustrated.

"Is Oscar going to be in trouble?" I'd asked.

"I lied and kept him out of it. And Leah's going to make sure he doesn't have access to the glass-bottom boat, or any other boat at night."

"What's the deal with the two cowboys? Was Ed involved in the liquor smuggling too?"

"No. But they talked their heads off to the deputies. Bad dudes for hire by whoever would pay them."

I nodded. I was finally convinced she was on our side. At least this time.

A knock on the sliding-glass door startled me back to the present. Rhett stood out there. Vivi looked long and hard. She glanced over at me. "Let him in."

Rhett said his hellos, settled in a stool across from me, and smiled. "I'm glad you're both okay."

I smiled back. I was happy to see him. I noticed everyone at the table was watching us and refocused on the conversation.

"Delores heard Ed killed Elwell right outside Vivi's door and made it look like she did it as another way to hurt the Sea Glass," Ralph said.

"Boone had his will prepared up in Chicago. The lawyer up there sent it to Ed at my suggestion. Ed must have been furious to find out you owned a quarter of the business when he read Boone's will to us." Vivi shook her head. "It almost ruined his plan. Well, it did ruin his plan."

Everyone gasped and looked at me. Vivi smiled. "Yes. You heard that right. Chloe and I are partners. Right?"

Rhett gave me a slow smile. My face warmed.

"Right," I said. "But I'll be a silent partner. I'm heading back to my job in Chicago tomorrow." I glanced over at Rhett. He stared down at his hands. Nothing to see here, folks. It made me sad. Maybe I'd been hoping he'd leap up and say, "Don't leave."

Not that that would have kept me here. It was for the best. Long-distance relationships rarely worked.

Vivi stood. "If this is your last day here, let's get this place opened up so you can earn your keep." She winked at me as she said it.

Winked!

I stood outside the Sea Glass at eleven the next morning saying one last goodbye to Vivi and Joaquín. I'd planned to leave earlier but stayed late last night, talking to Vivi, Wade, Joaquín, Michael, and Ralph. We'd sat out on the deck of the Sea Glass, talking like old friends. Funny how close you could get to some people in just over three weeks. Dorothy cried when she left the Emerald City, and I knew I'd cry when I left the Emerald Coast.

Rhett had been nowhere to be seen. He'd left the bar yesterday afternoon not long after I'd announced I was leaving today. All I got was a handshake and a good luck. Maybe Ann was wrong about who he liked, because it certainly didn't seem to be me.

I'd also taken one last run—well, hobble, considering my foot—on the beach this morning. I was going to miss those runs along with the sanderlings, pelicans, and dolphins. In Chicago it would be back to pounding the pavement or going to the gym to run on a treadmill. It didn't hold much appeal after my beach runs. But now my car was packed and I was ready to take off. I'd be back for visits when I had vacation time. The Sea Glass, the people, they'd become part of my heart, and I felt like I was leaving a piece of it with them.

Vivi, Joaquín, and I stood next to my Beetle—a bit awkwardly, no one knowing quite what to say. My phone rang. "Hang on a minute," I told them, "it's my boss." I'd sent her a text yesterday, saying I'd be back and ready to work in two days. I took a couple of steps away from them.

"Chloe, I have some difficult news."

"What?" I asked.

"There's been a hiring freeze. We were just briefed an hour ago. You don't have a job."

"But I never quit. I'm just on leave."

"The higher-ups said we did fine without you, so they cut your position."

"There's nothing you can do?"

"I fought for you, but there isn't anything else I can do. I'm sorry. You know once they lift the freeze I'll higher you in a heartbeat."

"Can I transfer to another library in the system?" I heard the edge in my voice.

"They are all in the same boat."

I thanked her and hung up.

"What's wrong?" Joaquín asked.

"I don't have a job or a place to live." I stared at my phone for a moment. "There's a hiring freeze. I've been frozen."

"That's the problem with the North. It's too cold," Vivi said with a dramatic shiver. She swung out an arm, gesturing to the beach. "Not here, though. Here you have a job, a place to live, and the only thing that's frozen are the margaritas. Stay?"

I looked out at the placid Gulf, then at Joaquín, who was nodding and bouncing on his toes like a five-year-old who was excited about the book he'd just found. I turned to Vivi. "Of course I'll stay. Thank you."

Joaquín squealed and gathered us in his strong, fisherman arms for a group hug.

"I have some ideas about changes we could make . . ."

"Shut up, Chloe," Joaquín said.

"I was kidding." My voice was muffled against his chest. Maybe, I thought. Maybe.

Acknowledgments

I have so many people to thank for helping me with this book. My editor, Gary Goldstein, has been amazing through the writing of this book. And thanks to all the other unseen heroes who work behind the scenes at Kensington. John Talbot, my agent, is always there when I need him.

Thanks to Tom DeAngelis, fireman, who answered so many questions. Curt Frost, who coined the term Redneck Rollercoaster for Jeep rides on their California ranch. Charlie and Kathy Minter for boating information and for being the best neighbors we could ask for when we lived on the Emerald Coast. Shannon Ponche, bartender extraordinaire in Brooklyn, for walking me through the bartender life. Shari Randall for talking to me about being a children's librarian and for being an amazing friend. Kristopher Zgorski and Michael Mueller for allowing me to use a story of theirs and inspiring a character or two. My beta readers, Jason Allen-Forrest, Christy Nichol, and Mary Titone. The three of you are fabulous, your support and honest feedback has made this book way better. Jessie Crockett—who writes an amazing series as Jessica Ellicott—helped me at the very beginning of the process by spending hours with me on the phone, plotting. It's something I'm not good at and she's great at, and she did it despite her busy schedule.

Barb Goffman, can you believe this is the eighth book we've worked on together? You are one heck of an independent editor and friend. You pushed me (and pushed me and . . .) to make this better, and I couldn't have done it without you. Any errors are on me.

To all the readers, reviewers, bloggers, librarians, and booksellers out there, a huge thank-you for your support of the Sarah Winston Garage Sale mysteries. I hope you like Chloe. A special shout-out to bookseller extraordinaire, Kelly Hebert Harrington. Her support of this series has been phenomenal. To the Wickeds. I love you all. And, of course, to my family, who take the brunt of my crabby, my-book's-due days—thanks for your love and support. I wouldn't be a writer without you.

If you like the Chloe Jackson, Sea Glass Saloon
Mysteries, you will love the Sarah Winston Garage
Sale Mysteries!

SELL LOW, SWEET HARRIET
A Sarah Winston Garage Sale Mystery
by
Agatha Award–nominee
Sherry Harris

"Bargain-hunting has never been so much fun!"
—*RT Book Reviews*

ONE WOMAN'S TRASH . . .
Sarah Winston's garage sale business has a new
client: the daughter of a couple who recently died in
a tragic accident while away on a trip to Africa.
Their house is full of exotic items from around the
world that need to be sold off. When Sarah learns
that the deceased were retired CIA agents, the job
becomes more intriguing—but when an intruder
breaks in and a hidden camera is found, it also
becomes more dangerous. And Sarah has enough
on her plate right now because she's investigating a
murder on the side at the nearby Air Force base,
where her status as a former military spouse gives
her a special kind of access.

. . . IS ANOTHER WOMAN'S TROUBLE
With so much work piling up, Sarah decides to hire
some help. But her assistant, Harriet—a former FBI
hostage negotiator—has a rare talent for salesman-
ship. Which is good, because Sarah may have to
haggle for her life with Harriet's assistance. . . .

Keep reading for a special excerpt, and look for the
Sherry Winston, Garage Sale
Mystery series, on sale now where books are sold.

CHAPTER 1

From the back of the base chapel I could see the large photo resting on an easel at the front of the church. Golden light from a stained glass window shone on a picture of a smiling, auburn-haired young woman, dead, murdered right here on Fitch Air Force Base.

I sat on a pew after a couple scooted over for me. The church was packed, standing room only even on a Tuesday morning. I wasn't sure if it was because they knew Alicia Arbas or were horrified at how she had died. Maybe it was a combination of both. When a tragedy hit a base, especially a smaller one like Fitch, military people pulled together.

I studied the picture of Alicia, her bright smile. She wasn't me, but she could have been. That's why her death hit so close to home. Why I was sitting back here listening to the prayers, eulogies, and singing hymns even though I hadn't known her all that well.

Thirty minutes later the service for Alicia was almost over. There had been a lot of laughter as people shared funny stories, but more tears because Alicia died at the hands of an unknown killer. Someone who lived on base or had, at the very least, been on base. People glanced at one another more often than normal. Were they trying to suss out if their neighbor could have been the one who committed a murder? I worried about what would happen to people, to a community such as this, when they couldn't trust one another.

We sang the last hymn as the casket was carried out. Alicia's husband, a young captain, followed, pale and uncomfortable-looking in his black suit. The pain in his face seared my soul.

A few minutes later I stepped out of the church. The January wind slashed at my tights-covered legs and pulled at my coat. I scraped at the blond hairs that slapped my face, so I could see where I was going. Lunch was to be served in the church basement, but I was headed to DiNapoli's Roast Beef and Pizza for food and comfort. I didn't know Alicia well enough to console anyone. I had paid my respects, said my prayers, so it was time for me to go.

I crossed the parking lot to my car.

"Sarah Winston."

I turned at the voice. Squinted my eyes in the sun. Scott Pellner, a police officer for the Ellington Police Department, called to me. I almost didn't recognize him out of uniform and in a suit. He was broad and muscled, a few inches taller than me. His dimpled face grim.

"What are you doing here?" I asked. I had scanned the crowd at the funeral, curious about who'd be there. There had been a large group from the base Spouses' Club, an OSI agent—the Office of Special Investigations—who I knew, lots of military folks in their uniforms. A few of my friends, but they were too far away to join. I hadn't spotted Pellner.

"Working the case," Pellner said.

The base and the town of Ellington, Massachusetts, had memorandums of agreement. When a crime was committed on base but involved a dependent—the spouse or child of the military member—they worked together.

"Do police really go to funerals to see if the killer shows up?" I asked.

"They do in this case," Pellner said. His voice was as serious as I'd ever heard it.

"No suspects?"

"There's suspects. But no proof."

From what I'd heard, at some point in the night almost a week ago, Alicia had gotten up to take their new Labrador puppy out to do its business. We'd had a terrible ice storm that day and a thick coat of ice caked everything. The house I lived in looked like it had been wrapped in glass. And when I'd gone to bed that night I had heard tree branches across the street on the town common snapping under the weight of the ice. Later chunks fell off the house as a warm front swept through from the south and I was grateful to be snug in my bed.

Early in the morning Alicia's husband woke to the sound of the puppy barking and crying. He found the sweet thing scratching at the back door—shivering but otherwise okay. After calling for Alicia, he found her sprawled in the backyard with a head wound.

Ice shattered around her. At first everyone had thought it was a terrible accident. But later the medical examiner discovered the wound might not have been an accident. When Alicia had first been found the scene wasn't treated as a crime scene, so any evidence had melted away. No footprints, no nothing.

"Who are the suspects?" I asked. I assumed the husband. He had to be on the list as the last person to have seen her.

"Did you know her?" Pellner asked.

Of course he wasn't going to answer my question. I shouldn't have bothered asking. "We occasionally crossed paths at the base thrift shop."

"Do you know who her friends are?"

I shook my head. "No. And I don't know who doesn't like her either." That's what he really wanted to know.

Car doors slammed. We turned to see the hearse pull away. Pellner shook his head. "I need to go." His face still grim as he hurried off.

Forty minutes later I pushed my plate away from me. I'd polished off the better part of a small mushroom and sausage pizza, today's special. Angelo DiNapoli, the proprietor and my dear friend, didn't believe in pineapple on pizzas and sneered at toppings like kale. According to Angelo those weren't real pizzas. He stuck to the traditional and was excellent at what he did. Me, on the other hand? Except for anchovies I'd eat almost anything on a pizza, especially if someone else made it.

I wished I could have a glass of wine to warm me,

but I was meeting a client who was interested in having a garage sale. That was a rare thing in January in Massachusetts, so I needed the business. I was still cold from talking to Pellner in the parking lot. And every time someone opened the door the wind nipped at my ankles like an overenthusiastic puppy.

I shuddered thinking again of Alicia.

"You haven't been in for a while," Angelo said. His face was warm, his nose a little on the big side, and his hair way past receding, not that he cared. By *a while* he meant five days. I'd been huddled at home.

I looked around the restaurant. It was almost empty. The right side, where I sat, was lined with tables. To the left was the counter where you ordered and behind it the open kitchen. I'd been in such a swirl of thoughts I didn't notice the lunch rush had left—back to wherever they had to go. That explained my cold ankles. Angelo DiNapoli pulled out a chair and sat down. He wore his white chef's coat, a splash of marinara on the pocket.

"Is everything okay?" he asked.

"I just left a funeral."

"For the woman who was murdered on base?" Angelo asked as he crossed himself.

I nodded. "She was like me. A younger version. Only twenty-five." Fourteen years younger than me.

"How so?"

"Active in the Spouses' Club, volunteered at the thrift shop, didn't have kids."

"You see yourself in her?"

"Yes. I know what it's like to have to move somewhere you don't want to live and far from everyone you know and love. Then do it over and over." I sighed.

"I didn't know anything about the military or military life when CJ and I met. And I was always afraid I'd do something that would hurt CJ's career." I had married my ex-husband, CJ, when I was only eighteen. "During our first assignment I asked a colonel's wife out to lunch because she was so friendly. We went to the Officers Club and ate. Then there was this huge brouhaha that a lowly lieutenant's wife was out with a colonel's wife. She didn't care. I didn't care. But a lot of other people did."

"That doesn't sound easy," Angelo said.

"It wasn't at first. It's hard enough to feel judged when it's just you, but then worrying about tanking your husband's career too? It feels like you're walking a minefield of rules no one gave you."

Angelo crossed his arms over his chest. "Are you reevaluating your life?"

"Maybe I have been. I've been a bit down since I heard the news of her death. It seemed like everyone loved her." I wasn't so sure everyone had loved me when I lived on base. CJ and I had lived on Fitch for a couple of years until we divorced two years ago. We had tried to work things out, but just couldn't manage it and split up for good last spring. "If the eulogies are any indication."

"They aren't," Angelo said, "any indication. Genghis Khan would sound like a saint at his own funeral. People gloss over. They forget that people are complex."

"You're right." I knew that. It's a lesson I'd learned over and over the past few years.

"Would you change the past?" Angelo asked.

I sat for a moment thinking over my decisions, how

life had led me here. I'd moved to Ellington right after my divorce and had started my own business organizing garage sales. My friends buoyed me and I was in a great relationship. I was proud of what I'd accomplished, but always feared failure. It was part of what I'd been obsessing about for the last week. I shook my head. "I wouldn't change much. Every decision made me who I am. Even though I'm still not sure who that is."

"Then what are you going to do? Sit around and feel sorry for yourself?"

I smiled at Angelo. He didn't pull any punches. "That's exactly what I've been doing."

"What have you been doing?" Rosalie, Angelo's lovely wife, joined us. Concern creased lines around her brown eyes. Her brown hair was cut short and suited her. Rosalie held three plates with pieces of tiramisu and passed them out. "We've missed you."

I almost laughed. It would keep me from crying. Jeez, I was one big ball of emotions. "You two are the best."

"At least someone recognizes that," Angelo said.

"Oh, Angelo," Rosalie said.

He held up both hands, palms up. "It's the truth."

We ate our dessert, chatted about things that didn't have to do with Alicia. They entertained me with stories of the early years of their marriage living in a small apartment in the bad part of Cambridge.

"Did you always want to open a restaurant?" I asked them.

"Yes," Angelo said. "My *nonna* and mama taught

me everything I know about food. I loved cooking from the day I set foot in their kitchen when I was three."

I turned to Rosalie. "And you?"

She smiled at Angelo. "I love him, so I supported his dream."

"She's a born hostess and a great partner," Angelo said. He took Rosalie's hand and kissed it. "Forty-five years almost, and I don't regret a day."

"Maybe one day?" Rosalie said with a wink. "Cooking is all about love for us."

Maybe I should learn to cook a dish and surprise everyone by having them over for a meal. It's not like I never cooked while CJ and I were married. It's just that when I tried I always seemed to leave an ingredient out or overcook everything. I blanched when I remembered the episode of the undercooked chicken. That was one dinner party no one would ever forget.

Even when I'd tried using a slow cooker, I seemed to end up with mush. Now there were Instant Pots and air fryers and pressure cookers. New appliances with elaborate recipes to try to master. It was terrifying out there.

"Have you two heard any local gossip about the murder?" Lots of military and civilians who worked on base lived in Ellington. There wasn't ever enough housing on base for all military personnel to live there, and for civilians it was a dream commute— only fifteen minutes depending on traffic. Even if they didn't live in Ellington they filled DiNapoli's at mealtime.

"Nothing here," Angelo said.

I looked at Rosalie.

She shook her head. "I was at the hairdresser two days ago. There was a lot of speculation but no information."

That was strange.

"You're going to take that pizza home with you," Angelo said, pointing to what I hadn't eaten.

No one left food behind at DiNapoli's. Angelo took it as a personal insult. Rosalie took the pizza, boxed it up, and brought it back over. After saying goodbye, I left DiNapoli's and drove over to meet my new client, pondering the lack of gossip about Alicia's death and what it meant.

CHAPTER 2

A tall, thick-boned woman met me at the one-story ranch on a quiet side street in Ellington. The street wasn't busy this time of day, but I knew at rush hour in the morning and evening it was used as a cut-through.

"I'm Jeannette Blevins." She had bushy brown hair held back with a sparkly headband. I knew from some of the paperwork she'd already filled out that she was thirty-three.

"Sarah Winston," I said. We shook hands. Her grip firm. We stood in a narrow hallway with a low ceiling that served as a foyer. What I presumed was a coat closet was to the right. We walked past it, took a left, and went into the living room. I was surprised to see a vaulted ceiling that made the room seem more spacious.

"Like I told you when I called, my parents died two months ago in Senegal. A tragic accident with a faulty gas line." She paused and sucked in a shaky breath.

"My brother and I need to get rid of all of this stuff."
She waved her hand around.

"I'm so sorry." She wasn't that old to have lost both
her parents. Jeannette had contacted me through my
website four days ago. Because of a past incident I
now requested documentation proving the party had
the right to sell the contents of the house. Since her
brother was the executor and lived out of town, I'd
also asked for and gotten a notarized letter from him
saying Jeannette could oversee the sale. When I was
satisfied that all was in order I agreed to meet with
her.

"Is there anything that you want to keep?" I asked.
There was so much left in here.

"My brother and I have gone through and taken
what we want. I live in a two-family house and don't
have room or the desire to take much. He lives in
New York City in a small place."

I scanned the living room. This would be a huge
job. Every bit of wall space seemed to have something
hanging on it. Paintings, mosaic tiles, mirrors, samu-
rai swords. It was an eclectic mix that gave me a bit of
a headache to look at. I stepped closer to study the
things hanging on the wall next to me. Everything
seemed to be excellent quality, at least in this room.

"Let me show you the rest of the house."

We walked through the three bedroom, two bath
house. One of the bedrooms had been converted
into a study. The house was filled with Japanese furniture, a Danish modern bedroom suite in the guest
room, framed maps, and shelves filled with figurines.
"Your parents must have traveled a lot," I said. I
snapped pictures with my phone as we went through

the rooms. It would help me organize, estimate how many hours this project would take, and maybe I could even do some pricing from home.

"They did. We all did." Jeannette stopped next to a family photo. Black and white, it looked like it had been taken in Egypt, since a pyramid and camel were in the background. She hesitated for a moment. "I guess it doesn't matter now that they are gone."

I wondered what was coming next.

"They were both in the CIA."

My eyes widened. "That must have been an interesting way to grow up."

"We didn't know it. We thought Dad worked for the agricultural department and that Mom was a translator. We took all the moves for granted."

"How did you end up here?" I asked.

"My dad was originally from Boston. They met in college at Georgetown. At least that was their story." Jeannette grinned. "I think Mom was my dad's handler, although they never admitted it."

"Wow." I thought about growing up in Pacific Grove, California. My childhood had been grounded, a bit boring even. It's one of the reasons why I'd gotten married so young "Are you . . ." I stopped. It wasn't any of my business if Jeannette was in the CIA or not. She wouldn't tell me if she was.

"CIA?" She laughed. "Oh, no. I'm a teacher. I loved all the places we lived, but I wanted to settle in one place."

Having moved all the time when I was married to CJ, I understood the need for roots. It's why I stayed in Ellington when we split up.

"Did you have a favorite place where you lived?" I asked.

"Japan. I was ten and it all seemed so exotic and amazing. For some reason my mom had more free time there. We spent lots of time baking and exploring. It was great." Jeannette took the photo off the wall. "I guess I should keep this. If you find anything else like this, will you let me know?"

I nodded.

"There's so much stuff that it's hard to spot everything."

"No problem," I said. "I'll keep an eye out. Am I going to find any spy gadgets?" My voice held a little more hope in it than I'd intended. This might be a very interesting sale.

Jeannette laughed again. "I think spy gadgets are overrated. Most work was done talking to people one-on-one."

Maybe I'd find a lapel pin with a camera or a pen with a poison dart. A girl could dream. Maybe I should be extra careful sorting things, though.

We discussed payment options. With a project this big I sometimes charged an hourly fee to price items, or I could take a larger than normal commission. The first option was better for me because there was no way to tell how much all of this would sell for. On the other hand I needed the business, so I was inclined to accept the larger commission. I'd toyed with the idea of starting an online auction site for this kind of sale. Maybe it was time to implement that. But before I offered it up as a solution, I wanted to double-check what kind of website I'd need to support it. And I would have to think about all the packing and shipping costs that would involve. It didn't seem like the right time for this idea.

We settled on a larger commission and signed a contract agreeing that I do the sale in two weeks. "I'm going to start promoting this sale online right away because we want to attract as many customers as possible."

"That's a great idea. Thank you." Jeannette gave me the keys to the house.

"I'll be back tomorrow to work."

Jeannette nodded. "The will stated that my brother gets eighty percent of everything." Her voice sounded brisk.

The way the will was split seemed unusual, but it wasn't my place to ask why.

"There was a reason, in the past, why they made that decision. I want to make sure we get top dollar for him."

"That's always my plan. And I've built a reputation for doing that."

She smiled. "I know. That's why I hired you."

Connect with U s

Visit us online at
KensingtonBooks.com
to read more from your favorite authors, see books
by series, view reading group guides, and more.

for sneak peeks, chances to win books and prize packs,
and to share your thoughts with other readers.

facebook.com/kensingtonpublishing
twitter.com/kensingtonbooks

Tell us what you think!

To share your thoughts, submit a review,
or sign up for our eNewsletters, please visit:
KensingtonBooks.com/TellUs.

Grab These Cozy Mysteries
from
Kensington Books

Available Wherever Books Are Sold!

All available as e-books, too!

Visit our website at **www.kensingtonbooks.com**

Sherry Harris is the Agatha Award–nominated author of the Sarah Winston Garage Sale mystery series and the upcoming Chloe Jackson Sea Glass Saloon mysteries. She is a past president of Sisters in Crime, and a member of the Chesapeake Chapter of Sisters in Crime, the New England Chapter of Sisters in Crime, Mystery Writers of America, and International Thriller Writers.

In her spare time Sherry loves reading and is a patent holding inventor. Sherry, her husband, and guard dog Lily are living in northern Virginia until they figure out where they want to move to next.

Website: Sherryharrisauthor.com
Blog: Wickedcozyauthors.com

*A whip smart librarian's fresh start comes with
a tart twist in this perfect cocktail of murder and
mystery—with a romance chaser.*

MURDE

With Chicago winters i̶ ̶ ̶ ̶ ̶ ̶ ̶ or, Chloe
Jackson is making good ̶ ̶ ̶ ̶ ̶ ̶ her late
friend's grandmother run ̶ ̶ ̶ ̶ ̶ ̶ on in the
Florida Panhandle. To Ch ̶ ̶ ̶ ̶ ̶ Vivi Slidell
isn't the frail retiree Chloe ̶ ̶ ̶ ̶ ̶ ̶ ald Cove.
It's less a sleepy fishing vi ̶ ̶ ̶ ̶ ̶ le hotspot
overrun with land develop ̶ ̶ ̶ ̶ it's a Sea
Glass regular who's mysteriously crossed the cranky Vivi.
When their bitter argument comes to a head and he's
found dead behind the bar, guess who's the number
one suspect?

In trying to clear Vivi's name, Chloe discovers the old
woman isn't the only one in Emerald Cove with secrets.
Under the laidback attitude, sparkling white beaches,
and small-town ways something terrible is brewing. And
the sure way a killer can keep those secrets bottled up
is to finish off one murder with a double shot: aimed at
Chloe and Vivi.

"AN INCREDIBLY ENJOYABLE BOOK."
—*Mystery Scene* on *Sell Low, Sweet Harriet*

$1.99
867797
AO—
443—G
No Exchange
Books
Mystery & Crime
savers

ISBN-13: 978-1-4967-2303-1
ISBN-10: 1-4967-2303-1

5 0 7 9 9

BKO451.7769

723031

KENSINGTON
U.S. $7.99
CAN $10.99
PRINTED IN USA